Marty pushed the door to his room open

Shannon lay on her back her face turned away from him, one arm at her waist, the other flung over the edge of the bed.

He approached quietly, taking her hand and folding it under the covers. With a muttered protest, she turned her head toward him and flung the arm out again. He smiled at the thought that even in sleep she could not be easily managed.

Shannon stirred and he stiffened worriedly, afraid of how she would react if she awoke in the middle of the night in a strange bed and saw him standing there.

But she opened her eyes slowly, took a moment to focus on him, then smiled and raised the wayward hand toward him. "Marty," she said sleepily, undisguised pleasure in her voice. "You're home."

Marty closed his hand around hers, sat on the edge of the bed and fell in love.

ABOUT THE AUTHOR

A native of Massachusetts, Muriel Jensen now lives in Astoria, Oregon, with her husband, who is also a writer, and their two calico cats. She also has three grown children.

Books by Muriel Jensen
HARLEQUIN AMERICAN ROMANCE

73–WINTER'S BOUNTY
119–LOVERS NEVER LOSE
176–THE MALLORY TOUCH
200–FANTASIES AND MEMORIES
219–LOVE AND LAVENDER
244–THE DUCK SHACK AGREEMENT
267–STRINGS
283–SIDE BY SIDE
321–A CAROL CHRISTMAS

EVERYTHING

MURIEL JENSEN

Harlequin Books

TORONTO • NEW YORK • LONDON
AMSTERDAM • PARIS • SYDNEY • HAMBURG
STOCKHOLM • ATHENS • TOKYO • MILAN

To Rita, Theresa, Claire and Lorraine—
and in loving memory of Estelle—
because they're the best sisters anyone ever had.
And because they're all *older* than I.

Published April 1990

First printing February 1990

ISBN 0-373-16339-8

Chapter One

"Aren't you the least bit interested in him?" Gale Hunter asked, hurrying to keep up with her friend's long-legged, New York-marathon pace through the department store.

"Of course I am," Shannon replied. Walking down the cosmetics aisle, she stopped to indicate an almost empty tester bottle of Dreams, the holiday season's most popular perfume. "Replace this please, Hilary," she said to the beautiful blonde behind the counter.

"Yes, Miss Carlisle."

Running her eyes the length of the spotless glass counter and seeing every display freshly dusted and placed with artful precision, Shannon smiled and nodded her approval at the clerk before moving on.

"I meant in a personal sense," Gale said, picking up the thread of their conversation.

"Of course not," Shannon replied. "The deal we're considering is business." She paused in the junior department to stare at a mannequin that was dressed in several layers, including lace, denim and fur. The alarming ensemble was accessorized with a tiny beaded purse slung from shoulder to opposite hip, and dark tights and boots that looked perfect for an expedition to the jungles of Borneo.

Gale folded her arms and whispered to Shannon, "Would you be caught dead in that?"

Shannon tilted her auburn head, considering the mannequin and the question. "Ten years ago I might have."

Gale turned to frown at her.

"Okay, fifteen."

Gale laughed. "I wasn't questioning your age, but your
taste."

Shannon looked back at the mannequin with a wistful
little smile. "At sixteen your taste runs to the outrageous, to
making a fashion statement that tells the world you're finding yourself and it's just got to have patience with you."

Gale, whose first job had been in Carlisle's shoe department in the summer between her junior and senior years in
high school, had known Shannon in those days. "You were
never like that."

"I know." Glancing at her watch, Shannon pushed her
friend toward the parting elevator doors. "I was too busy
learning to manage Carlisle's to try on clothes. And we had
a dress code then, left over from my grandmother's day.
Remember?"

Gale rolled her eyes. "Do I? Women couldn't wear slacks
on the sales floor, and men had to wear three-piece suits.
Thank goodness you changed all that." As the old elevator
sailed unsteadily toward the top floor and the administrative offices, Gale smiled at Shannon. "You have been a be-
nevolent dictator."

Shannon inclined her head, feigning grand modesty.
"Why, thank you."

The elevator doors opened onto the fourth floor, and Gale
followed Shannon across the gray and burgundy carpet into
her office. Walking through to a small lounge at the back of
the room, Shannon flipped a switch and studied her reflection in the harsh honesty of the fluorescent light. She sighed,
leaning across the counter to freshen her makeup.

"That little Hilary in cosmetics makes me feel like a
warthog."

Gale laughed. "She is young. I think Bradley Cummings, our director of personnel, has a taste for sweet young things. Fortunately for Carlisle's, they do look good behind the counter and he knows you'd hang him from the mezzanine if he ever behaved improperly toward them."

Gale sat on the edge of the counter and watched Shannon run a brush through her hair. "This way there are lots of pretty young things for him to look at, and to keep you and me on our toes."

"On our toes is right," Shannon said, turning sideways and straightening her posture. "Age and gravity are at work here. How did we get to be in our thirties, Gale?"

Ever practical, Gale shrugged. "We finished all there was of our twenties."

Shannon dropped her makeup in a drawer and laughed at her friend and assistant manager. "You're such a wit. Now." She flipped off the light and went to her desk, glancing at her watch as she collapsed into her chair. Gale followed, taking the chair in front of the desk. "I have ten minutes before I meet with Henry and Martin Hale. What do you think I should ask for besides everybody's jobs?"

Gale looked into Shannon's brown eyes and shook her head. "Don't worry about us. Just make sure you come out of this with enough to be comfortable, and to buy yourself your own personal carousel."

Shannon sighed and leaned her head against the tufted back of her chair. "If that was all I cared about, I'd have simply sold out the stock and let everybody go. I'm not wild about a modern chain taking over our wonderful mahogany anachronism. But—" she made a sweeping gesture with one hand "—there are two hundred jobs at stake here. I can't turn my back on that."

"Your father would have."

Shannon cocked an eyebrow. "I take after my grandmother."

Gale questioned that conclusion with a laugh. "You're not stodgy."

Shannon sat up, grinningly defensive. "She wasn't stodgy. She was . . . responsible, determined, and maybe a little too forceful. But she meant well. And she did well. Five minutes, Gale. Any advice?"

Laughing, Gale reached down to take Shannon's hand and pull her to her feet. "Yes. We're going to look at my poster of Martin Hale one more time."

Walking into her office, Gale led Shannon to the miniscule closet where she stored her coat and purse. Opening the door, she stepped aside to let Shannon admire the advertising poster that adorned the back of it.

The poster had been a promotional tool for Daring, last year's hottest-selling men's cologne. It was a full-length shot of a man leaning against a Mediterranean-style bedroom dresser. Reflected in the mirror over the dresser was the figure of a woman, clad in a negligee, reclining on a bed. The man wore only black briefs and a smile that was at once impulsive and dangerous. Across the bottom of the poster, the copy read: "Daring and my woman are all I need."

Gale had begged the poster from the cosmetics department the moment they'd taken it down, and she used it as a sort of morale builder—an inspiration in her relationships.

Shannon studied the poster and expelled a ragged breath, feeling for a rare moment more woman than executive. She admired the long, muscular legs, the neat hips and formidable shoulders. She emitted a sigh. "That is some body," she said, her tone laced with respect. She turned to Gale. "We know Martin Hale went from quarterback for the Rams to modeling. What's your point?"

"Did you know that his ex-wife is Monica Hale, the movie star?"

Shannon frowned. "I've heard that somewhere. Why?"

"I just thought if he tries to give you a hard time, it might help you to remember that you've seen him in his underwear, and that he's been dumped by one of the world's most beautiful women." Gale took one last, lingering look at the poster and said with a shake of her head, "The woman must be nuts."

She closed the closet door and walked with Shannon to her office. "Knowing he has his vulnerabilities, too, will help you stand firm and even gain the upper hand. Gotta get that." Responding to the ring of the telephone, Gale ran back to her office. "Good luck," she called, closing the door that adjoined their offices.

Sitting on the edge of her desk, Shannon picked up a Baccarat paperweight that had belonged to her grandmother and turned it in her hand, considering her options. They were very few.

If she didn't sell Carlisle's Department Store to the Hale chain, she would be out of business in a year. Located in the downtown area of Portland, Oregon, the store had been established by her grandfather in 1936, two years before he died of a heart attack. Eugenie Carlisle, Shannon's grandmother, only twenty-six years old at the time of her husband's death, had held on to the store with grim determination through the severe shortage of goods created by World War II.

Albert, Eugenie's son and Shannon's father, had been at the helm of Carlisle's during the economically healthy fifties and sixties. He'd been a ruthless businessman. Though the store had prospered, Albert had done little for his employees. Even longtime employees worked for low wages, and there were few benefits and no insurance plan.

The store prospered until the increasing popularity of malls and the growing inconvenience of shopping in a heavily trafficked downtown area took their toll in Portland as they had in many other metropolitan centers across the country. Sales were down, goods were more expensive, and Carlisle's prosperity declined.

Shannon had taken over three years ago after her father was killed in an automobile accident. Having grown up in the store, first pestering the employees then, when she was old enough, working among them, she understood their needs and was determined to see to them despite the store's other problems.

She supposed the economic climate hadn't been right for all the changes she'd made on behalf of her staff, but many of them were her friends as well as her employees and she felt a responsibility to them.

All in all, she was pleased with what she had accomplished during her three years in charge of Carlisle's, but if she was to save it from the ignominy of becoming another empty big-city storefront, she'd have to deal with the Hales and hope they would be merciful.

Suddenly the door connecting her office with Gale's burst open and Gale ran across Shannon's office to the window. "I think they're here!"

Following her to the window, Shannon looked down onto the street. Below them a long white limousine gleamed in the winter sunshine.

"There?" she asked.

"No." Gale pointed across the street to where two men emerged from a red Jaguar convertible with its top down. "There. See? That's him!"

A white-haired man in a dark overcoat had stepped from the driver's side and was putting coins in the parking meter. His passenger, however, was having a little more difficulty getting out of the car.

Shannon watched with interest, and Gale giggled while the second man, apparently despairing of folding his long legs to disembark the conventional way, boosted himself onto the back of the seat and leaped lightly over the side to the pavement.

He paused a moment to straighten his tie and adjust his jacket, then fell into step beside the older man as he crossed the street.

"I'll bring them up here," Gale said, already halfway out the door, "while you put on the coffee." She paused to give Shannon a thumbs-up. "Remember. You've seen him in his underwear."

"DAD, I WISH you'd get a real car," Marty Hale said as he pushed the large glass door open for his father. "Or at least one that doesn't have the top stuck down. It is late October, you know."

"I thought it was an invigorating drive. Besides, the company limo didn't seem right for this trip." Henry Hale stopped inside the store and drew a deep breath. His eyes scanned the luster and sparkle of a well-tended store decorated for Christmas and nodded, as though something he'd suspected had been confirmed. "God, does anything smell as fine as quality retail goods? Perfume, good wool, leather. What do you think, Martin?"

Marty looked across Carlisle's large ground floor and found it hard not to be swayed by its charm. Artificial Christmas trees decorated with chunky gold garlands and miniature lights hung from the ceiling. Red and green plaid cloths covered the small feature display tables, and the long glass counter surfaces were covered with bright seasonal displays.

Mahogany pillars and the gold garlands twined around them shone warmly, the parquet floor was spotless, and everything the eye fell on showed the mark of care in selection and treatment.

But it was old. He knew that if his father and T. Shannon Carlisle struck a deal, the expense involved in elevating this store to Hale standards of convenience and safety would be enormous.

Though he'd spent fifteen years away from the family business, he had grown up in it, and all he'd learned was still a part of him. He saw all the obstacles to efficiency and an immediate show of profit, which was what business was all about.

But he'd learned more than business sense under his father's tutelage. Henry Hale always said that a good family conducted its business in the same way that it conducted its life. It strove to get ahead, to make its mark, but if it found no beauty and no fun along the way, the venture simply wasn't worth it. Money was good, it was important, but it wasn't everything.

He turned to his father and replied with all sincerity, "It's beautiful. I'd restore rather than remodel."

Henry nodded again, that same gesture of a truth confirmed. "You've got a good head on you, son—as impressive as your career stats."

Marty laughed. "Good breeding. Is that T. Shannon Carlisle coming our way?"

The dark eyes that could take in an entire floor of merchandise in seconds, then list them in order of turnaround speed, peered nearsightedly at the figure coming their way.

"Is she a redhead?" Henry asked.

"Brunette. And where are your glasses?"

"In my pocket. Tall?"

"Small. Put them on. What if you have to sign something?"

"I'll let you do it." The woman was in focus now and offering Henry her hand. Henry saw that she wasn't T. Shannon Carlisle, but an attractive woman could claim his attention, whoever she was.

"Mr. Hale?"

At Henry's nod, Gale introduced herself. "I'm Carlisle's assistant manager, Gale Hunter. Miss Carlisle has coffee waiting upstairs if you'll follow me."

"I'm sure following you will be a pleasure." With a gallant and mildly wicked bow, Henry fell into step behind Gale, gesturing to Marty to follow him. With a cautioning frown, Marty took up the parade.

If he pinches her, Marty thought, I'm going back to football. The man was a good businessman and had been a great father, but where women were concerned he was getting worse instead of better. What had begun as a cautious exploration into the field of man/woman relationships a year after the death of his wife of thirty-eight years was turning into an intimate case by case study of every woman between the ages of twenty and dotage.

"Pardon me?" Suddenly realizing that Miss Hunter had spoken to him, Marty smiled apologetically. They were on an ancient elevator with an iron gate that slid into place before the doors closed. As it bucked slightly, he tried to look relaxed.

"I asked if you'd driven all the way from your headquarters in Bend with the top down?"

"Yes, the top is stuck down."

"Fresh air is rejuvenating," Henry said, smiling with great charm as he studied Gale's small but round proportions appreciatively. "Of course, a young thing like yourself doesn't have to worry about that."

Marty closed his eyes.

The elevator jolted to a stop. Gale pushed the creaking gate aside, then the doors opened and she led the way to Shannon's office.

"I think she likes me," Henry whispered over his shoulder.

"She's just too well mannered to slug you," Marty whispered back.

Henry sighed with paternal disgust. "You have a good head, Martin, but sometimes the rest of you is really dull."

They were led into a large office that reminded Marty of a commercial he'd done for French champagne. It had been staged in a turn-of-the-century tearoom full of chintz and lace and potted palms.

Here the accents were blue and pink, but the effect was the same. On a cold morning in October, in the heart of the city, he felt as though he'd walked into a French country cottage.

At a glass-topped wicker table across the room, a woman looked up from pouring coffee and smiled a greeting. She came toward them as Gale began introductions.

"Hello, Mr. Hale," she said. "Welcome to Carlisle's."

During his brief stint as a model, Marty had learned that movement and speech could be taught, but nothing could create or duplicate the natural grace that emanated from a well-mannered, good-natured woman. He observed that phenomenon in the woman who extended her hand to his father.

T. Shannon Carlisle had hair the color of a dusty desert sunset. It was fairly short, skimming the line of her jaw, but full of movement as she walked. One side was caught back with a gold clip, the other rippling in a deep wave against her cheek. Her eyes were brown and direct, her nose and chin aristocratically defined, her complexion pink and freckle-free.

As Henry reached for her hand, she squared her shoulders in a gesture of self-confidence and Marty knew instinctively that there was a difference, however subtle, between good-natured and sweet-natured.

"Miss Carlisle," Henry said as his hand closed over hers. Marty braced himself, expecting his father to kiss it, or hold it too long, or bow over it. But apparently his father saw that this wasn't a woman to be trifled with.

Although Marty had met a lot of women as a celebrity, had even been married to one, there were many things about women that still remained a mystery to him. But he had learned that no matter who the woman was or where you found her, one quality about her was usually clear. Either you could con her or you couldn't.

He wasn't the kind of man who ever tried, but he'd seen many men who did and observed the women on whom they worked their spells. This one would sprinkle liars on her breakfast cereal.

"And, Mr. Hale." She turned her attention to him. Her grip was firm, though her skin was soft and her smile was genuine. That was something a camera always caught, he thought absently. Honesty.

"For the purposes of our discussion," his father said, moving to the small chintz-covered sofa she'd indicated before she crossed the room to pick up the tray of cups and coffeepot, "I'm Henry and my son is Martin."

Sitting across from them in a chair that matched the sofa, she poured. "I'm Shannon."

As she offered a cup to Henry, he asked irrepressibly, "May I ask what the *T* is for?"

She smiled and shook her head, the gesture indicating self-deprecation rather than an unwillingness to answer. "Tiffany."

Henry raised an eyebrow.

"I know." She passed a steaming cup to Marty. "It's disgraceful to name a child after a jewelry store, but like Truman Capote's Holly Golightly, my mother loved Tiffany's." She smiled again, sitting back with her own cup. "Actually, I've always been grateful she didn't have fond feelings for Van Cleef and Arpels."

Henry laughed and, with an artful combination of charm and seriousness that Marty admired, sat back and began to talk business.

He asked questions for which he already had answers in the very complete file Marty had helped him compile before they'd even approached her about the purchase. Marty didn't wonder what he was doing. He knew the poker-playing posturing was a part of all business negotiations.

Listening intently to Shannon's answers, Marty noted that she was honest and accurate. She exaggerated nothing, inflated no figures, minimized no problems. Sales were only moderately good, the building needed extensive work, the bookkeeping and inventory systems had to be updated.

Henry nodded. "I'm sure," he began slowly, looking into his coffee cup, then up at her, "that it's hard for you to let Carlisle's go."

Shannon took only a moment to draw a steadying breath. That observation wasn't something she'd expected. She knew Henry Hale's reputation as a shrewd businessman. His expression of concern over her loyalty to the store widened her eyes and straightened her spine.

"So far, Mr. Hale," she said quietly and with a smile, "I'm only considering letting it go."

With a large hand, Henry turned his cup in its saucer, then spoke a figure that was considerably in excess of what he had originally planned to offer. "Would that help you decide?"

With that generous offer hanging between them, Shannon found her mind running in two separate directions. Half was thinking that there would be enough to retire her father's personal debts, set her up in a small boutique and still leave her in comfortable circumstances.

But the other, more skeptical, half was wondering if he was playing some game with her that she didn't understand, or if that overly generous offer included a stipulation that she never set foot in Carlisle's again, leaving him the clear field that was so important to a store undergoing a change in its image.

"Are you trying to buy me out of your hair, Mr. Hale?" she asked directly.

"Actually—" he put his cup on the table, stood, walked to the lace-curtained window, then turned around "—I'm trying to buy you into it."

As he turned back to the view of the busy Portland street, Shannon swung her gaze to Marty, looking for an explanation.

He simply shrugged and smiled. "I don't get the point, either," he said, "but it's bound to be interesting."

"My point," Henry said, casting a quelling glance at his son before leveling dark eyes on Shannon, "is that if we can come to terms, I'd like you to stay on as assistant manager. That figure included your salary for next year."

Shannon did some quick mental calculations, subtracting the market value of Carlisle's from the figure Henry Hale had proposed. She concluded that she would be making as much as her father had when Carlisle's was in its prime—and she'd always thought him overpaid.

She controlled her delight at the prospect of staying on at Carlisle's, and made herself remember all the other things for which she had to fight.

"I would love to stay here," she admitted, the truth of that softening her negotiating stance, "but so would everyone else. I have an excellent staff, from Gale Hunter, my assistant, through every department, to the janitorial team."

"They would stay, of course," Henry said, riffling through a file he'd brought with him. Finding the sheet he was searching for, he ran his index finger along a column of figures. "As long as they prove themselves good employees. They do have benefits seldom found in department store personnel, however. That's heavy overhead."

"It pays off."

Henry looked up at her. "Loyalty can't keep a store in business."

Shannon looked at Henry. "Then why did Hale Stores add retirement benefits to their personnel package two years ago? I checked. Hale people are treated very well."

Only an inclination of his head betrayed Henry's surprise. "It was good business."

"Inspiring loyalty by letting your employees know you care about them *is* good business," Shannon said, putting her cup down. "I wouldn't consider turning Carlisle's over to someone who wouldn't take care of my people."

Henry nodded slowly. "I don't pamper my staff quite as much as you do, but I respect them and see that they're well provided for. All right. The benefit program would stand."

Shannon smiled and offered her hand across the table. "Then you may buy my store, Mr. Hale."

Giving her a firm handshake, Henry turned to his son. "You could learn something from this woman, Martin."

Having observed the exchange between his father and this unusual woman, Marty despaired of ever understanding business. "I gather that's the plan."

Shannon turned her attention to the younger Hale, remembering something Henry had said earlier that hadn't quite registered at the time. Martin Hale looked at her with a reluctance that seemed to contain an element of amusement. Confused, she turned back to Henry. "You said I would be *assistant* manager."

Henry nodded. "Martin will move out from Bend to take over as manager of the Portland Hale's."

Chapter Two

"Can you live with that?" Henry asked, noting her less than delighted expression.

For the first time, Shannon took a long, hard look at Martin Hale. She remembered Gale's injunction to think of him in his underwear, but found it impossible. All his considerable physical attributes so enticingly revealed in the poster were now sheathed in a Perry Ellis three-piece suit of gray wool—and in their concealment were strangely even more enticing.

Or they would have been had she been able to concentrate on them. Instead, she looked into blue eyes under thick, straight, sun-streaked brows that matched a rich, slightly curly head of hair, and into a smile that was boyish and reached into one's soul like every good Madison Avenue smile. She observed that his chin was as square as his shoulders, whose considerable proportions balanced the length of his legs. And she thought, with a moment's indignation, *A football jock with a Marlboro Man face is going to tell me how to run my business.*

Then she remembered two things. Firstly, it would no longer be her business—sad but true. And secondly, she had gotten more out of her deal with Henry Hale than she had dared hope. She had no right to balk or to complain. Besides, if Martin Hale remained as quiet as he had been this morning, she might be able to work around him.

Shannon nodded. "Of course."

Henry turned to his son. "And you, Martin?"

Marty smiled into Shannon's carefully neutral expression, his guileless blue eyes flickering with some deep down clarity that made her shift in her chair, startled, feeling as though her private thoughts had been glimpsed.

Then Marty turned to his father. "I can live with her." His gaze swung back to Shannon, his smile innocently apologetic as he amended, "Pardon me. I meant that I can live with *it*. The situation."

"Of course," she said again, her expression as bland as his.

Henry looked from Marty to Shannon and stood. "Yes, well, if you can round up that nice little Miss Hunter to show me around the store, Miss Carlisle, I'll leave Martin with you to talk over the details of administration. And you'll have to find him some office space."

Shannon tried not to panic. This was all moving faster than she had imagined. In the space of half an hour she'd gone from a nearly penniless proprietor of a department store to a high-income assistant manager of a store in the West Coast's major chain. But with the new security came the complete disruption of her work life. She was moving down a peg, and would probably have to wet-nurse a superior who assuredly knew more about touchdowns, first downs, and all those other strange statistics football fanatics kept than he did about the business he'd be running.

"Very well." Shannon went to the phone and paged Gale, explaining Henry Hale's wishes. Sounding delighted, Gale rapped on Shannon's office door a moment later.

"Well, Miss Hunter." Henry put an arm around Gale's shoulders in a gesture that was supposed to convey harmless, avuncular attention, but made Shannon wonder if her co-worker was safe.

Gale, however, taking the man's arm, didn't appear the least concerned as she led him out the door with a wave over her shoulder for Shannon and Marty.

"I can't promise that he won't pinch her," Marty said, taking note of Shannon's concern. "But she's in no more serious danger than that."

Shannon turned to him, wondering if there was some kind of readout in her eyes that told him what she was thinking.

He shrugged with an expression of amused innocence, confirming her suspicion. "I've learned to read the defense and get right through it. I guess it's like a sixth sense."

"Yes." Shannon folded her arms and sat on the edge of her desk, the skirt of her dress swirling, then settling around her shins. "I understand you were a football star."

Unbuttoning his jacket, Marty took the wicker chair that faced her desk. "Actually, I never quite achieved star status. I was more of an astronomical disturbance."

"Gale tells me your team won the NFL championship."

He nodded. "But not because of me."

"You played for eleven years. You must have been doing something right."

He frowned at her. "You do your research as thoroughly as my father does. I suppose you know about my three years of endorsements and modeling."

"When your face has been in a national advertising campaign," she said, "you can't expect to hide it." It wasn't his face one remembered, she thought absently, though it *was* rather perfect. As he studied her face from his chair, she had a sneaking suspicion he'd read that thought, also.

"If you're blessed with a sixth sense," Shannon said, walking around the desk, trying to get the conversation back on a business level, "you'll be grateful for it. The demands on a manager are—"

About to sit behind her desk, Shannon remembered what Henry Hale had said about finding office space for his son. Since the man facing her would be taking over as manager, it was logical that this office should be his. She wondered if she should be sitting behind her desk. "Do you...?" she began, indicating her chair.

"No," he replied before she could finish. "I don't want your chair or your office. I'm sure we can find something else suitable. Please sit down."

Shannon complied, thinking that for a man with such a look of unassuming innocence, his manner of gaining control of a situation was insidious. Beside his forceful and gregarious father, he appeared quiet, almost uninterested. But she suspected that he was quiet out of respect for his father's position. When he was alone, Martin Hale was certainly, however charmingly, assertive.

"What makes you think I can't do it?" he asked.

She pulled her chair in and crossed her legs. "What?"

"Manage the store."

Shannon sighed. She could deny she'd thought that, but she was now convinced she wouldn't fool him. She replied as evenly as she could, "Because football and modeling can't have prepared you for what you'll face here."

He took that dose of honesty without the hurt feelings she expected. Actually, he seemed quite amused by her observation; the blue eyes that observed so much also revealed a lot.

"You're right, I'm sure. But I might have skills heretofore untapped, some business genius built into the Hale genes."

Shannon let her eyes run over him and saw only the handsome model. "I suppose that could be possible," she lied.

He laughed, the sound genuine, not at all strained. "Then take comfort in your being here to guide me along, and my willingness to do my best. If you show me a little patience, extend me the courtesy of having a little faith in me, I'm sure you'll find me an able pupil."

Shannon fought the guilt he stirred in her. There was too much money at stake here, too many people involved, too much of herself at risk to trust the store to a man who didn't know what he was doing.

Then she remembered how her father had thought that about her, how imprisoned she had felt by his refusal to recognize her skills, how selfish she had thought him because he would never give her a chance.

She looked up at Marty, parting her lips to speak.

"Apology accepted," he said. "Any suggestions as to where I can find a place to live?"

Shannon gave up being surprised by his intuitiveness and concentrated on his question. Remembering his divorced status, she suggested, "There are some beautiful condos near the river, apartments all over the place..."

"I'm looking for a house. A nice neighborhood."

A little surprised by that preference when he'd probably be spending most of his time at the store, Shannon nodded and made no comment on it. "Gale's mother is a real estate agent. If you'd like, I can give you her number. I'm sure she could find something for you. Ah... when... will you be taking over?"

"In about two weeks." Marty got to his feet and wandered around the office, pausing to study a grouping of watercolors hung over the sofa. They were all of carousel horses. He moved to the window and studied the traffic below for a moment before turning and slowly walking back across the carpet. "I wish you wouldn't think of it as my 'taking over.' It's obvious from my father's research and the visible product on the three floors below us that you're an excellent manager. I look forward to learning a lot from you." He settled into the chair again and gave her that guileless smile. "But not if you continue to look at me as though I've fumbled on the five-yard line."

Even Shannon, who'd never watched a complete football game in her life and only caught the fever at Super Bowl time like other Americans, could understand his reference.

She leaned back in her chair, more unsettled by his good-natured serenity than annoyed by it. "I apologize again," she said without hesitation.

When he drew a breath that made her suspect he might feel as frustrated as she did, she went on. "Please understand that it's nothing personal. I grew up in this store. I've clerked in every department and done every job from receiving to cashiering. I lived for the day when it would be mine."

She gave him a dry grin that was more a gesture of acceptance than complaint. "When you've wanted something your whole life, three years is a very short time to live that dream."

Knowing that better than most people, Marty nodded. "That's easy to understand."

"Not that I have a right to complain," she went on. "I'm delighted that a company with such a fine reputation as Hale's has bought Carlisle's and that I've been allowed to stay on." She paused and added with a graceful tilt of her head that asked him to continue to understand. "It's just a little hard to step down for you."

"You don't have to step down," he said, "just...aside...to give me a little room. If the title of assistant is bothering you, we—"

"It isn't!" she said more harshly than she'd intended.

Appearing unconvinced, he began again, "We could—"

"It isn't!" Getting to her feet behind the desk, Shannon frowned down into his mildly surprised expression and slapped a pencil she'd been holding on to the desktop. "If I gave you that impression, I'm sorry. I don't care about the title. I only care about the store. I'm having a perfectly normal, emotional reaction to...to..."

"To knowing that it now belongs to somebody else," he finished for her. "I understand. I didn't mean to imply anything with the suggestion that we change your title."

Shannon merely nodded, knowing she'd felt petty about her reservations before he'd even suggested the title change. His offer had simply confirmed for her that her reaction was selfish.

"Nobody wants to go backward in a career," Marty said. "Personally, I'm getting used to it. Starting over is getting to be what I do best." With a smile that was more charming than innocent, he got to his feet. "Want to show me around?"

Shannon stood, too. "Of course. We'll start with this floor to see if there's a suitable office for you."

"WE STORE OUR NEW ZEALAND wool rugs, linens, and wool coats in here because it's drier than the basement, even though we make a special effort to keep the temperature constant."

Shannon flipped a light switch to reveal a room slightly larger than her office. Plastic covered a tier of rugs and several rolling racks of coats. A doorless closet across the room was filled with packaged linens.

She waved a hand toward the wall of curtained windows that protected the merchandise against the danger of fading by the sun. "You'd have a wonderful view of the hot dog stand across the street." She smiled. Marty noted that Shannon was relaxing as she moved around the store she loved so much. "That ought to remind you of your days on the football field."

Returning her smile, he crossed the room to look down to where she had pointed. Under a brightly colored umbrella, a vendor passed a hot dog to a waiting customer. Letting the drapes fall closed, he surveyed the well-protected stock and shook his head.

"I'd hate to take a chance on risking such high-ticket items by moving them elsewhere." He indicated that she should pass before him out the door, and he flipped off the light. "And I have enough aches and pains to remind me of my days on the field."

His comment had an ironic sound, but in the dim hallway Shannon couldn't see his expression. Wondering about that remark, she led the way down another corridor and went into a room that was half the size of her office. Being on the corner and behind the large Carlisle's sign that identified the store at quite a distance, it had only one window.

Marty walked to the middle of the room and looked around.

"No view of the hot dog stand," Shannon said, leaning against the doorjamb. "But it is right over the store's restaurant. A couple of years ago I did our inventory analysis in this room. On *Potage Parmentier* day, it's enough to send you into an eating frenzy."

Hands in his pockets, the tails of his jacket thrown back, Marty turned to her with a questioning look. "How's that again?"

"Our chef is French. Every Thursday during the winter she makes French potato soup with leeks, carrots, celery and lots of onions and cream. It's fantastic. The shoppers love it, and so do I. I always switch lunch hours with Gale so I can get there before it's gone."

He smiled at the chink in her armor of elegance. "A passion for onions and high-calorie food, huh?" Frowning suddenly, he walked back to her. "Why didn't you use your office to do the inventory analysis?"

"I didn't have it then," she explained, turning off the light and closing the door. "My father did and his assistant had Gale's office. Gale and I worked on the sales floor."

He followed her around a corner and down another corridor. "Then how did you end up with the ugly task of inventory analysis?"

She stopped to look at him in surprise. "Why ugly? It's exciting to organize the figures we keep all year and to analyze them. If you do it correctly, you can read them as clearly as words on a page."

Marty, who found his family's business interesting, and even exciting from the standpoint of promotion and presentation, had always hated the numbers, though he understood how important they were.

He started to move on, grinning at Shannon over his shoulder. "Like I said earlier, you'll have to stick by me. Especially when it comes to figures. What's in here?"

"Stock return."

A quick glance into the room of stock that was either damaged, outdated or being returned for credit revealed a space so filled with goods, paperwork and boxes that it would have taken days and probably a government edict to clear it out. He quickly closed the door.

"It has no windows, anyway," she said.

He studied her as she walked beside him. "A passion for potato soup *and* windows?"

She smiled. "When you're in charge of something, you should have a view of the world. Prevents you from making narrow decisions."

They had reached the elevators. With a melodic *ping*, the doors parted, freeing Gale and Henry, who were both laughing uproariously.

"Oh, good," Henry said, composing himself, his arm still around Gale's shoulders. "There you are. Are you two ready for lunch?"

"We were just going to tour the store," Marty said.

"You can do that after lunch. Gale says there's a great Scottish place down the block."

Marty looked doubtful. "Scottish? Haggis and stuff like that?"

Gale laughed. "No. Sandwiches and salads mostly."

Marty turned to Shannon. "All right with you?"

"Of course." She pointed across the hall to her office, where her phone was ringing. "I'll answer that and get my coat."

"We'll meet you two there," Henry said, pressing the elevator button again. "Find an office, son?"

"There's a room down the hall," Marty explained, pointing in that direction. "It's behind the sign, but I think—"

"Oh, Mr. Hale," Gale protested, "that's too small."

He smiled. "I don't need that much room."

"But you'll be meeting with salesmen and suppliers." Gale frowned in the direction Shannon had left, then her smile ignited. "I know!"

"I'm not taking Shannon's office," Marty said, second-guessing her, or so he thought.

"No, but my office would be perfect. You'd have Shannon nearby, you could share her files and not clutter the smaller office with—"

The elevator doors parted, and Henry pulled Gale into the tiny car, interrupting his son's protest. "That idea has merit," he said. "We can discuss it at lunch."

Suddenly longing for the comparative quiet of a fourth down and nine, Marty wandered to Shannon's office door. Finding her hanging up the phone, he entered.

She walked toward him with her coat over her arm. "So you're afraid of haggis, are you?" she teased.

Taking the coat from her, he held it open. "A pudding made out of sheep innards has absolutely no appeal for me."

Shannon slipped her arms into the sleeves, laughing. "I quite agree. Despite my Scottish name, we had a French cook while I was growing up."

"Of course, there's a lot to be said for shortbread cookies."

"And scones."

Well, they did have food in common if nothing else, Marty thought as they waited for the elevator. As the doors parted, Marty held them open with one hand and reached for Shannon's arm with the other. It was a purely instinctive gesture of courtesy, a gentlemanly attempt to help her onto the rickety car, but she drew away. The slight movement of her arm put it beyond his reach, but it was deliberate nonetheless. The gesture was so at odds with her poise and self-assurance that he was surprised.

Confused about whether the source of her mild rebuff was personal or professional, Marty was further mystified when she glanced at him and said jokingly, as though nothing had happened, "The Scots also make excellent marmalade."

Thinking that their association looked as if it would certainly be interesting, Marty replied, "Their Chivas Regal isn't bad, either." And maybe he was going to need some.

Chapter Three

"So, it's settled." Gale pushed her empty plate away and smiled across the table at Marty. "You can have my office and we'll have Shannon's father's old desk and office furniture brought up from the basement for you. We'll have everything ready for you when you arrive." Then she frowned at Shannon, who sat beside him. "What'll we do about the walls when I take my floral prints with me?"

Shannon turned to Marty. "Do you have your own things you'd like to put up? Trophies? Awards?"

"I'd really rather Gale kept her office and I'll take—"

Caught up in Gale's enthusiasm, Shannon didn't hear his protest. She pointed at him with her teaspoon. "Downstairs with my father's things are some photographs of the old store—a sort of history of Carlisle's. I've wanted to do something with them for ages. They'd be appropriate in your office."

Marty nodded and spread his hands, abandoning his objections. "I give you free rein." Smiling across at his father, he said, "See how effectively I've taken charge?"

"Good work, son." Henry laughed, then sipped from his mug of coffee. "Delegating is the real art of management." He sobered and focused on Shannon. "Our initial plan was for Martin to take a good look around during the holiday season and assess where we should make structural changes. Then we were going to redecorate the store in theme with the rest of the chain. But now that I've seen it closely, I'd rather not do that. That mahogany would cost a mint these days, and the chandeliers that you have in the jewelry and fur departments are classic."

Shannon smiled. When she had toyed with the idea of simply selling out the store's stock, rather than selling the business, she'd been determined to find a place in her life for those chandeliers, even if she had to buy a house to do it. "We do have an elegance you can't find in a mall."

"That's true, and we want to preserve it. You and Marty can set up plans for the changes, and come January, we'll get it all under way. What do you think?"

Shannon nodded, finding nothing with which to disagree. "It sounds like a reasonable plan."

"Good. I'm leaving tonight, but Marty's staying an extra day to house-hunt. Gale's already called her mother, and she'll be meeting him this afternoon. He'll be back the second Monday in November."

Shannon thought Marty looked a little harassed as he nodded confirmation. She supposed, for someone who'd spent most of his adult life as a celebrity, the prospect of moving his residence and taking up an even more confining job than the usual nine-to-five would be demoralizing if not downright depressing. While smiling bracingly at Henry Hale, Shannon thought with a mental sigh that Marty appeared to be a nice person, but she had her work cut out for her to make him into a manager.

"SHANNON, I'M HERE." Ten-fifteen in the morning on the second Monday in November, Shannon sat on the corner of her desk and listened to the slightly distracted quality in Martin Hale's voice coming over the telephone. In the background a dog barked.

"You're supposed to be *here*," she pointed out, her emphasis on the word indicating the store.

"I know." He laughed with soft charm, but Shannon refused to be softened by it. An employee who was late on his first day made a bad impression. An employer who was late on his first day made no impression at all, and that was worse. Had she imagined the sincere, hard-working, honest man she'd thought she'd seen under the gloss of a great body and good looks? "Something's come up, and I can't come in today. Can you get along without me?"

A dozen sharp answers came to mind, but she bit them back.

He laughed again. "Go ahead and say it. You've been getting along without me for three years. You're thinking it so hard I can hear it."

"Actually, it's been longer than that." Her voice was amiable even if the words weren't. "Don't worry, I'll manage. Come in when you can."

"Thank you." His slightly ironic tone indicated that he'd heard the hint of sarcasm in her voice. "And I need a favor."

He was really pushing it, Shannon thought, but she was making a good salary, and her store and her sales force were intact. "What can I do for you?" she asked politely.

"Gale's mother was supposed to send in some papers with Gale, related to the closing of the deal on the house. I have to get them to the title company today."

Shannon had seen them on his desk that morning when she'd gone into the newly renovated office to see that every thing was in order. "They're on your desk."

"Good. Can you have someone bring them by?" He gave her an address in an old, upper-income-bracket neighborhood.

"Of course."

"Thanks, Shannon."

Shannon cradled the receiver and groaned aloud. She conceded to him that making a move was an exhausting, exasperating ordeal, but did it prevent him from driving to the store to pick up the forms he needed? She had always made a point of never asking an employee to run her personal errands. But she was no longer in charge here, she reminded herself as she reached for the ringing telephone.

A crisis in the glassware department resulting in several aisles full of shattered crystal kept Shannon busy until early afternoon. When she remembered that Martin Hale was waiting for his papers, she had to admit to a little retributional satisfaction. Then she hurriedly tried to find someone to make the delivery. But Gale was occupied with a new group of part-timers hired for the holidays, the store was too busy to justify taking anyone from the sales floor, and the stock people were overwhelmed with preholiday deliveries. Shannon was amused to find herself the most dispensable. Seeing that the clock now read 2:00 p.m., she took a cellophane wrapped basket of fruit and candy from the confections department and ran to her car.

Marty's house was a white post-Victorian, a plain but large two-story with a deep front lawn surrounded by a split-stake fence. In the driveway there was a dusty Dodge minivan. Shannon climbed six steps to the porch and stood amid a fortress of empty moving boxes while she rang the bell. The door opened, but she saw no one. Then a voice in the vicinity of her hipbone said, "Hi."

She looked down into a cherubic but pale face with a red nose and big blue eyes made even more enormous by their soupy quality. "I have a code," the boy said, carrying a battered stuffed monkey and a box of tissues. He was wearing fuzzy blue pajamas with feet, and Shannon guessed his age at about four. "What's that?"

"Ah . . ." Completely off guard, Shannon lowered the basket so that he could see inside. "Fruit and candy."

The boy looked from it to her hopefully. "For me?"

Suddenly the door opened wider and Marty appeared in jeans and a smudged gray sweatshirt with a tear at the neckline. For a moment Shannon had difficulty equating the man in front of her with the man with whom she'd talked business several weeks ago. Then he smiled, and he was suddenly very familiar. "Hi, Shannon. It was nice of you to bring the papers yourself." He swept the boy up onto his hip and urged her inside. "The place is an absolute disaster. Don't touch anything or you'll ruin your clothes." Furniture and boxes cluttered the large room. Shannon felt a pang of guilt at having had no sympathy for him this morning. To the boy, Marty said, "I thought you were in bed."

Ignoring that false assumption, the child pointed to the basket in Shannon's hand. "There's candy in there."

Shannon shifted and smiled. "A little welcome gift."

Marty looked pleasantly surprised. "Thank you." With his free hand, he pointed to the kitchen. "Want a cup of coffee? The chairs are safe to sit on. I wiped then down this morning for breakfast."

The large kitchen was slightly less chaotic than the living room. Boxes stood around, but the counters were clear and she saw when he opened a cupboard door for cups that the shelves were full. He poured expertly with one hand and put a yellow mug in front of her. "This is Joshua," he said, gently pinching the stomach of the child in his arms. The boy doubled over, giggling. "Josh, this is Shannon. She works at the store."

Josh gave her a moment's close scrutiny, then pointed a stubby finger at the basket. "Can I have some candy?"

Marty smiled apologetically and took the chair opposite her. "He has a one-track mind. An orange would probably be better for you, Josh, but let's see..." He removed the decorative bow, peeled back the cellophane and found a Toblerone bar. He opened it, snapped off a piece and handed it to Josh, who now straddled his knee.

Then he turned his attention to Shannon, and she felt the full impact of it with a start. His eyes were so blue. "Sorry about today. Josh was feverish this morning. Our housekeeper's moving out with us from Bend, but she's driving her own car and she needed an extra day to stop at her son's on the way. She's about to become a grandmother for the first time. I enrolled Josh in preschool, but I hated to leave him with strangers when he wasn't feeling well."

"Of course." Shannon wondered if the guilt she felt showed in her face. "Moving's such an ordeal anyway. I didn't realize you had a child. Do you want me to take these to the title company for you?"

Marty wondered at the slight flush of color in her cheeks. She'd probably thought he was goldbricking. He smiled at the thought, remembering his chaotic morning. "Thanks, but I should go myself. I've got a couple of questions to ask them. How are things at the store?"

"We had a crisis in Glassware this morning," she said, sipping from the mug. She paused and closed her eyes appreciatively as she swallowed the strong, hot brew. "Good coffee. Looks like one of your first duties will be filing an insurance claim."

He nodded, happy to not have to deal with that until tomorrow. "And how have you been?"

She was surprised by the question. "Fine. I'm always fine."

He smiled teasingly. "No traumatic reaction to having sold the store?"

She shrugged. "So far no one's been around to remind me that it's sold. Maybe once you're on the scene on a regular basis, trying to push me around, I'll snap and snarl at you. But so far no problem." Trying to redeem herself now that she knew he had a child, she heard herself suggest, "Look, do you want me to stay with Josh so you can get to the title company? I'm sure you don't want to take him outside with that cold."

He glanced at the clock. It was well after three. "God!" He put Josh on his feet, then stood, patting his pant pocket for keys. "I almost forgot. Are you sure you don't mind?"

"No, go ahead." Josh had chocolate all over his face, and Shannon busied herself by wetting a paper towel and wiping him off. Children usually made her nervous. It wasn't that she didn't like them, but she'd never been around them, and her own father had been cold and distant. Children were so physical, and she wasn't demonstrative by nature. Something painful jangled in her mind as that thought formed, but long practice allowed her to push it away before it could take shape. She could handle Josh for an hour or so. At the moment, he was less disturbing than his father.

"I'll be back in forty-five minutes," Marty promised, pulling on a jacket he'd taken from a row of pegs next to the kitchen's back door. "That okay with you, Josh?"

Josh, having his face washed, simply nodded. Marty watched the awkward way Shannon handled the task and frowned at her. "You sure you'll be okay?"

She straightened and frowned back at him. Josh took the opportunity to run to the television in the living room. "Do I look that inept?" she asked with a faint smile.

He grinned apologetically. "Frankly, yes."

She folded her arms. "Thank you and goodbye."

Tossing her a wave, and stopping to bestow a kiss on Josh, who was seated in an overstuffed chair, his gaze glued to cartoons, Marty loped out to the van.

"You want to sit with me?" Josh asked as Shannon wandered out from the kitchen. He pushed his tiny body into one corner of the chair and invited her to join him. When she looked doubtfully at the space left, he said confidently, "Dad sits here with me. There's lots of room."

Shannon squeezed into the space and watched the Ghostbusters save a small community from being slimed. By the time *Duck Tales* was over, Josh had made himself comfortable in her lap and was telling her in detail the various traits of the cartoon characters. She now had chocolate on her blouse and smudges from his feet on her skirt, but he was so sure of her willingness to hold him that she felt relieved. She seemed to have earned his friendship without having to do anything.

A sudden thump at the back door frightened her out of her complacency. "That's Tulip!" Josh scrambled out of her lap and ran for the kitchen. Shannon followed the boy, arriving in time to see him open the door to a mass of gray-and-white fur the size of a compact car that dived into the kitchen. It pranced with the enthusiasm of a ballerina and the grace of an elephant. Tulip was apparently a facetious name. After covering Josh with kisses, it leaped up on Shannon to do the same. She found herself looking into the eerily transparent gray eyes of a love-crazed malamute.

"Down!" Shannon said firmly, deciding that showing weakness in the presence of incisors three inches long would be fatal. Tulip, apparently sensitive to the tone of her voice, got down and stood behind Josh, whining.

"She gets a dog biscuit when she comes in," Josh told Shannon. Then he pointed to a high cabinet. "I think Daddy put them up there."

Shannon opened the cupboard and craned her head back to look all the way up. The dog barked. Nothing immediately identifiable as a box of dog biscuits was visible. She closed the door. "Well, you just moved here, Josh," she said, shooing the boy toward the living room. "Maybe Tulip will understand that we don't know where they are."

Tulip barked twice, a sound Shannon interpreted as "Fat chance!" The dog sat, staring at the cupboard, and barked again. Josh scampered off to his place in the big chair, leaving Shannon to deal with Tulip.

WHEN MARTY CAME HOME, Josh was contentedly watching cartoons, another piece of chocolate in his hands and on his face, and Shannon was standing on the countertop in her stockinged feet. Unaware of his presence, she rummaged through a top shelf on tiptoe. Distracted by her well-turned ankle in sheer black hose, and the soft curve of her calf that disappeared invitingly into the folds of her plaid skirt, Marty stared at her.

"Who's that?" "Radical, Dad!" and "Outstanding genetic engineering!" came simultaneously from behind him, jarring him out of his lazy perusal.

Startled, too, Shannon spun around, forgetting the narrow space she was standing on, and pitched forward. As Marty reached up quickly to get a firm grip on her waist and swing her to the floor, she saw three young boys behind him, staring up at her in surprise. "What are you doing?" he asked when she was safely on the floor.

His hands still at her waist, the fingers widespread and warm, and three faces so much like his peering over his shoulder made it difficult for her to answer.

But Tulip spoke for herself. The taller of the three boys reached into the overhead cupboard on the other side of the sink and tossed a large biscuit to the dog. Plumy tail wagging, biscuit proudly in its teeth, the dog pranced into the living room.

Shannon smiled thinly, pointing to the cabinet she'd been ransacking. "Josh thought they were over here."

Marty took in her stained and rumpled clothes, her disheveled hair. "What happened?"

"Nothing, I...Josh was in my lap. Then the dog jumped on me..."

She looked out of her element, he thought, like a rose in a pot of ivy. "I'm sorry." He put a finger on a smudge of chocolate on her shoulder. "I'll have it cleaned for you."

She waved away his offer with a sweep of her hand. "Oh, Joanie in Alterations can get rid of anything."

"Put a tissue under it and rub it with talcum," the boy to his right said. "The magnesium carbonate will absorb the stain."

Shannon blinked at the scientific explanation. Marty put an arm around the boy's shoulder and pulled him forward for an introduction. "This is Jarrod, my second son. A science freak, but also a scientific genius. He's fifteen."

Jarrod mimed a theatrical bow, turning right and then left, murmuring, "Thank you, thank you." His hair was darker than Marty's but he had the same blue eyes.

"That's Evan, sixteen." The tall boy who had thrown Tulip the biscuit looked Shannon over once with open suspicion. A replica of Marty, his approaching maturity gave him strong, angular features. He appeared more intense than his father, less relaxed. He put his hand out. Though Shannon sensed he'd taken an instant dislike to her, she had to admire his manners. "He's going to Stanford next year, and he's working on the great American novel.

"Grady, here, is thirteen," Marty went on, pulling the third boy from behind him. Grady was already showing signs of being thickly built. His hair was honey-colored and there was a trace of green in his blue eyes. "He hopes to take over for Bobby Unser in about ten years."

Bobby Unser, Shannon thought, trying to identify the name. Bobby Unser . . .

"He's a race car driver," Grady said helpfully, apparently reading her expression. His smile was warm, like his father's. Shannon saw Evan and Jarrod exchange a pitying shake of their heads.

"I hope I didn't keep you too long," Marty said. "I thought I'd pick the boys up. They were going to come home by bus, but we weren't sure about the schedules and I was near the school."

"Don't make a habit of it, Dad," Jarrod said, clapping Marty's shoulder. "You're going to have the guys think we're dorks."

"We are dorks," Grady said.

Jarrod turned to him patiently. "But we should try to keep it to ourselves as long as possible."

To Shannon, the small room seemed suddenly, overwhelmingly male. She took a swift look around, saw four faces looking at her with varying degrees of perplexity and felt as though she had blundered into a men's locker room. The only species that made her more uncomfortable than children was men. "Well..." She smiled, trying hard to hide her discomfort. "Welcome to Portland, all of you." Then she focused on Marty. "And you'll be in tomorrow morning?"

"Right." The boys began to move around the kitchen, opening the refrigerator, throwing open the cupboards in what looked like a desperate search for food. Marty pulled her into the living room. "When they get into a feeding frenzy, you could be killed. You're sure you're okay?" He ran a hand lightly up and down her back in a solicitous gesture. She arched her back to relieve the contact, then stepped out of his reach.

At the door Shannon turned to face him, forcing a smile in place. "Well, welcome to Portland," she said, then remembered she'd just said that. She cleared her throat and tried to appear businesslike. "Your office is ready, and I think everything's in order for you."

"I'm sure it is." She had hoped he'd wave her off from the porch, but he walked her down the steps as he spoke. "I'm sure you've been very efficient." Marty watched her over the top of the car as she went around to the driver's side and opened the door. He simply couldn't figure her. Just as she had that morning on the elevator, she'd deliberately withdrawn from his touch. Yet her manner was warm. She'd become a little nervous when he'd arrived home with the boys, but that was understandable. Sometimes they were enough to make *him* nervous.

Before getting into the car she looked at him over the roof as though she were about to say something. Then she apparently changed her mind and got into the car. Marty ducked down and waved. "Thanks again for the basket," he called.

She nodded, waved and drove away.

Shy or cold? he wondered as he strolled back up the walk. As closely as they'd be working together, he imagined it wouldn't be long before he had an answer.

Chapter Four

"Poole pretends to be a dragon," Shannon warned quietly as she and Marty approached the books and stationery department. "She's been here for forty years and seems to feel she's entitled to speak her mind. If she says something rude to you, try to remember that she's the one who always makes it to work whatever the weather, that she submits the most accurate inventory of any department, and that she offered to work for me without pay for six weeks when my father died and I had to deal with payables that were five months overdue. I didn't take her up on it, of course, but that's the way she is."

Clarissa Poole weaved her way toward them through table displays of sale books and standing racks of marked-down office items. Her plain, long-sleeved dress in an unfortunate shade of green served to seal Shannon's image of a dragon in Marty's mind. The picture was reinforced by dyed blond hair pulled back into a bun whose disheveled construction gave it the look of the jagged crests on a dragon's head. She had a formidable bosom, spindly ankles and a blue gaze so direct that Marty knew she would challenge rather than greet him.

Shannon made the simple introduction and Marty offered his hand. Clarissa Poole shook it in a sturdy grip and took his measure. "Pleased to meet you, Mr. Hale. I hope you're not planning to turn Carlisle's into a rubber-stamp image of every other glitzy mall department store."

Shannon stood back, interested to see how the new manager would perform here. With his good looks and innocent charm he had devastated all the pretty young things in Cosmetics, Junior Wear and Lingerie this morning at the beginning of his introduction tour. Even the young men in the Rogue Shop had fallen victim to the appeal of his easy manner. But he had dealt with them using his old locker room, before-the-camera skills. Those would do him little good in a confrontation with the Dragon, and Shannon waited, prepared to step in and rescue him should that prove necessary.

Marty smiled at Clarissa. "I'm not. That would be a crime." He wandered through the department, critically studying the racks and displays. "Carlisle's uniqueness is one of its most valuable assets. That—" he turned to Clarissa, who had followed him "—and the supportive attitude of its staff."

Clarissa glanced at Shannon. Deep in Clarissa's sharp eyes, Marty saw the apparent affection. "Shannon has earned loyalty and respect." Clarissa turned back to him, and he could easily read in her expression what she left unsaid. He would have to earn it, as well.

He nodded, leaning back against the edge of a table. "I can see that." He folded his arms, prepared to linger a while. "Well, Mrs. Poole, if you had free rein to make changes in this department, what would you do?"

"That's easy," she replied. "I'd take a thousand more feet of space. The front covers of books should be displayed, and I haven't enough room to do that. I'd put in a rack of classics, more category fiction, and another, less formal, line of greeting cards." Clarissa sighed, enthusiasm blunted by reality. "But I'm flanked by Leather Goods on one side, and Glassware on the other, both carrying higher ticket items than my department. I know there isn't room for that."

Marty straightened, looking around, then up. Shannon and Clarissa did the same. "What if we built you a gallery?" He went to the wall that flanked one side of the department and put a long, slender hand against it. Both women came up beside him. "Do you have an in-house carpenter, Shannon, or do you hire out?"

"Frankly, we haven't had much of a budget for carpentry," she replied. "But the few things we've done we've hired out."

"We'll ask Gale about it. Her mother could probably recommend someone." Marty turned to Clarissa. "What do you think, Mrs. Poole? The gallery could even run the length of the wall from Glassware all the way over to Leather Goods. Would the stairs be a problem for you?"

Clarissa, flushed with enthusiasm, squared her shoulders and gave him a sudden, sturdy smack on his forearm. "And I was just beginning to think you'd work out. I swim from six to seven every other morning at the Y, and on alternate mornings I use an exercycle. You build me that gallery," Clarissa said, "and I'll slide down the banister."

Marty turned to Shannon. "Make a note to put a nurse on staff," he said with a straight face.

"What do you read?" Clarissa demanded suddenly.

Knowing that the answer to that question would probably make or break him in the Dragon's eyes, Marty considered tossing out some erudite author, then bravely told the truth. "Robert Parker. Dick Francis."

She considered him for a long moment, then a small smile formed on her bright red lips and she nodded. "Welcome to Carlisle's, Mr. Hale."

Marty returned the smile. "It's the Portland Hale's now, Mrs. Poole."

She looked at him another moment, then nodded at that, too. "Call me Clarissa."

"That'll cost a bundle," Shannon warned as they rode the escalator to the coffee shop.

"We've got a generous remodeling budget. Do you think it's a bad idea? Shannon?"

She stood a step above Marty and looked downward slightly into his eyes. For a moment their color and clarity made her lose track of her thought.

"No," she said quickly, looking away from him. "I think it's a brilliant idea. I've wanted to do something to expand that department for years, and a gallery never once occurred to me." She gave him a quick glance and a wry smile before turning to step off the escalator. "Even if it had," she added as he stepped off beside her, "I wouldn't have had the capital to do anything about it. Ready for lunch?"

"I'm famished." He grinned and followed her to the dining room decorated in floral patterns of pink and green. Tied-back ruffled curtains revealed a wall of windows that looked onto downtown Portland. "Taking on dragons uses up one's reserves."

As the pretty dark-haired hostess led them to a table, Shannon gave him a dry glance. "You could have done it with one hand tied behind your back. I fully expected her to eat you alive or, at the very least, that I'd have to support your singed body back to your office. Yet here you are, topping her list of heroes."

Marty stopped a lazy perusal of the menu and glanced up at her, half amused, half confused. "You're still not sure about me, are you?"

She shrugged, smiling to soften the honesty. "I've just never seen anyone operate with such charm. My grandmother was a lot like Poole, straightforward and outspoken, but she knew what she was doing. My father didn't really care about anyone, so he used people and rode over them as it suited him. He made no pretense of caring or being kind. Unfortunately, he *didn't* know what he was doing. If he hadn't died when he did, he'd have killed Carlisle's. And I..." Shannon shrugged again. "I haven't a grain of charm in me. I know what it takes to get the job done and I do it. I'm usually too busy to think about every word and to try to make my orders appealing rather than demanding."

"If that were true," Marty said, "you wouldn't have a store full of people who smile at you behind your back, and Clarissa wouldn't give a damn about you."

Shannon smiled at that, closing her menu. "No one's ever called her Clarissa. She's been Poole for as long as I can remember, or the Dragon. You've made an important conquest there."

"Good." He leaned back as a waitress set gold-rimmed white china cups before them and filled them with coffee. "I'm sure I'll need friends. Are we touring upstairs this afternoon?"

"Right. Linens, Kitchen Shop, Furniture and Appliances. How is your office, by the way? Do you have everything you need?" Shannon watched Marty study his menu with concentration.

"I think so. I didn't spend much time in it this morning before we started touring the store." He spoke absently, then closed the menu and focused on Shannon. "I like the old Carlisle's photos, though. I presume the rather sober lady in the big hat and the ankle-length dress is your grandmother?"

"Yes." A reflective smile curved Shannon's lips. "Eugenie Beulieu Carlisle. She was only twenty-six when my grandfather died and she took over the running of Carlisle's by herself. She held it together and made it through the war when it was so hard to get goods to sell, then turned it into *the* place to shop during the boom years."

The waitress returned to take their order, then Marty leaned back to study Shannon. "So you get your business acumen from your grandmother?"

"I get the love of it from her." She sipped at her coffee. "I had classes in all phases of business, but she had instinct. Some inherent propensity for second-guessing the customer guided her all those years, and I don't think she ever made a wrong move, at least not a serious one."

Remembering what she'd said earlier, Marty asked cautiously, "But your father didn't inherit that gift?"

Shannon sighed, coming out of the pleasant memories, apparently making a choice not to indulge the unpleasant ones. "He was spoiled and selfish and probably somewhat ignored. He grew up with the best of everything, but my grandmother was very busy during those years and my father spent a lot of time away at school. He told me he resented having to work summers in the store. He came to hate it."

"Why didn't he pursue some other career?"

Shannon shrugged. "He'd have probably hated that, too. Who knows? He wasn't a particularly happy individual, either with his circumstances or the people in his life. He finally drove my mother away when I was seven."

Marty digested that information in silence, remembering how important his mother had been to him when he'd been seven years old, how important she'd remained to him throughout his teen years. Even as an adult, as a husband and a father, he'd turned to her for the unqualified love and patient wisdom he could find nowhere else. Her death had taken something from him that nothing and no one could replace. But Shannon's mother had simply walked away. That must have been doubly painful.

"I'm sorry," he said sincerely.

She sighed philosophically. "Even at seven I understood her choice. Had I had the option to leave, *I'd* have taken it."

Marty was sure it had to hurt more than that, but the coffee shop during lunch was not the time or place to press the issue. "Did the stains come out of your skirt and blouse?"

It took her a moment to catch up with him. "Stains? Oh, from Josh. I'm sure they will. I left it with Alterations. I presume Josh was better today?"

Marty nodded, laughing. "Definitely. He was up at five-thirty. I called the preschool, told them he had a cold, and they said to bring him down anyway, that they have a couple of rooms set aside to separate sniffly kids from those who are well. Every single parent's dream."

Their food arrived, a spinach salad for Shannon and *poulet à la crème* for Marty. His eyes widened at the elegantly presented dish as he inhaled the aroma of the rich cream sauce redolent of brandy and nutmeg.

Shannon grinned at him as he cut a bite and closed his eyes over the exquisite flavor. "You're going to want to nap this afternoon instead of tour two more floors."

"Have you *tasted* this?" he asked.

"Yes, that's why I stick to salad. I'd be buying my clothes in the Big and Beautiful Shop in no time."

Half an hour later, after short, stout Emelienne had come out of the kitchen to introduce herself to the new manager, been praised elaborately for her elegant dish and had kissed Marty on both cheeks and returned, glowing, to the kitchen, Shannon shook her head at Marty. "Now that you've also conquered the dining room, can we go back to work, sir?"

He heaved a satisfied sigh. "I feel like I've been awarded the Croix de Guerre by General de Gaulle." He warned Shannon teasingly, "Don't call me 'sir,' or you'll find yourself scheduled for Sunday afternoons."

Downing the last of her coffee, Shannon dismissed the threat with a wave of her hand. "I always work Sunday, anyway."

He frowned at her. "Can't you delegate that?"

"I don't want to. Those who have families like to be home with them. It's just another day to me."

Marty studied her, thinking how sad that was. On Sunday afternoons in Bend, he and the boys went skiing, or played football, or baseball, or whatever the season would allow. In the evening they made sandwiches and sprawled around the television. Invariably the easy intimacy brought out some small problem one of the boys had had during the week and allowed him to offer a solution or, when he couldn't come up with one, to give at least his support and understanding. Sundays were family days, but Shannon Carlisle was all alone in the world.

"This Sunday," he suggested casually, "I think you should trade hours with someone and spend it with me and the kids."

She looked shocked and a little horrified, but he held her gaze, unimpressed. "I couldn't do that," she said after a moment. "I mean, it's kind of you, but...we...we just can't have that ... in the store."

His confused frown deepened. "Have what?" he asked. "I was thinking of lunch and a few hours of Trivial Pursuit, not mud wrestling."

Feeling silly, she leaned back against her chair with an affronted look, blaming him. "I wasn't suggesting anything of the kind. I just mean that it isn't ... healthy ... for store morale if the manager and the assistant manager spend time together after hours."

Marty grinned. "That sounds like something your grandmother with the forbidding look and the big hat might have said."

Shannon patted her lips with her linen napkin and drew her dignity around her like a shield. "It's only good business sense."

"Oh, come on," he said gently, pushing his plate away. A glance up at her as he signed the tab told her he didn't believe her. "It's fear of the unknown, isn't it?"

She walked ahead of him out of the restaurant, stiff-backed, until they reached the elevator. "It isn't fear of anything," she insisted in a reasonable voice as they waited.

"You don't want the staff talking about you when you've just arrived."

The elevator doors parted and a gaggle of girls from Cosmetics and Lingerie got off. As Shannon held the door, they swarmed around Marty, talking and laughing until he extricated himself to get onto the elevator, shooing them toward the dining room. The doors closed and Marty pushed the fourth-floor button.

"They wouldn't find you half so appealing if you weren't eligible," Shannon said, watching her feet as the elevator rose. "You wouldn't want to do anything to botch that, would you?"

As a man who'd been plagued by groupies most of his life, Marty had learned early to dismiss what they thought. The attention was flattering, sometimes even fun, but if he had to behave in a particular way to earn it, he could easily do without it. He didn't see why life as a department store manager should be any different.

Still, he decided to change tactics. Shannon did have a more formal approach to business than he, but he wasn't convinced that she believed everything she'd told him. There was an attraction between them, or perhaps whatever it was couldn't be that clearly defined. He liked her, and he knew that her appeal for him was more than intelligence and good business sense. He was fairly sure that she found him interesting but was determined to keep the store between them to insure against any kind of involvement. Something or someone had made her skittish. Under that businesslike reserve, he was beginning to see loneliness and an occasional glimpse of fear. The loneliness was easy to understand, but he wondered what motivated the fear.

Well, reverse psychology sometimes worked on his boys. Shannon was more mature and smarter, of course, but children or adults with a problem tended to have the same vulnerabilities. Perhaps he could work that to his advantage.

"You're probably right," he said finally. The doors parted on the fourth floor, and he and Shannon stepped off side by side. He saw her quick glance at him as he headed toward their offices.

"Of course I am," she said with a little less conviction than she'd expressed when making the argument.

Marty opened her office door and stepped aside to let her through. "I'm going to call home to see if Edie's gotten there yet, then we can resume our tour."

"Sure." Shannon headed toward her private lounge. "I'll call Mrs. Hunter about carpenters."

"Good." Marty disappeared inside his office and closed the door.

In the privacy of her bathroom with its long mirror surrounded by makeup lights, Shannon bent at the waist and brushed her hair over her head. The vigorous exercise was temporarily therapeutic. For a moment she didn't feel as though something potentially rewarding had been denied her, as though she'd made yet another personal mistake.

She looked into the mirror to smooth her hair and saw the same face that had looked back at her for the past three years. It was her businesswoman face—controlled, serene, steady. But it was backlit by a small undercurrent of excitement. She'd seen that in her reflection at home this morning when she'd contemplated coming to work on Martin Hale's first day on the job. She studied it now in concern.

"You can't have those things," she said aloud to herself as she went about repairing her makeup. "Men make you nervous, you're awkward with children, and you're not . . . warm. This is where you belong, in the administrative office of Carlisle's—Hale's, Portland. And if you keep your distance with this man, let him see only the things you do well and not the things for which you aren't prepared, maybe you'll remain here for a good long time."

Sighing, she tugged her suit jacket down, did a quick turn in the mirror, and satisfied that the business woman was once again in place, went into her office.

"HALE RESIDENCE."

The strong, competent voice on the other end of the line allowed Marty to breathe a sigh of relief. "Hi, Edie," he said warmly. "How's your son?"

"Hi, Mr. Hale," Edie replied. "He's great. I'm going to be a grandmother in about a month. How are you and the boys? This place is a disaster!"

"We've been hanging by a thread, Edie." He laughed. "Waiting for you to catch up with us. Don't worry about dinner. I'll bring something home."

"I've already got a roast in. Where's Josh?"

"I'll pick him up tonight, then you can follow me to the preschool in the morning. Portland's a little bigger than Bend. It'll take you a little time to learn your way around. Anything you want me to bring home?"

He heard her open the refrigerator door, then Tulip's enthusiastic bark as the dog requested something from the refrigerator shelf. "Milk, popcorn...I guess that's it."

"The boys should be home about four. Here's the store's number if you need to reach me."

Edie repeated the number.

"Right. I'll be home with Josh about six."

"I'll try to have things organized by then."

"Don't overdo it. It'll take time. Bye."

Marty hung up and sat there for a minute, absorbing the precious, comfortable feeling of having things under control at home. There were bound to be crises as the boys adjusted to their new environment, but at least Edie was there to minimize the damage until he got home.

It was important that he be able to concentrate on the store for the next few months, that he learn all he could from Shannon and find the best way to apply what he learned. This job was crucial to him. He was tired of starting over. Where he had once turned away from the family business, eager to make it on his own, he now embraced it as the only way he could manage his life. He had to succeed for his family, his father, and for himself. For one reason or another, there had been too many failures in his life lately. He wanted this change to take.

He pushed open the connecting door to Shannon's office. She stood over her desk, looking through a folder. "I want to make a few notes before we leave. Do you mind waiting for a few minutes? I presume there are supplies in my closet?"

"I stocked it for you," she replied. "There should be yellow pads and steno pads in it."

Shannon sat on the edge of her desk, idly flipping through a china catalog in the folder while small sounds of activity came through the open door from the next office. Then she heard a muted oath and walked to the door. She peered around it, wondering if the new manager had stapled himself to something. Her mouth fell open, and she took a step backward, intent on retreating.

"Miss Carlisle," Marty said, his back still turned to her.

Pulling herself together, Shannon stepped inside the door and stared at the window, refusing to look where Martin Hale's eyes were fixed—at the nearly naked poster of himself tacked to the inside of the closet door.

"It's Gale's," she said traitorously. "She must have forgotten it. And that's your coat closet. Your supply closet is over there." Without turning, she pointed to the door on the other wall.

Marty closed the door and walked to Shannon, shrugging back into his suit coat. "Maybe I'll leave the notes until later. If the picture's Gale's," he asked quietly, "why are you blushing?"

Feeling the heat rise from her throat, Shannon chanced a glance at him and found his blue eyes alive with amusement, his mouth poised on the brink of a laugh. Laughter she couldn't contain erupted, and she put a hand over her eyes, vainly trying to recapture a businesslike posture. "Because I enjoyed looking at it, too, I guess," she admitted, succumbing to the blush. "When you and your father came to discuss the purchase, Gale told me that I should imagine you the way you look in the poster, that I would have an edge in the negotiations because I'd seen your... vulnerability."

There was feigned indignation in his expression, but laughter behind it. "So you two plotted against me?"

Shannon considered the question and decided that was probably fairly stated. "Yes."

"And what would the employees think of this, do you suppose?" he asked with apparent gravity. "If we leave it here," he mused, "then I have a poster-sized photo of myself in my closet." He shook his head with a wince. "That has an unsavory sound. If I suggest that Gale move it to her new office or take it home, that would smack of the fraternization you feel is so destructive to the morale of our staff."

Shannon pursed her lips in disapproval of his gibe, but felt too guilty to object to it. When she'd put up pictures in his office, and had seen that his desk was filled with what he would need, it had never occurred to her to check the coat closet, that Gale might have forgotten her poster.

"I'll call her about it this afternoon," she promised. Eager to change the subject, she tried to look more sober. "Ready?"

He, too, sobered, though that laugh behind his eyes never quite disappeared. "Of course, Miss Carlisle. Lead on."

Straight-faced, they walked to the elevators. Shannon pushed the Up button, and they waited, careful not to look at each other. Then Shannon glanced up, caught his eyes on her and let out another laugh.

"Are you going to fire her or kill her?" he asked, laughing, too.

"First one, then the other," she replied as the doors parted and they stepped into an empty car.

Chapter Five

"Thanksgiving won't be the same without Grandpa," Grady said, pouring more milk into his glass, then passing the carton to Jarrod. "I miss him already."

"He'll probably spend it with that stripper," Jarrod said, filling his glass.

"She's not a stripper." Marty held his coffee cup across the table. "Add a little milk to that, will you? She's an exotic dancer." He spoke with a straight face and looked up to see three worldly wise pairs of eyes looking back at him.

"What's that?" Josh wanted to know.

"A lady who takes her clothes off while she dances," Evan replied, filling his glass, then Josh's.

"Doesn't she get cold?"

Grady frowned and turned to his father. "I've always wondered about that, too. I mean, those places can't be that warm, and in the winter..."

"There're usually lots of people crowded around her," Jarrod considered scientifically. "Between the internal body temperature raised by her exertions, and the body heat surrounding her, she—"

"I'm sure if she was uncomfortable," Marty put in, quickly, knowing it wasn't always safe to let Jarrod analyze, "she'd find another line of work. So what do you guys think of your first week in Portland?"

Grady smiled broadly. "I like it." Marty couldn't help but smile back at him. The boy liked everything and adjusted to almost any situation like a sturdy dandelion. "Our class went to the port docks today. You wouldn't believe the size of some of the ships, or how busy it is. I'd love to captain a big boat some day."

Jarrod frowned at him. "I thought you were going to drive race cars."

"Well, I'll need something to do when I'm too old to race," he pointed out. "Like Dad started a second career when he got too old for football and modeling."

Marty gave him a glance as he put his coffee cup to his lips. "You're grounded for the next three years."

While his brothers laughed, Grady reached out to punch Marty's arm. "You know what I mean."

"He could have kept on modeling," Jarrod said. "He quit to spend more time with us when Mom left."

"She had important things to do," Evan said with an aggressive edge to his tone, as though expecting argument or contradiction.

Jarrod turned to him impatiently. "Nobody said she didn't, but somebody had to take care of us. That's why Dad's back at Hale's even though he'd rather be doing something else. Right, Dad?"

"Partly. It was time to do something more permanent."

"Before you got flabby and it started to show in those Daring ads." Grady smiled innocently as Marty's gaze swung his way again.

Marty had a fleeting image of Shannon's flushed cheeks and confused expression when she'd found him studying the poster of himself on the closet door, but he pushed it aside. He was making a conscious effort not to think about Shannon, though his mind seemed to have plans of its own. "You bucking for four years, Grady?"

"Just trying to keep you humble, Dad."

"You're doing an excellent job."

"Actually, you're young for a parent of kids our ages. Wow!" Jarrod exclaimed, distracted. Edie, short and spare in a utilitarian white apron, with graying dark hair in a short, frizzy style, put a chocolate cake and a stack of dessert plates on the table. She cut the cake in thick wedges, and Jarrod distributed pieces while he continued. "Most of our friends' parents are in their fifties and you're only thirty-six."

"Didn't Grandpa try to stop you from getting married so young?" Evan asked. "I mean, you're always warning us to be careful, that the decisions we make now will affect our lives forever."

Marty nodded, passing a piece of cake to Joshua who waited with his fork poised and a greedy gleam in his eye. "He reasoned with me, but I was sure I knew what I was doing. I loved your mom and I'd already been tapped by the Rams. I felt invincible."

"What's that?" Grady asked.

Before Marty could reply, Jarrod turned to his brother. "Like you're Superman." Then he looked at Marty, his brow furrowing. "So how do you think it worked out, Dad? I mean, all in all."

Marty took another sip of coffee and answered honestly. "All in all, I think I came out on top."

Evan's gaze was level, challenging. "But Mom's gone."

"That wasn't his fault," Jarrod said.

"It wasn't anybody's fault." Marty raised both hands in a silent order to stop a potential argument. It always came to this, and he didn't know how to control it. If there was one thing he truly hated about his divorce it was that it had pitted his two oldest sons against each other, one defending his mother's position, the other, his father's. "Life changes and people change with it. Sometimes what seems perfect in the beginning just doesn't fit anymore. But I loved your mom and she loved me for a large part of our lives. I had a career a lot of men can only dream about. And now I've got you guys and I'm back in business with Grandpa. Your mom's getting more and more famous all the time and she's happy. Considering the way things turn out for some people, we're pretty lucky.''

"So, what are we going to do for Thanksgiving?" Evan asked.

"I thought maybe we'd go out to dinner." Marty took a bite of fudge cake and wondered briefly if Grady's prediction of flab taking over his life might not come true sooner than expected, with Emelienne's cooking at work and Edie's at home. "Edie's been working hard to get the house in order. I'd hate to ask her to fix such a big dinner when she's got extra work on her hands. What do you think? I know it means no leftovers, but maybe she could fix a turkey dinner when things aren't so hectic for her."

The boys nodded, reluctant but understanding.

"Maybe the lady could come with us," Josh suggested, chocolate frosting surrounding his mouth.

"What lady?" Evan asked.

"The one who brought the candy."

When Evan still looked confused, Grady added, "The one who was standing on the counter looking for dog biscuits."

Jarrod grinned. "The one with the radical body."

"Oh, yeah." Evan frowned at Jarrod. "I don't think she liked us. She looked anxious to leave."

Marty laughed. "You guys would make Conan the Barbarian anxious to leave. Her name is Shannon Carlisle. Grandpa bought the store where I work from her. She liked you. She's just kind of . . . shy."

"You like her?" Grady asked.

"Sure," Marty replied. "She's a nice person and she's very, very smart."

Evan grimaced. "Smart women are frightening."

Jarrod looked up in surprise, a bite of cake halfway to his mouth. "Why?"

"I guess because they make me feel dumb."

"You are," Grady said quickly.

Marty turned to him with a firm look. "No shots when we're talking seriously, okay?"

Grady blinked. "I didn't know girls were serious."

Evan grinned. "And you called me dumb. Dad, I think Grady meant, do you like her . . . seriously?"

"I don't know her that well yet," Marty evaded, confused himself about his feelings. "We've only been working together a week."

Evan studied him for a moment, then nodded, apparently satisfied. Grady sparkled, Jarrod was probably closer to genius than Marty cared to consider, and Joshua was all charm. But Evan was astute. He'd guessed about the divorce before a word was said about it, and despite all of Marty's and Monica's efforts to be careful in front of the children. He saw and understood subtle things that escaped the other boys. Except those things he didn't want to understand and carefully ignored.

Marty couldn't help wondering if thoughts of Shannon lingered in his eyes, or if Evan would have looked suspicious at the mention of any woman entering their male stronghold, even on the fringe of it. Evan adored his mother, and Marty felt sure he still expected her to come home.

"If you found a smart wife," Jarrod said to Evan, "she could support you while you wrote your books."

Evan shook his head at his brother's naïveté. "It doesn't work that way. Smart girls marry smart guys."

Grady looked worried. "Well, a dumb girl won't be able to support you. You'll have to live at home."

Marty pushed away from the table. "He's going to have a bestseller first time out and he'll be able to support all of us. Come on, let's clean up so you guys can get to your homework."

Evan and Jarrod carried their plates into the kitchen, still arguing about girls, and Josh followed behind, balancing his plate on his arm while he speared the last bite with his fork.

"So, are you going to ask the radical body to have turkey with us?" Grady asked, trailing Marty with his plate.

"Her name is Shannon," Marty said, passing his things to Edie, who was rinsing the dishes in the sink. "And she may already have plans."

Josh, who was helping Edie fill the dishwasher, looked up and shook his head knowledgeably. "Uh-uh!"

"How do you know?" Marty asked.

Josh's eyes widened. "I ast her when she was here. She tole me."

Leave it to a four-year-old to take the direct approach. "Well, we'll see."

"Evan wouldn't like it," Grady warned, suddenly serious.

"Don't borrow trouble," Marty advised, pointing to the stairs. "Your homework's waiting."

Grady sighed over life's injustices and headed off in that direction.

"You didn't tell me about a radical body." Edie fitted a pot into the dishwasher and slid the drawer closed. Then wiping her hands on her apron, she looked up at her employer, waiting for an answer.

Marty poured himself another cup of coffee. "She's the woman my father bought the store from. She *is* gorgeous. Josh thinks we should take her along with us for Thanksgiving dinner."

Edie raised an eyebrow. "Do I see a light in your eye, Mr. Hale?"

"The light's out, Edie." Marty added a shot of milk, then put the carton in the refrigerator.

Edie snorted. "The light's never out. Just ask me. If a tall, handsome bon vivant came along with retirement income and Medicare supplemental insurance, I'd leave you in a minute." She turned to tend to the dishwasher, then asked over her shoulder, "It doesn't matter, you know."

"What doesn't matter?"

"Whether or not Evan likes it," she replied.

Marty looked down, saw Josh looking from one adult to the other with lively interest and asked, "Isn't it time for your bath?"

Josh shook his head. "I had one already."

"When?"

"Yesterday."

Marty put his cup on the counter and swung Josh onto his hip. "You have to have one every day. Go ask Evan to start the water for you and I'll come up and help you."

"I'm not dirty."

"You have chocolate all over your mouth."

"Can't we just wash my mouth?"

"No." Marty put him on his feet and shooed him toward the stairs. With a martyred look over his shoulder, Josh started up.

"Evan hasn't objected to the suggestion," Marty said, turning back to Edie. After two years in the same household, they'd perfected the art of holding on to the interrupted conversation.

"And I'm sure he won't. He'll just behave like injured royalty if you do invite her along."

Marty grinned. "Of all the kids, he reminds me most of Monica, and he reminds me of her particularly with that look." Then his grin dissolved and he said quietly, "But his feelings for his mother are all he has left of her. You shouldn't make fun, Edie."

Edie sighed, putting a covered bowl into the refrigerator. "I'm not making fun. But you've been supporting his feelings long enough. Maybe it's time someone told him the truth about his mother."

"Nobody's hiding the truth from him," Marty replied. "He just doesn't want to see it. But one day he will, and life will lighten up for him a little."

"And in the meantime he loves the woman who abandoned you and him and his three brothers, and he blames you that she's gone."

Marty raised a shoulder. That fact had caused him considerable pain until he'd finally understood it. "It's easier than admitting to himself that the mother he adores didn't love him enough to stay. Nobody can make him see that until he's strong enough to look it in the face, decide that it wasn't his fault or anybody else's but hers and live with it."

Edie looked up at Marty sympathetically and shook her head. "Well, I don't think you should pass up the opportunity of having a new relationship with an interesting woman because Evan can't face the truth about his mother."

"I wouldn't." Marty stared into his cup and looked up to find Edie still watching him. "Shannon wouldn't work out around here, anyway," he said with an absent shake of his head.

Edie leaned against the counter beside him. "You've given it some thought."

"A little," he admitted. "You know, there are some people you feel something for even before you know them well enough to know if you'd be compatible. Chemistry, or something. Anyway, something about her appeals to me— a kind of sweetness and quiet you don't see much anymore. And it's all woven into this great mind. But..." He shrugged and took another sip of coffee. "She's not sure she likes me and she's afraid of kids."

"Maybe she's never been around them."

He laughed a little, remembering how Shannon had looked when he left her with Josh his first day in Portland. "That's true. But most women have some instinctive link with children that helps them know what to do. She doesn't. And I've got a houseful of them.''

Edie looked up at him. "Did you ever think you'd be able to manage the boys all by yourself and work and keep your head together?"

Marty remembered clearly the complete panic of the first few months after Monica had left. "No," he said.

She nodded. "Well, it's been my experience that good people rise to the occasion. Don't write her off before she's had a chance."

The sounds of splashing water, a high, excited giggle and an impatient, stronger voice came from upstairs. At the same moment there was a loud thud at the back door followed by a demanding bark. Edie opened the door, and Tulip ran inside and up the stairs, eager to be a part of the disturbance.

Marty headed for the noise, sure he was going to have to restore order in a moment. "What woman in her right mind would willingly *want* a chance to be part of this chaos?"

"With you thrown in," Edie muttered to herself as she sprinkled cleanser in the sink, "you might be surprised."

"THANKS, BUT MOM and I are going to the coast to have Thanksgiving dinner with my sister and her family. I'm bringing Pete along. Why don't you come with us?" Gale sat on the corner of Shannon's desk in a cranberry wool suit with a nipped-in waist and a flirty peplum. She held a long, cylindrical package.

Shannon studied Gale longingly for a moment, thinking how easily feminine her friend had always been, how comfortably warm and womanly. While she was always on guard against the little everyday assaults on her armor—a man's casual touch, a glance that saw what she didn't want revealed. There were moments when she'd have given anything to be like Gale, and other times when she wouldn't have been that vulnerable for the world.

Shannon leaned back in her chair. "You mean Pete Forrester, the Men's Wear buyer? Is it getting that serious?"

Gale shrugged mysteriously, then dropped the pose and laughed. "Shan, he's so wonderful. He opens doors for me, calls me when he can't see me, brings me flowers and chocolates." She sighed heavily. "I hope I don't blow it."

Shannon swatted Gale's hip, which was situated beside her calendar. "If this doesn't work out, he's the one blowing it."

"Well, I'm trying to relax and not think about it too much. I'll just let what will happen happen." Gale raised a corner of her lip in a grimace. "But it isn't easy." Then she put her package on the desk and shifted to look at Shannon more closely. "How's it going with the boss? He's made a good impression. General scuttlebutt is that you made a good move." She laughed. "The girls in Cosmetics and Lingerie think he's a big improvement over you." Gale sobered suddenly. "Incidentally, did the cashier's office call you about Cosmetics' register bag being ten dollars short? That's the third time in two weeks we've had a ten-dollar shortage."

Shannon nodded, frowning. "I know. We're watching it."

A small smile broke Gale's sobriety. "We're?"

"Mr. Hale and I." Shannon smiled wryly in response. "Actually, I can't find a thing about the boss to complain about, either. He asks my opinion about everything, and he's got some pretty good ideas of his own. He defers to me in front of the staff, something I never expected, and he's nice to be around." She frowned. "I like him."

Bracing her weight on her hand, Gale leaned toward her friend. "Shannon, why does deciding that you like him make you glower? He's not Keith."

Shannon sat up a little straighter, a shiver running along her arms under the concealment of her thick pale blue sweater. The very sound of Keith's name made her body revolt. She forced a smile for Gale, trying to hide the reaction. "I'm not glowering. It would have been so much more comfortable to dislike him." She went on in a theatrically dramatic tone, clutching a fist to her chest. "To curse my fate and the nasty turns of a life filled with pathos."

Gale was unmoved by Shannon's attempt to distract her with humor. She put a hand out to cover Shannon's on the desk. "He isn't Keith," she said again. "Keith's gone. This is a kind, nice man who'd never treat a woman like—"

Marty shouldered the administrative office door open with a preoccupied shove, a white bakery bag in one hand and his briefcase in the other. He was unprepared for Gale's concerned attitude as she leaned toward her friend, and the hollow, frightened look in Shannon's eyes.

Marty stopped inside the door, wondering what he'd interrupted. "Can I help?" he asked quietly. "Or would you rather I disappeared into my office?"

Gale raised an eyebrow at Shannon. "See?" she whispered. Then she leaped quickly off the desk, picking up the package for which she'd come. Her cheeks colored as Marty's eyes noted the rolled-up poster in her arms.

"Mr. Hale, I . . . I'm really sorry about this." She headed for the door in a sideways motion, as though unwilling to turn her back on him. "I . . . I forgot it. I mean, I can't believe I did that because I've been staring at it for . . ." Her blush deepened, and she glanced helplessly at Shannon.

Marty took a few more steps into the office as Gale continued to crabwalk toward the door. Shaking off the tension of a moment ago, Shannon decided her friend needed help. "What she means is that she was so concerned with seeing that the office was cleaned out in time for your arrival that she just . . . forgot . . . the poster."

Gale nodded. "That's it."

Marty put the bag down on Shannon's desk. "Do us all a favor, Gale," he said over his shoulder as he headed toward his office. "Take it home and burn it."

"Do I have to?" she asked. "Hilary in Cosmetics offered me twenty dollars for it."

In the process of opening his door, Marty turned to Shannon, his eyes stunned. She bit furiously on her lip, offering him a sympathetic widening of her eyes.

Marty raised his gaze to Gale, his voice quiet. "I trust you to do the sensible thing with it, Gale. But if it shows up anywhere in this store and I find out about it—" he smiled benignly "—you'll be working for the Bon."

"Yes, sir." With a quick glance at Shannon, Gale hurried off.

Still laughing at the memory of her friend's expression, Shannon poured two cups of coffee, put the doughnuts on a plate and carried the tray into Marty's office for the brief conference that had become a daily ritual.

"How are the kids?" she asked, setting the tray on a side table.

"Great," he replied absently, looking over notes on a yellow pad in the middle of his desk. He pushed it aside to allow her room to place his coffee and the plate of doughnuts. She took the chair that faced his desk. "They're settling in well enough at school, Josh already has a best friend at preschool, and my housekeeper has turned the jungle of boxes into a comfortable, livable home."

"What are you going to do about Thanksgiving?" she asked. Shannon sat erect on the edge of the chair, her cup balanced on her crossed knee. She resisted the urge to look around in wonder at where that voice had come from. It had been her voice, but she hadn't known she was going to say that.

Marty concentrated on breaking a buttermilk bar in half, considering the significance of her question. Had it simply been a conversational inquiry, or a prelude to an invitation? Glancing at her, he couldn't tell. He could see only that she appeared as surprised by her comment as he was. As straightforward as she was, reaching out seemed to be difficult for her.

It was on the tip of his tongue to tell her what he and the boys had discussed and that Josh had suggested inviting her along. But football had taught him that strategy was more valuable than impulse. He decided to lay a little groundwork and wait.

"Not much," he said, leaning back to cross his ankles on the corner of his desk. "We used to go to my Dad's, but that's out of the question, of course. And I hate for Edie to fuss when she's been working so hard getting us settled in." He bit into the bar and sipped at his coffee. "We'll probably just have sandwiches or something."

"Why don't you all come to my place?" Shannon asked. That suggestion didn't surprise her as much as the sudden rush of enthusiasm she felt for the idea after she'd spoken it aloud. She quelled it in an attempt to maintain dignity and a professional quality to the discussion. "You're welcome to bring Edie and Daisy, too, if you want."

He smiled and corrected gently. "Tulip."

"Right, Tulip." His watchful eyes were playing havoc with her efforts to sustain a professional remoteness.

"Wouldn't that compromise your attitude on fraternization?" he asked.

"No," she replied, reaching for her croissant. "Since your family is hundreds of miles away and your only contacts at this point are business ones, it's my responsibility as your assistant to see that your children don't have sandwiches for Thanksgiving dinner." She glanced up with an offhand smile. "Simple as that."

He grinned. "Can you cook?"

He half expected her to reply indignantly, but she seemed to consider the question logical. "Very well," she replied.

Then she added candidly, "It's probably my *only* domestic accomplishment. You have my address. Two o'clock?"

Marty nodded solemnly. "Two o'clock." Then he lowered his eyes to the notes he'd made the night before, trying not to betray his satisfaction with his skillful handling of the situation.

Chapter Six

"It looks like a hospital," Josh said of the plain, square building with its rows of windows looking out onto the Willamette River.

"It's a condominium," Marty explained while he stopped in the middle of the parking lot to offer Grady his comb. "Like an apartment."

Evan, holding Josh's hand, nodded approval. "Great place to hole up and write a book."

Marty took the comb from Grady and worked on the stubborn hair himself. "I think you're supposed to do that in remote places in primitive surroundings so that you're not distracted by comfort. Best I can do, Grady. You still look a little like Alfalfa."

"It's part of his charm," Edie said, pushing the boy forward. Evan and Josh followed, but Jarrod lingered behind with Marty.

"This dinner important to you, Dad?" he asked.

Marty looked down at him in surprise. "Why?"

"Well, look at us," he said, indicating their fairly formal appearance. "We look like a bunch of paid escorts with a house mother. Except for you, of course. You look like the...whatever the male equivalent of a madam is."

The others had gone into the condo's lobby, but Marty held Jarrod back, outside the doors. His boys all challenged his ability to stay abreast of and guide their development, but Jarrod often made him feel that the effort was futile. "This dinner is important to me because this is a very nice lady who went out of her way so that the six of us wouldn't feel alone and lonely on a holiday. Please don't bring up your observations on madams and paid escorts, okay?"

"You're tense, Dad," Jarrod observed gravely. "You know you can trust me."

Marty nodded, not entirely convinced. "And if I can't," he said mildly, threatening with a smile, "you know I can hurt you." He opened the door.

Shannon admitted them to a spacious, modern living room in subtle shades of pink and gray. She looked flushed, a little harried and charmingly out of place in a floral apron and low shoes.

"I think you've met everyone but Edie McIntyre," Marty said, "our housekeeper and good friend. Edie, this is Shannon Carlisle."

Shannon took her coat. "I'm glad you could come, Edie. Where's Tulip?"

"We left her home." Marty looked around at the pale carpet and plump, low furniture. "I think it was a wise decision. She'd have made herself comfortable on the sofa by now."

Shannon laughed. "Gale has a spaniel who's slept there more than once." She surveyed the group. "Any of you good in the kitchen besides Edie?"

"Dad taught us all to cook," Jarrod said.

Evan qualified that statement by adding, "Omelets and goulash. We won't starve, but Julia Child never calls us for advice, either."

Shannon laughed again, a little of the edginess she'd been feeling all morning easing away.

"I need someone to mash potatoes, someone to mash carrots and turnips, someone to stir the gravy and someone to toss salad."

Grady folded his arms. "I'm not touching turnips."

Shannon pointed Marty and the older boys toward the kitchen, then led Edie and Josh down the few steps into the den, turned on the television and prepared the VCR. "My taste runs to old movies, so I hope you'll be able to find something you like. Make yourself comfortable and I'll bring you a glass of wine. Josh, would you like some milk or a Coke?"

"Coke," he replied, then, at a glance from Edie, added quickly. "Please. Thank you."

Shannon hurried back to the kitchen to find it filled with males with their sleeves rolled up. Evan had found a colander and was washing lettuce while Jarrod mashed potatoes and Grady stirred the gravy she'd prepared.

Shannon leaned around Marty's arm to look into the pot in front of him, then smiled up at him. "I see you got the carrots and turnips."

He returned her smile, and her edginess disappeared completely. "You've got to be quick around these guys. Does this need more butter?"

Shannon took a fork from the drying rack near Evan and dipped into the smooth concoction. "More salt maybe."

"I've got it." Jarrod passed it across the island they worked over.

"This has big lumps in it," Grady complained of the gravy. Shannon went to investigate.

"That's giblets," she said.

He turned in puzzlement to Evan. "Guts," Evan explained.

Grady dropped the spoon. "Dad, want to trade guts for turnips?"

"No." Marty turned him back to his chore. "It's not guts. It's the edible inner organs of the turkey."

Evan shrugged as though his point were proven. "Guts."

Shannon put her hand on Grady's shoulder. "Would it help if I gave you a longer spoon?"

"It would help," he replied, "if you told me I can pick them out when it comes time to eat it."

"Of course."

"Ah, excuse me…" Marty watched her pour a single glass of wine, then a Coke. "Who's that for?"

"Edie and Josh."

Marty glanced up at Jarrod. "They're resting while we're working with guts and turnips and they get drinks."

"Am I facing a strike?" Shannon asked.

Marty looked around at his sons, who all nodded agreement. Shannon pulled down more glasses. "Three Cokes and one wine?"

There was a murmured protest for a different distribution of the numbers that Marty quelled with a look.

Shannon smiled at Marty. "I wouldn't want to face these guys across a bargaining table."

He laughed. "It isn't even easy across a dinner table."

By the time they sat down to dinner, Shannon was impressed with Marty's children. They were handsome, intelligent, capable and as eager to tease as their father. Evan was quieter than the other three, but less cool than her first impression of him. Jarrod and Grady provided a relentless barrage of jokes and stories during dinner while still managing to consume their fair share of the turkey. Grady meticulously picked the giblets out of his gravy but happily ate everything else, even the carrot and turnip mixture.

When they all finally sat back in their chairs, the twenty-two-pound turkey was little more than a carcass and most of the bowls on the table were empty. Shannon felt inordinately pleased with herself. "Edie, if you'll take everybody into the den, I'll clear the dishes away and bring the pumpkin pie in there."

Edie stood. "This time I insist on helping."

"Sorry." Shannon shook her head firmly and shooed everyone from the table. "I'll take care of it. Go and sit down."

"C'mon." Josh pulled Evan toward the den. "She's got lots of movies, huh, Edie?"

Shannon looked up from stacking plates. "Evan, there are some game cassettes in the closed cabinet under the television."

"All right!" Jarrod and Grady followed along enthusiastically.

"You're sure I can't help?" Edie asked again.

Shannon smiled over her shoulder as she headed for the kitchen with a tower of plates. "Positive. I'll bring coffee and dessert in a few minutes."

When Shannon disappeared through the bat-wing doors, Edie looked across the table at Marty, who was picking up the turkey platter. "If you married her and kept me on," she said softly, "I could die a happy woman."

"If she hears you say that," he warned, "you'll die before your time. Don't let the guys break her television, okay?"

Marty shouldered his way into the kitchen with the platter and placed it on the counter. Shannon came from the refrigerator with a pumpkin pie on the flat of one hand and a carton of vanilla ice cream in the other. She put both on the counter and frowned at him. "I thought I told you to go sit down."

"I didn't listen," he replied. "Where will I find dessert plates?"

She pointed to an overhead cupboard. "Forks are in the drawer in front of you." The large, airy kitchen suddenly seemed to shrink. He remained beside her, pulling down plates and taking forks from the drawer while she concentrated on cutting the pie into even pieces. She could smell his cologne, the crisp, clean cotton of his shirt, the scent that once used to fill her with fear, but now only served to make her unaccountably nervous—the scent of a man. Her earlier edginess began to invade her once more.

Sensing the tension in her, Marty moved to check the coffee maker. "There are about two cups in here," he reported. "Want me to make another pot?"

She breathed in, as if she'd just been given oxygen. "Please. You want the boys to have Coke again or milk?"

"It's a holiday," he said, working over filters and fragrant ground coffee. "If you have enough Coke for another round, let them live it up."

Shannon found herself smiling at his reply. He was so warm and easy, she thought, so unlike the rigid, uncommunicative parent her father had been.

"My father could have learned a thing or two from you," she said, carefully serving up the pie.

Marty cast her a surprised, sidelong glance.

"Your boys seem to have a lot of fun," she explained. "To be at ease with you. That must be nice."

He fitted the filter basket onto the glass pot and plugged in the coffee maker. He turned to face her but kept his distance. "I always had that from my father. And I'm sure I get more out of our relationship than the kids do. There have been times in my life when I might have given up if I hadn't had them. They've restored my perspective and sense of humor many times."

She laughed, resting the knife on the now-empty pie plate. "I don't think I'll ever look at giblets in quite the same way again."

"Fair exchange," he said. "Grady hasn't eaten turnips since he's been old enough to make his wishes known. You may have converted him."

"Will they all want ice cream with their pie?"

"Yes, but you'll have to put Grady's on the side. He eats them separately."

Shannon carried pie out on one tray and Marty took drinks on another. Hands reached out for the food, but the adults were otherwise ignored as the boys carried on a cut-throat game of Space Invaders. Edie sat apart from them, contentedly looking through a magazine.

"Keep the food off the carpet, guys," Marty cautioned.

Four voices replied, "Sure, Dad," but four pairs of eyes never left the television screen.

Marty smiled at Shannon, transferring the two remaining pieces of pie and the two coffees to one tray. "Do you want to stay and play the winner, or sit in the other room and tell me your life story?"

"They'd murder me, I'm sure," she said, leading the way up the three steps to the living room. "Have you noticed my view of the river?"

"No. You put us right to work, remember?" He followed her to the sofa and placed the tray on the light wood coffee table in front of it. Then he knelt on one knee on the cushions as she did and looked out at the water, busy even on Thanksgiving with tugs and freighters and longshoremen loading logs.

She acknowledged his teasing with a quick smile, then turned back to the scene. "When I was little, we used to live on the hill, and I had the same view, though from a longer distance. I used to think about stowing away on one of those ships. All lit up at night they look so inviting."

Marty read the wistful look in her eyes. "If you're still thinking about it," he said, "I'll need at least two weeks' notice."

She laughed lightly and turned to sit properly on the sofa. She was happy she'd followed her impulse to invite him and his family to dinner. He was as easy to talk to and to be with socially as he was at the store. "When I got a little older, I came to love the store even more than the thought of going to sea. I guess I found the warmth there that I couldn't find at home, so it became less important to sail away."

Marty sat and took the pie she offered him. "Did you ever hear from your mother after she left?" He hadn't been sure how Shannon would take the question, but she seemed more relaxed than usual today, without the armor that was always in place at the store.

"She died in a train accident the year after she left." Shannon sighed and Marty found it difficult to translate the gesture. It seemed to carry more acceptance than grief. "I saw very little of her when she was home, so I didn't miss her that terribly when she was gone. I had a nanny, Miss Kimball. She was a tall, spindly tyrant my father had selected, probably because she was as humorless as he was."

Frowning, Shannon paused to take a bite of pie. After chewing it thoughtfully, she surprised Marty by laughing. "There's an old mannequin in the basement from the Twiggy period in the sixties that reminds me of her. The face is pretty, of course, and hers wasn't, but the body is flat and angular. I can remember her so clearly, pulling herself up to her full height and refusing me something simple..." As she spoke, she sat up straight and squared her shoulders in imitation of the subject of their discussion. She raised an imperious eyebrow and tilted her head back to look down at Marty. " 'No, Tiffany, you may not have a soft drink. You may not leave your light on to read. You may not go to a party with all those undesirable children.' Those offensive children were my classmates at school."

Sighing, Shannon shook her head and leaned against the sofa. Her expression was one of confusion. "My father hated my mother for whining and clinging to him, then he hated her for leaving him." She amended with a bleak smile, "For leaving him with me. I could almost understand why he disliked me. But what did I ever do to Miss Kimball?"

Marty resisted the urge to stroke the frown from her face. "The world is full of petty tyrants who love to lord it over the defenseless. I'd like to see her try it with my kids."

Shannon's frown disappeared and she laughed. "So would I. Grady and Jarrod would have her suicidal in a minute."

Marty rested an elbow on the back of the sofa and asked quietly. "How did you ever get through it all to become a gentle, gracious lady?"

Shannon felt warm surprise color her cheeks. Did he really think that of her? "I had my grandmother," she replied, glancing away from his watchful blue eyes. "She saved my sanity and my belief in kindness and caring."

Grinning, Marty looked astonished. "The sober lady with the big hat?"

"She had a heart of gold," Shannon said, defending her staunchly. "She just didn't know how to share it with everyone. She picked me up every Saturday afternoon and took me to the carousel in the park." She looked out the window at the lowering sky, a small smile forming. "She'd let me ride it for hours. I'd get lost in the music and the color and the companionship of other giddy children and imagine myself on my trusty steed on a personal crusade for love and justice. Then it was time to go home again, and I'd live through another dreary week knowing that the following Saturday I'd be able to ride the carousel again."

Shannon came out of her reverie to find Marty's watchful blue eyes still on her. "My grandmother died when I was ten, and now I can't see a carousel without wanting to get on it, or see a carousel ornament of any kind—" she swept a hand to the tall shelf that occupied the wall at Marty's end of the sofa "—without wanting to own it."

He turned to look and saw that every spot on the shelf held a carousel horse, or one of the other whimsical animals that often decorated them. There were tall figures, miniatures, framed, cross-stitched pictures on easels, prints and one small, complete carousel. Shannon pointed to it. "That's a music box. Poole gave it to me when I took over the store."

"Bribery?" Marty teased.

"Friendship," she replied. "My first job in the store when I was fourteen was in her department."

They were silent for a moment. Sounds of the boys' laughter and the electronic noises of the video game came from the other room. On the river an anchor being lowered grated noisily, then splashed.

"You've never married?" Marty asked.

"I'm divorced."

Her expression was completely neutral. He found it difficult to decide if she regretted her status or was satisfied with it. "And you're still relying on the carousel to get you from day to day?" he asked.

That was true. She lived by holding on to the few bright spots in the past—her grandmother and the Saturday afternoons in the park. She ignored everything else—her father, Keith—and gave little thought to the future, except when it related to the store. Her brief foray into reaching for love and a personal life that would give some substance to her as a woman had almost destroyed her. She had long ago opted to settle for less.

"Well," she said philosophically, folding a corner of the paper napkin on her knees. "It's my theory that we're not supposed to have everything in life."

With a suddenness that surprised her, Marty pulled the napkin from her fingers. She looked up at him wide-eyed. "The pursuit of happiness is your right," he said. "It's in the Constitution."

She smiled at him as though he were young and innocent. "There are some things we can't have despite the guarantees of a sovereign power."

He saw it then in her eyes, behind the lingering memories of the grim childhood she had let him glimpse, behind the newer pain involving something he didn't know about and couldn't understand—the ashes of anticipation, the death of hope. In the darkest hour of his own misery, he'd never known the personal despair he saw in her eyes.

He felt angry with her, with himself for not knowing how to help her. "How can someone so in love with carousels," he asked, "ever stop dreaming?"

Shannon looked at him, wondering why she felt as though she had somehow failed him. Before she could find an answer for him or for herself, there was a thud from the other room followed instantly by a high-pitched wail.

Edie was untangling a screaming Josh from the low stool from which he'd fallen. "Jarrod pushed me!" Josh accused, reaching for his father.

When Jarrod opened his mouth to deny the accusation, Evan came quietly to his defense. "No, he didn't. Josh got excited about the game and was bouncing around on the stool. He fell all by himself."

Grady grinned at Jarrod. "He was beating you, though. You did have a motive."

Jarrod rolled his eyes at Marty. "Dad, you've been promising me for twelve years that you'd give Grady away."

After a quick check of the child in his arms assured Marty that Josh's pride was more injured than his body, he glanced at Grady with a grin. "Sorry, Jarrod. It's been harder to find a patsy than I expected."

Grady went to stand beside Shannon. "Did you hear the way I'm treated?"

Shannon nodded sympathetically. "Shocking."

"I could stay with you," he suggested.

She reminded him soberly, "I cook guts and turnips."

Grady dismissed that with a shrug. "Dad says you have to overlook some things when a woman comes into your life."

Shannon smiled at Marty, the tension of a moment ago dispelled by the small crisis. "Is that so?"

"That's been my experience." He smiled back at her. "We're going to help you clean up the kitchen and be on our way."

"I told you..." she began to protest. But Marty had pointed to the kitchen, and the three older boys, with Edie in pursuit, headed for it. As she continued to sputter, Marty put Josh down and led him toward the kitchen. "If you don't lend a hand," Marty threatened over his shoulder with a grin, "I *will* leave you Grady."

Chapter Seven

The condominium had never seemed so quiet. Shannon carried a balloon glass of brandy from the liquor cabinet to the sofa where she had sat with Marty, feeling stifled by the silence. Pulling up the long skirt of her gray silk dressing gown, she sat on her knees on the middle cushion and looked out at the lights of the ships and small boats below.

Marty's presence only inches away from her was still fresh in her memory, alive in her senses. Moving her eyes from the river to the place beside her and finding it empty was almost painful. She sipped the brandy and felt its mellow fire slip down into the knot in her stomach.

The apartment rang emptily. She still had a strong impression of a tableful of boys eating hungrily, her big kitchen crowded with elbows that needed room, voices that couldn't be contained, laughter that didn't stop. Yet when she looked, she was alone again. She had expected to feel relief when Marty and his family had gone, but instead she felt . . . restless, curiously lonely.

Strange, she thought, that she'd grown up unloved and practically ignored, and though she'd longed for affection and attention, she'd learned to deal with the loneliness and overcome it. She'd taken a backward step today, she realized with alarm. Inviting Marty and his family to spend the holiday with her had been a mistake. It had challenged the emptiness for which she had settled after Keith.

"PALM SPRINGS?" Shannon placed a stack of mail on Marty's desk and turned to stare at him. He hung his jacket on a brass coat tree near the table and ran a finger inside the collar of his shirt as he walked around his desk. Shannon's eyes tracked him as though he were crazy. "What do you mean we're going to Palm Springs? We can't go anywhere. It's the end of November. We're into the Christmas rush. It's out of the question."

"Please sit down," he said, glancing up at her as he inspected a large manila envelope postmarked Bend, Oregon. His tone was deliberately administrative, and he saw her comply with a resentful lift of her eyebrow. She'd been remote and a little cool in the week since Thanksgiving dinner, and he'd decided to change tack in dealing with her. She was afraid to let a personal relationship develop between them, and he'd decided to deprive her of it completely, to be all business and hope that she missed the natural camaraderie between them. "It wasn't a suggestion, Shannon," he said, reaching for the silver letter opener that had been a gift from the boys. He slit the envelope and removed its contents, waiting for Shannon's reaction.

"You mean it's an order," she said evenly after a moment.

"The Hale's in Palm Springs has an inventory system that's a model of its kind." He spoke absently, looking through the printed material and photographs. "My father wants us to look it over and be ready to update our own next year. I have to be at a board meeting in Bend week after next, so next week is the ideal time for us to check out Palm Springs."

"And what does the Portland Hale's do while we're gone?"

He glanced up at her, his expression professional. "Gale's perfectly capable of handling things for four days. If there's a serious problem, we're only a few hours away." He gathered up the material spread out on his desk and handed it to her. "Here's some information my father sent on the system. Please look it over. We leave on Monday." He made a point of scanning his desktop, then the top of the table near the wall. "Where's my coffee?" he asked. He noted with satisfaction that the color in her cheeks was a little redder than it had been a moment ago.

Shannon folded her arms, the papers clutched in her hand. She gave her head a little toss he'd come to recognize as an indication of temper. "Where's my croissant?" she countered, playing right into his hands.

"You've been absenting yourself from our morning meetings," he said. "There seemed little point in bringing it."

"I've been busy."

"Hiding in the stockroom. I checked."

Her color now flamed. "I wasn't hiding. The holiday rush is on, and I was making certain we had enough bags to see us through."

Unimpressed, he leaned back in his chair and looked at her evenly. "You'd have done that in July. I know you. You were hiding."

"You don't *know* me." He'd never heard her raise her voice to a customer, or an employee, or a salesman, but she was shouting now. Someone else might have considered it insubordination. He saw it as an important chink in her armor. "You waltz in here with your good looks, oozing charm and affability and turn everything your way in less time than it took you to tour the store. You have more instinct than knowledge, and more flair than sense, but don't think that means you can bully me around. If I want to count bags, I'll count..." Suddenly she heard herself. The strident tone of her voice and the aggressive quality of her words surrounded her and she sat, leaning an elbow on the corner of his desk and resting her forehead in her hand. "If you'd brought the damn croissant," she said, "I wouldn't be making an idiot of myself."

"If you'd shown up for meetings—"

"I know, I know," she interrupted, dropping her hand to look across the desk at him. She looked pale and tired. Still, a wry smile came and went. "Strange what self-control hinges on, isn't it? Croissants and coffee."

His voice gentled. "Why did you stop coming?"

Because my apartment has been empty since you were there, because I think of you all the time, because I look forward to the time every morning when we closet ourselves in here with coffee and doughnuts and you talk and laugh and we discuss things equally, like I always wanted to do with my father—with Keith. Only my father never wanted to listen and Keith never wanted to talk. All that sat on the tip of her tongue and couldn't be spoken. He'd think she was crazy. *She* had for a long time.

That look that made Marty feel helpless, that touching loneliness, that complicated fear, were back in her eyes. He wanted to change the subject, let her off the hook. But it seemed to him that she'd been pushing away whatever haunted her for some time, and while it saved her from looking back, it also prevented her from looking forward. He'd found that in dealing with fear, confrontation was usually best. "You're afraid of being attracted to me, of my attraction to you."

Somehow that candid assessment of the situation didn't surprise Shannon. She'd worked with Marty long enough now to know that whatever he lacked in experience in retail, he made up for with an uncanny ability to understand his position and face it, good or bad, with a positive outlook. He seemed to apply the same principle to his personal life.

"All right." She crossed her forearms on the corner of his desk and leaned toward him, her brown eyes direct. Marty saw vulnerability under the firm pose and was touched by it. He often bluffed himself. "I understand that this is presuming a lot," Shannon said. "But in the interest of seeing the possible end result, let's just take for granted that our appeal for each other developed, became serious, and we tried to plan a life together. You have four children who need a mother, and I don't know the first thing about...about cuddling, or soothing, or encouraging, or all those other things mothers do."

In the awkward way she spoke the words, Marty saw verification of what she'd told him in her living room—she'd never had those things. He pushed aside sympathy and concentrated on what she was saying. "They're not in my experience and therefore not part of my makeup. And you...you would want those things from me, too. I'm not a warm person, Marty." She slightly stiffened at the thought. "I'd only hurt you."

He studied her determined expression and the dark emotion under it that seemed to cry out for relief despite her insistence that she hadn't any. Under the calm she looked mildly frantic, and he decided that he'd probably pushed enough. "I think you mistake inexperience for inability," he said, "and underestimate my capacity to deal with frustration, failure, even pain in pursuit of what I think is best for my kids and myself."

He held her eyes for a moment, and Shannon found herself without argument. Ruthless selflessness was too complicated a concept in her present state of mind. While she stared at him, he picked up the telephone and dialed an extension. "Gale. Hi, it's Marty. Would you run down to the bakery and bring back a croissant and a buttermilk bar? And something for yourself. Right. Bring it to my office." He cradled the receiver and grinned at Shannon. "Do you have a bathing suit?"

HUSTLED FROM A PLANE to a cab to a motel room to the Palm Springs Hale's, Shannon wandered moodily through the gleaming first floor of the store while Marty and the manager followed. A native of the Northwest, Shannon had been prepared to find the desert community gaudy and pretentious, to dislike the glitzy store, and to remain politely removed from the man who had insisted she come. But she soon discovered that in the brilliant desert heat, even the prickliest life-forms bore flower and fruit.

She pushed through the big glass doors and stepped from the air-conditioned store out onto the sidewalk. The hot breath of the desert wrapped around her, seduced her. She spread her arms and breathed in. The fragrance of citrus and other exotic vegetation filled her nostrils.

"I'll expect you back at 10:00 a.m. tomorrow." Marty and the manager, a beautiful woman in her forties, had joined Shannon on the quiet sidewalk of Palm Canyon Drive. It was midafternoon and there were few cars or pedestrians. People were probably lying by swimming pools, Shannon thought longingly, sipping iced tea on patios, absorbing the lovely sun.

She turned her attention to the woman. "Thank you for lunch, Mrs. Goodwin."

The Palm Springs Hale's had a thin, highly strung young man as chef of the dining room, and lunch had been shrimp vinaigrette on a bed of cappelli. The thought of a cooking duel between the young man and Emelienne was a thought Shannon would like to entertain later, when she wasn't feeling so decadent.

Marty shook Mrs. Goodwin's hand. "Thank you for your hospitality. Tomorrow we'll get down to serious business."

The manager sealed the handshake with her other hand, then backed into the store with a gracious smile. It had been a simple, innocent gesture, Shannon thought, but it served to undermine the delicious sense of irresponsibility that was beginning to overtake her. All morning and through lunch she'd noticed the careless touching, the little excuses to stand near Marty, to lean over his arm to point. Mrs. Goodwin wanted him, and Shannon was surprised to find how vehemently she resented that.

She started off down the street, the sigh of a breeze ruffling her hair away from her face, molding her yellow blouse against her, swirling her skirt. Marty caught up with her, removed his jacket and slung it over his shoulder, holding the collar by one finger.

"We have a few hours before dinner," he said, pulling at his tie and unbuttoning the top button of his shirt. "What would you like to do?"

She glanced at him as she walked. There was amusement in her eyes and a little concern. "I know what Mrs. Goodwin would like to do."

Marty laughed softly and kept pace with her. "So do I."

"Isn't she married?"

"Widowed."

Shannon snickered. "Probably wore him out."

When she stopped to look in the window of a chocolate shop, Marty took her arm and pulled her around. She looked up at him guilelessly, her smile easy. "You needn't feel as though you have to spend the afternoon and evening entertaining me. I mean, if Mrs. Goodwin—" The increased pressure on her arm made her think twice about finishing the sentence.

He leaned over her. "Hale's has a store in Myrtle, Montana," he said quietly, his expression only partially amused, "where the snow falls from October to May. You could be transferred there." They stood in the shade of a pink and gray awning, blue eyes gently threatening, brown eyes filling with satisfaction. "Now," he said again, "what would you like to do?"

"I'd like to buy some chocolates and some champagne," she said, "and sit on a lounge chair by the pool and absorb the sun."

Marty quirked an eyebrow. "The chocolate will melt and the champagne will get warm."

Shannon rolled her eyes. "Don't be so stuffy, Hale. Those are minor problems easily overcome. Come on." She pushed her way into the shop, expecting him to follow.

LYING ON HIS BACK on a lounge chair, Marty rolled his head sideways and let his eyes roam slowly over Shannon. Her eyes closed against the sun, her arms resting loosely on the arms of the chair, her long-fingered hands dangling to the side, she breathed evenly and made him remember things he'd lived without too long.

The gentle rise and fall of her small breasts in the black low-cut suit drew his attention and held it for longer than he deemed reasonable. His eyes traveled past the smaller jut of ribs, the concavity of her stomach, the delicious length of thigh accentuated by the French-cut leg of her suit. He followed the bend of one shapely knee, the mildly muscled calf and the neat ankle.

With a ragged sigh, he reached for the bottle of champagne in the ice bucket between their chairs. In another bucket, sitting in an ashtray on the ice, was the bag of chocolates.

"Me, too, please," Shannon murmured languorously without opening her eyes.

"Which?" he asked. "Champagne or chocolate?"

"Both."

He looked into the bag. "There's one piece left. You've eaten all the rest."

A little frown appeared on her forehead. "You could get dressed and go buy more."

"I'm satisfied. You're the one who wants more. Here."

Reluctantly Shannon opened her eyes to sit up and take the wineglass. Marty reached over and pushed the back of her chair up.

She smiled her gratitude for the small kindness. "I guess it's almost time for dinner, anyway. I feel like lobster."

Marty readjusted his own chair and sipped at the bubbly wine. "You're going to look like a lobster if you don't put your shirt back on." He was thinking of his own sanity as well as her comfort.

Shannon prodded her upper arm with a finger and saw how red her skin was against the resulting white spot. She leaned sideways to put her glass down and pulled on her lacy cover-up. Then she retrieved her glass and stretched her legs, settling comfortably. "Where did you live when you played for the Rams?"

"In a ranch-style house in a pretty canyon not too far from Los Angeles." He waited for the little stab of pain that always came when he thought of those days. He'd felt so all-powerful then, so secure. He'd had a beautiful wife, three healthy sons, an impressive career. The ease and swiftness with which it had all fallen apart had frightened him, almost disabled him. But for the first time since his divorce, he felt nothing.

"I can't imagine leaving this wonderful climate for rainy Oregon." She laughed softly. "The northwest is in my blood, but you spent so much time here in the sun."

"The Hale Corporation's offices are in Bend and I needed the job."

"That was after...?"

"My divorce? Yes."

Shannon studied him for signs of tension, but found none. "You don't mind talking about it?"

He glanced at her, smiling wryly before taking another sip of champagne. "To a point. What do you want to know?"

She curled her knees up and turned sideways in the chair to look at him. "I just wondered... I mean, you'd been married quite a while."

"Thirteen years."

"What... happened?"

"I spent a whole year asking myself that," he replied. "I think we just weren't focused on the same things anymore."

"She became an actress."

Marty nodded. "That wasn't a problem for me. She's very beautiful. When she got the opportunity, I was as excited for her as she was. Even when she became an instant hit and received more and more offers, I tried to change my life to accommodate what was happening in hers. One of us had to be with the children, and I sincerely wanted her to enjoy her success. I got a modeling offer that kept me home more than traveling with the team did, so I took it."

Shannon waited.

Marty downed the rest of his champagne swiftly and put it beside his chair. Now she could see the tension and the pain. "Then she began to pass up work closer to home for roles that took her away for months at a time. We became less and less important to her. I saw it happening and became desperate to hold our lives together. She came home from a two-month shoot in Paris, and I told her how I felt. She'd always wanted a house in Bel-Air, so I bought one and promised I'd do whatever it took to keep home and hearth together if she'd work closer to home, spend more time with us. She promised. That compromise resulted in Josh."

The breeze began to cool, and Shannon held her cover-up more tightly around her. Marty didn't seem to notice as he sat up, dropping his feet to the patio and straddling the chair. "Trying to hold on to something that's over is such a mistake. Before she delivered Josh, we both knew it was over. She left before he was three months old."

Shannon had little experience of love and couldn't hold back the question. "How could she have loved you and been happy with you for thirteen years, then just leave you and her children—one of them an infant?"

He shrugged. "She did it. *How* she was able to do it doesn't really matter. Anyway..." He looked over his shoulder to smile at her. "As hard as it was to adjust to her leaving, to get myself and the kids through it and over it, it was better than settling for less than what I wanted."

"What do you want?" she asked.

He considered that a moment, looking up at the cloudless sky. "Stability for myself and my kids. Like you, I grew up in the family business, but unlike you, I had a need to prove myself outside of it. And I did. But when Monica left and I had to do something with my life that would allow me to spend evenings and weekends at home, I discovered there was precious little work for jocks or models that fitted that schedule. I turned to my father for help, and he gave me a job without a smirk or even an implied 'I told you so.'"

"You're a lucky man."

He nodded, then leaned back in the chair. "But I can't shake the feeling that my kids are being shortchanged. I'd like them to come home from school to a mother instead of a housekeeper. Edie's wonderful, and I don't know what I'd have done without her, but she's not their mother."

Shannon considered the injustice of that and suggested philosophically, "You can't have everything in life. I keep trying to tell you."

He rolled his head to smile at her. "I'm still not listening."

Shannon saw the movement out of the corner of her eye as she reached down lazily for the last chocolate. Something green and scaly skittered past her hand, and she tossed the bag, screaming as fear of anything reptilian supplanted common sense. The sudden movement collapsed the rickety chair and dumped her on her bottom with a thud.

"Shannon, what . . ." Marty got to his feet, torn between laughter and concern. He reached down to pull her up, holding her arm while she untangled herself from the chair's plastic webbing.

"It looked like an alligator," she said, looking up into the smile he was trying hard to hold back. "It ran under my chair!" she added, indignant over his amusement.

"It was a lizard," he said, losing control of the smile. "About this big." He held his thumb and index finger two inches apart.

"They can be poisonous."

"It was a garden lizard."

Shannon sighed, embarrassed. "It frightened me. Ouch!" As she dusted herself off, she gasped at a stab of pain on the side of her thigh, above her knee.

Marty knelt, noticing for the first time that her wineglass had broken. He ran a thumb lightly over the long, freely bleeding scratch, feeling for glass.

Shannon's pulse began to quicken, and the familiar, suffocating fear began to rise. "I'm all right," she said, trying to behave normally as she pushed at his shoulder to free herself.

He glanced up at her and saw that the usually well-concealed fear was now in her eyes as she looked down at him. He straightened and, taking hold of her arm, eased her around the broken glass and toward his room. "I'll wash it off for you, make sure there's no glass in it and put some antiseptic on it."

"I can do that." She tried to pull away toward her own room.

"I can do it better," he insisted. "Relax. You know I wouldn't hurt you."

"I'll do it!" With that, Shannon gave a final, determined yank.

Marty could have held her fast, but chose not to because now he realized that she was afraid of him. Being feared was new to him, and he didn't like it. He took a step back, out of her way. With anger that seemed directed at herself rather than him, Shannon hobbled off to her room.

MARTY TURNED HIS SHOWER on full force, peeled off his trunks and stepped under the water. Planting his feet against the strong, hot spray, he threw his head back and let it beat at his body. He remembered Shannon looking frightened, pulling away from him, and thought with grim determination that he didn't need that. In the last few years of his marriage to Monica he'd had enough of a loveless woman to last him a lifetime. Since then he'd been offered love by starlets, models and groupies eager to share the fringes of the limelight. He'd accepted a few, but it had never replaced what he'd lost, the love he and Monica had shared before the seduction of fame and power had lured her away. Perhaps he was a man out of time, but he didn't want to settle for sex or convenience. He wanted a warm, willing woman in his arms who longed for him the way he longed for her, who would give comfort as well as take it, who would be there in the morning to share his demanding world of children and a new career.

So why did his subconscious keep putting brown eyes and auburn hair on the woman who lived in his mind as the ideal who would be everything he wanted? Shannon was beautiful and sweet, but she had a problem she seemed unable or unwilling to share, and it was putting a lid on what was growing between them. He was stretched in too many directions at the moment; he simply didn't have the energy to deal with someone else's trauma.

Marty turned the hot water off with a decisive twist and stood under the barrage of cold. The sudden, violent shock cleared his mind of all thought, then, as his body adjusted, he continued to reinforce his argument. In football he'd been noted for his guts, in modeling for his endurance. But now he didn't know if he had either anymore. He could take the abuse to his body, and he could take the exhaustion, but he couldn't take failing one more time.

Turning the water off, Marty reached past the shower curtain to snatch a towel off the rack. He pressed his face into the nubby, sweet-smelling softness. As tempting and promising as a relationship with Shannon appeared on the surface, he knew pursuing it would cost him more than he had to give. He would have to turn away from it.

SHANNON BRUSHED HER HAIR in the bathroom where the light was better than in the outer room with its bigger mirror. She needed a good, hard look at herself.

Fear no longer lingered in her eyes, but anger was there, crackling and alive. "You can turn away from him," her brave voice told her as she pulled the brush punitively through her hair. "Like you've turned away from every man who's ever approached you since Keith, and you can turn into a crusty old woman, or you can take a stand here, show some character and try to turn your life around."

Shannon put the brush down and picked up a gold filigreed banana clip. "He has four children," her sissy voice said. "Four boys."

"You have a deep-seated emotional knot in your make-up and he's not throwing it in *your* face."

"I'm afraid."

She smiled and fitted the barrette. "Welcome to the world of real people."

Fluffing her bangs in place, tugging at the loose curls at her ears, Shannon wondered idly if she was going crazy. Walking back into the bedroom, she checked her white, off-the-shoulder cotton dress in the bigger mirror. Doing a turn, she considered that she'd just spent several minutes talking to herself; her insides were trembling like pudding, and she was actually considering putting an end to the past.

In all the tedious days and nights since Keith, she'd lived with the unnatural fear underlying every moment. It was so strong, so woven into her being that she'd never once considered taking steps to escape it. She'd simply tried to shut it out, pretended it wasn't there, learned to live with the diminished human being it had made of her.

Tonight she wanted to change that, and she didn't know where the courage was coming from. It was simply there—nothing large and heroic, only a small, persistent need that demanded attention.

Before it abandoned her, she stepped out onto the stone patio, slid her door closed and walked the few steps to Marty's door. He was already waiting for her, hands in his pockets, ankles crossed as he leaned against the low stone wall that surrounded the pool.

"Hi," she called, covering the distance between them with a light, quick step. The sweet smell of flowers cascading over the patio walls filled the evening air.

His resolve not to get involved with her lasted as long as it took her to walk toward him. She was graceful and elegant, white cotton flirting below her knees and molding her breasts, her bare shoulders creamy and round, her hair glowing like a remnant of the sunset in the deepening dusk.

His heartbeat quickened at the sight of her but rose to his throat when he saw the little flare of courage in her eyes, the naked trust. She was trying to fight whatever fear had taken possession of her that afternoon.

He straightened away from the wall in an instinctive need to support her resolve—whatever it was.

Shannon saw that and felt the little germ of bravery take a cautious stretch. After all the times she'd pulled away from him, after her reaction this afternoon, he was still there waiting, ready to do whatever she needed of him when he didn't even understand the problem.

She tucked her hand in his arm and held on. He didn't move. She felt tensile strength under her hand, the warmth beneath his white cotton jacket, the smooth gold of his watchband, the crisp hair on the back of his wrist. Fear made one halfhearted attempt to surface, but she tightened her grip, took a breath and it disappeared.

She smiled into Marty's eyes. "Ready?"

He looked down into hers, his own cautious. "Yes. Are you?"

She nodded, a little surprised, a little pleased with herself. "Yes."

He smiled then and started toward the steps that led to the street.

Chapter Eight

Marty couldn't stop staring into Shannon's eyes. He'd never seen them so bright, so self-satisfied, so completely untroubled. She'd just finished a plate of lobster that might have given Evan or Jarrod pause, and now picked at a parfait glass of chocolate mousse.

He leaned back, pulling his demitasse of espresso toward him. "Palm Springs is doing things to you," he observed lazily.

It did things to him, too, she thought. His fair good looks were burnished and dramatized by the candlelight, and the ready humor that always made him look so youthful seemed to have been replaced by a thoughtful, mature concentration. And its focus was her.

Not certain how powerful her little shot of courage was, she tried to keep the atmosphere light. "It's given me an appetite."

He laughed softly. "You always have an appetite. It's given you a sort of..." His blond brows drew together as he studied her for the right word. "I don't know...a kind of abandon that's a refreshing change from the always responsible businesswoman."

"It's the warmth," she said, glancing at him as she spooned into the mousse. "It makes me all—" she wriggled her shoulders in a gesture meant to define the word she finally blurted "—languid."

Marty had to concentrate on sipping and swallowing.

She pushed the empty goblet aside and said as though she'd given it careful thought, "And I think it's the aura of the sheikh."

Marty raised an eyebrow. "Excuse me?"

"The sheikh," she repeated. "You know. The desert lover who stole women from their humdrum lives and carried them off to his tent."

Despite his surprise, he was interested. "That appeals to you?"

"The tent does," she admitted, leaning against the back of her chair and smiling dreamily. "A bank of silk pillows, a bowl of dried fruit, palm trees outside and a warm pool of water, lush fabrics from the caravan. Why don't I have one of those?"

"Because we're staying in a motel."

Shannon rolled her eyes. "Not the tent. The espresso."

"Because you had dessert," he replied, then warned. "It'll be a little rich on top of chocolate mousse."

"I have a strong constitution," she insisted.

Marty called the waiter over and ordered a second espresso.

Shannon sipped from it and rolled her eyes again, appreciatively this time. "The inventory system looks complicated. Do you think . . . ?"

"Let's not talk business." Marty dipped his spoon into the mound of cream on her cup and added it to his own.

Shannon made a face at him. "This is a *business* trip."

"We're on our own time now."

"Have you called the kids?"

"Let's not talk about them, either."

"What do you want to talk about?"

He stirred the cream into his espresso, then sipped and leaned back once more. "Let's get back to the tent. I think there's something revealing there. Despite your firm grasp of business and your no-nonsense approach to management, I'm beginning to see another side. The youthful wish to run away to sea, the fascination with carousel horses that could represent a latent wish to run away with the circus, and now a revelation of a fondness for the sheikh. Are you whimsical at heart, Miss Carlisle? Do you seek to escape your retail prison?'' He ended the question on a dramatic note, his smile playful and taunting.

Shannon felt more carefree than she had in years. It was almost as if she were someone else, some lighthearted creature, buoyant of spirit, who'd never known the dark years she'd experienced. "Maybe it means I should have gone into the hotel/travel business rather than retail."

Marty laughed. "You certainly know how to squash a daydream. Want to dance?" He said the words quickly, before either of them had too much time to think. He was taking advantage of her giddy mood, but he was sure that was the only way she would do it—on the impulse of the moment, riding the crest of her earlier success.

For one brief moment she looked terrified. Then the resolve she'd depended upon earlier that night formed in her eyes and she put her napkin on the table and pushed her chair back. He stood and offered his hand, and she didn't hesitate to take it.

Her hand was cold in his as he led her to the small dance floor at the far end of the spacious room. Mellow music with a lot of strings and enough horn to add pathos came from the glittering orchestra.

Shannon's heart pounded. I can do this, she told herself as she turned to him. It will be more difficult than taking his arm or holding his hand—this is body contact we're talking about. Holding. Legs touching. My breasts in contact with his chest. His arm around me. The color drained from her face, and she looked up at Marty in mortal fear that she would scream.

He didn't touch her. She had deliberately walked them to a back corner of the floor, where other couples danced by them, shielding them from the people eating dinner. They remained inches apart, looking at each other.

"Change your mind?" he asked gently.

If you'll let it happen just once, the therapist had told her over and over, *just once, it'll be easier the next time, and you'll drive the fear away.*

"I . . ." Her voice was hardly a whisper, she tried again. "I haven't danced in . . . years."

Marty smiled. "Neither have I."

She swallowed. "I wasn't very good at it then."

"Me, neither."

"Do you wonder why we're trying it now?" she asked.

He shook his head. "I know why," he said significantly. "Different partners."

That was the clue, Shannon knew, the reason she'd taken his arm, the reason she'd enjoyed dinner so much—and, indeed, every moment since he'd come to Portland—the reason she was standing here, willing to make an effort to conquer the black beast of her existence. Marty wasn't Keith.

She put a hand on his shoulder, and without ceremony he placed a hand at her back, took her other hand and began to move with the music. He left inches between them. They danced with the circumspect posture of long ago, she acutely aware that she had freedom to move, he feeling keenly the distance that separated them. His splayed hand was warm against the thin cotton of her dress, her waist felt small and fragile under his fingers.

When the music stopped Shannon heaved a sigh as though she'd been relieved of a great weight. I did it, she thought in amazement. I did it.

"All right, Carlisle," Marty said, leading her off the floor, sensing without understanding that she'd accomplished something important. "Big day tomorrow. Can't play all night, you know. You're going to have to be sharp in the morning to absorb all that inventory stuff and save me from the clutches of Mrs. Goodwin.''

The waiter returned Marty's credit card, and he signed the slip as Shannon reached under the chair for her purse.

''Do you want a big breakfast, or shall I pick up something from the bakery?'' Marty asked. They walked the four blocks to the motel hand in hand under a fat yellow moon.

''Big.''

''Silly question.''

''Mrs. Goodwin's bigger than I. If I have to handle her for you, I'll need fuel.''

''You should have enough in you now to keep the lights burning in Manhattan until April.''

''Smarty.''

''That's 'Marty,' '' he corrected. ''No *S*.''

Shannon burst into laughter that lasted all the way back to the motel.

BY WEDNESDAY AFTERNOON Shannon's brain burst with figures, categories, computer codes and input departments. She tossed things into her suitcase with an uncharacteristic lack of care, then walked desultorily to the sliding screen door and opened it. The fragrance of the wisteria that cascaded over the walls assailed her and her sense of responsibility.

Marty's screen door slid open, and he leaned out to smile at her. ''You're supposed to be packing.''

''You have influence at Hale's,'' she said, breathing in the delicious air. ''Couldn't you transfer Goodwin to Portland and send me here?''

He leaned against the doorjamb and crossed his ankles. ''You'd abandon me to such a fate?''

''You could come, too,'' she said magnanimously.

He was silent for a moment. "Then we wouldn't be playing here. We'd be working. Wouldn't that stunt the romance for you a little?"

Shannon stepped out onto the patio and spread her arms as she had that first day on the sidewalk. The sun seemed to fill every pore in her body. "It's not the romance," she said, pulling her arms in to hug herself. "It's the warmth. It's like being plugged in all the time, as though your power source will never be cut off. As though you'll be warm forever."

That was probably what the child she had been had hoped to find by running away to sea, Marty thought, or with the circus, or the sheikh—the warmth that had been missing in her life. But that had been an emotional warmth, and she now talked about a physical one. Perhaps, in the tangle of human thought and emotion, they had become one.

He wanted to go out on the patio and join her. He wanted to wrap his arms around her and watch the sun set over the hills. He wanted to be close to her, but he knew better than to push. "What do you feel like for dinner?" he asked.

She turned from her perusal of the horizon to give him a smile that melted his backbone.

"Dancing," she said.

FOR TWO NIGHTS in a row they had danced like instructors from the Arthur Murray studios, harmoniously but precisely, as though an audience of students watched. Marty had ignored the surprised glances of the other dancers who watched the beautiful woman holding herself so stiffly in his arms. Though he didn't understand why, he knew what she had conquered to remain under his touch.

But tonight he felt the difference the moment he touched her. She was pliant, warm, relaxed. When she placed both of her hands at his neck, he joined his behind her waist, careful to hold her loosely, to allow her room to escape. When she inclined her head against his chin, he resisted the effort to tighten his grip.

"Thank you," she said softly. Violins and trumpets filled the air with "Isn't it romantic?"

"For what?" he asked.

She leaned back to look at him, her eyes warm, her small smile bright. "You know 'what,'" she said. "I know you don't understand why, but you know what you've done, what you've helped me do. Thank you."

Though he thought desperately of what he'd give to have her explain it, he simply nodded, making no demands.

She relaxed against him again, feeling the wonder of the proximity of their bodies and the total lack of fear in her. Her arms embraced his sturdy shoulders, her breasts bumped familiarly against his broad chest, the sensitive skin at her temple rested against the warm, faintly scratchy angle of his square chin, and her nostrils were filled with the scent of his after-shave and brandy, and she didn't feel one ripple of panic. She felt comfortable, secure, content.

As Shannon's breasts swelled against his chest with a little sigh of satisfaction, Marty drew a fortifying breath and let himself wonder what he had done.

She'd been right, of course. He didn't understand the trauma behind Shannon's reaction to touch, but he knew that he'd helped her overcome something cataclysmic because she'd trusted him to be gentle, undemanding, patient.

At the moment, with his arms full of her, he was hard put to find that chivalry within himself. He wanted to pull her closer, to turn her head until he could see the warmth in her eyes, the startled parting of her lips that always came before a laugh, and kiss her until all fear and caution were gone.

But that would terrify her, and she trusted him to know that. God, Hale, he thought grimly. How in the hell do you always find yourself in an impossible situation?

"ARE YOU MANAGING all right, Clarissa?" Marty asked, approaching Poole as she put a new roll of tape in the cash register. The sounds of power tools and hammering came from behind a temporary frame wall constructed to separate the small army of carpenters from the customers.

"Oh, yes." With a pencil tucked into her haphazard bun, Poole smiled up at him. She closed the top of the register, pushed a button and watched the new tape emerge. "Moving everything away from the wall has crowded us as you can see, but there's plenty of room to move, and the inconvenience is a small price to pay for ultimately having more space."

Marty looked around and saw a fairly respectable distribution of customers. "It's not affecting customer traffic?"

She smiled. "If I see them frown at the noise and walk away, I chase them down and find them what they want."

Marty laughed and patted her back as she came around the counter to lean against the front of it. "Good girl, Clarissa. The job foreman told me they expect to be painting by the end of the week. That'll be a little quieter, anyway."

"We're doing fine. How was Palm Springs?"

"Fine." He couldn't help the reflective smile that underlined the word. Since he and Shannon had returned two days ago, it was business as usual between them. But the subtle change that had taken place in her in the desert remained. She was a little softer, a little less tense, a little more interested in him as a man.

He turned to Poole to find her watching him with a curious expression. "How fine?" she asked.

He went into a brief account of the inventory system, avoiding the question in her eyes. "The new cash registers we're bringing in after the holidays will keep track of everything for us—practically think for us."

The telephone rang, and Poole reached behind her to answer it. Marty went around the wall to discuss the gallery's progress with the foreman, but Poole's urgent shout called him back.

With a hand over the receiver, she raised her voice to be heard above the noise. "They've caught a shoplifter in Men's Wear and they can't find Security."

He reversed directions. "I saw Zak on my way down. He was heading for the dining room. Tell them I'm on my way, then call him."

Marty took off for the department at a run. Shoplifters were seldom dangerous, and they almost always ran, but he knew that the young Men's Wear buyer was off today, his assistant was his father's age, and the rest of the clerks were from the new crew hired for Christmas.

He reached Men's Wear to find a frightened, petite blonde waiting for him. She pointed to the back door around which employees and customers were crowded.

"She's got him in the parking lot!" she said, her eyes wide as she ran with him. "Hurry!"

Great. Now he knew the shoplifter was a man and the clerk who'd chosen to stop him was one of the new, inexperienced girls who didn't know or hadn't followed store policy on shoplifters. He peeled the barrier of onlookers away from the door and emerged into the parking lot, then stopped in his tracks.

Shannon, in pink slacks and a belted pink sweater, had a man larger than himself pinned against the door of a pickup truck by the back of his leather jacket.

"Look, lady!" the man shouted over his shoulder, but Shannon only pushed him harder against the truck. As Marty sprinted the distance that separated them, he was sure it was only surprise that prevented the man from backhanding her and sending her flying across the pavement while he made his escape. Fear and fury rose inside him, equally hot and volatile.

Pushing Shannon aside, he grabbed the back of the man's collar and started toward the store. "What's with her?" the shoplifter demanded, still unresisting. He glanced at Marty with troubled, bloodshot eyes. "She having some kind of identity crisis or something? I mean, it's cold and I need a coat, so I figure I might as well bag a nice one, you know? Geez! Then Red Sonja chases me down!"

"I've got him, sir," Zak said, appearing at the door. He was tall and lean, a retired Portland policeman. "Sorry about that. I—"

"No problem," Marty said, handing the shoplifter over. "Take care of him." With considerable effort he smiled at the employees and customers still clustered at the door. "Everybody back to work. Or back to spending." There was a titter of laughter and the crowd dispersed.

Then Marty turned to Shannon, who still stood in the parking lot. He hadn't said a word to her, but she'd felt his anger when he'd shoved her aside to assume control of the shoplifter. It was bright in his eyes now as he strode toward her. She folded her arms and waited calmly. This was a side of him she'd never seen, and she was more interested than frightened.

"An employee doesn't try to apprehend or to chase a shoplifter," he said, stopping inches away from her. His voice was quiet, but she could hear the strained breath underneath. "You call security and wait for them to handle it."

"He had a three-hundred-dollar jacket," she replied reasonably. "I tried to call Zak when the girls first noticed him and called me. I couldn't find him, and by the time I got there, the shoplifter was—"

"He was bigger than I am!" Marty's voice raised a decibel as he pointed a thumb at his chest and looked down a good eight inches at her. "If he'd fought back, you'd have been oatmeal."

Sufficiently impressed with Marty's temper, Shannon smiled in the interest of appeasing it. "I have a black belt in bluffing. I talked tough, and he didn't struggle once."

Unimpressed with her attempt at humor, Marty continued to stare her down. "You work for me now," he said quietly. "The next time, wait for the guard."

"Look!" she demanded. The adrenaline rush inspired by her saving a high ticket item and catching one of the banes of every retail businessperson's existence began to turn to anger. "When I ran this place, a three-hundred-dollar jacket meant a lot to me. I couldn't afford to let one walk out the door and neither can you. The three hundred bucks might not even make a percentage point's difference on Hale's profit and loss, but let word get around that you take a soft stand on shoplifting and they'll be coming in here with wheelbarrows!"

"Well, you don't run it anymore! Now you do what I say."

"Or what?" Unconsciously she wrapped her arms around herself against the penetrating chill of the forty-degree weather, though her tone remained hotly aggressive. "Or Myrtle, Montana? Are you threatening me with that again?"

"No," he said quietly, deliberately, unable to calm down. "I'm wondering why it takes an Act of Congress for you to make yourself touch *me*, yet you were throwing the shoplifter around without any apparent distress."

Shannon paled but didn't flinch. "My mistake. I didn't know you wanted to be thrown around."

He shifted his weight impatiently. "You know what I mean."

"Yes," she said, "but you don't know what you mean, so back off."

"Well, maybe I'd like to know," he said, flinging his arm out in a gesture of helplessness.

Shannon stared at him for a long moment, then finally sighed. "Maybe one day I'll tell you. May I get back to work now?"

"In a minute." Marty swung his jacket off and dropped it onto her shoulders. "Hale policy," he said, his voice quieter, though no less authoritative, "has always been that the clerk is more valuable to us than the item lifted. I don't care what you *used* to do. Don't ever chase down a shoplifter again."

"I second that," Henry said appearing beside Marty, looking dapper in a dark three-piece suit.

"Henry!" Shannon smiled, distracted from her annoyance by surprise. "What are you doing here?"

"I've just come from the Seattle Hale's, so I thought I'd pick Marty up for the board meeting. I'm driving, and it's such a long, dull trip. Get inside, girl. It's cold out here."

With one last glance at Marty, Shannon ran into the store.

"You, I presume," Henry said, following as Marty wandered to the walk that led around the store, "need time to cool off."

Both hands jammed into the pockets of his pants, Marty looked down at his father, his temper rearing again in his eyes. "You should have seen the shoplifter she collared out here."

Henry nodded. "I did."

"He was bigger than I am."

Henry grinned. "She didn't appear to be afraid of you, either."

Marty snickered, then glanced at his father and laughed openly, his good humor easing back. "No, she didn't."

"You having trouble working with her?"

"No. In fact, it's going much better than I expected. She's been very supportive, and I've tried to give her latitude. But this morning she took too much."

"You care about her," Henry guessed.

"I'm supposed to."

"I mean as a man, not as her boss."

Marty groaned and stopped at the rear entrance to the stockroom, leaning his shoulder against the white stone wall. "She's very complex. For once in my life I'd like to meet a woman who wasn't."

Henry leaned against the wall, facing his son. "You aren't under the misconception that *you're* uncomplicated?"

Marty sighed. "I was a jock and model. Hardly heavyweight endeavors. I am what I appear to be."

Henry shook his head as though summoning patience. "Why do you do this to yourself? Everything you gave up, you did for your family. You came back to Hale's because you found yourself a single parent who needed a more normal work schedule." Henry jabbed a finger into Marty's white shirt. "You didn't fail at those things, Marty. Monica failed you. How many men do you know are willingly raising four kids and have turned their lives around to be able to do it well?"

Marty put a hand on Henry's shoulder, restored once more by his father's love and unqualified support. He grinned. "Is this where you give me a lifesaver?"

Henry shoved him into the stockroom. "No, it's where I kick you in the butt."

Chapter Nine

Shannon was lonely. Not a new feeling. She'd lived her whole life apart from those who should have mattered to her, to whom she should have mattered. But she'd never known this restless dissatisfaction before, this longing for something that wasn't there. Or someone.

As she helped Poole and her staff push racks back into place and carry books up the stairway to the new mahogany-railed gallery, she guessed that the void in her childhood had been easier to bear because it had been a case of not missing what she'd never had.

Since Marty had arrived a month ago, she'd enjoyed the companionship of someone who cared about her. They were only friends, but the warmth he'd brought into her office seemed to have affected her tremendously. Now she dreamed of things she'd given up long ago.

"He's only been gone two days," Clarissa said, handing Shannon two large pictorial books. From the top step of a small folding ladder, Shannon reached down to take them.

"Who?" she asked.

Poole held the books a moment longer until Shannon was forced to look at her. "You know who. You've been sighing all morning. Miss him, do you?"

Shannon snatched the books. "If he were here," she said, "he'd be doing this and I'd be having coffee."

Poole looked around at the newly finished gallery with its stock of new books and sighed with satisfaction. "I can't wait for him to see how beautifully this has turned out. Why didn't we ever think of this?"

"I don't know. I guess sometimes it takes new blood to show us what's in front of our noses. Come on." She pointed to the box of books at Poole's feet. "Pass me something."

Poole handed up two coffee table books on Impressionist art. "Kathy Baker called me this morning," she said with a frown. "Our cash bag was short again last night. I don't understand it. We try to be so careful. That's twice in the past three weeks."

"Just between you and me," Shannon said, reaching down for another handful of books, "it's happened in other departments, too. I think someone's Christmas shopping at our expense."

"But no one's been—" Poole was interrupted by a call from under the gallery. "Telephone, Miss Carlisle!"

"Be right there!" Shannon called back, placing the books she held before stepping carefully down the ladder and grinning at Clarissa. "I'll be glad when you get a phone up here." Breathlessly Shannon accepted the receiver at the bottom of the gallery. "Shannon Carlisle."

Edie's voice sounded frantic. "Miss Carlisle, I don't know what to do. My son called and their baby's coming. My daughter-in-law is having complications, and her family is three thousand miles away. Mr. Hale is in Bend and I can't reach him. The board's gone to this place Mr. Henry owns in the mountains. It doesn't have a phone, and they go there when they don't want to be disturbed. I could send the police for him, but I hate to do that."

Shannon knew what the woman was asking. Edie knew no one else to call for help. I can't do this, she thought with a panicky chill. Four children. With Marty gone I'm responsible for the store.

Her brave inner voice reminded her that she could run the store in handcuffs if she had to. They're only kids. Most women deal with them every day of their lives and still get other things done. Buck up!

"Make your plans to go, Edie," Shannon said, hoping to inspire confidence in the other woman. "I'll come over this afternoon. What time do the boys get home from school?"

"About four, and each of them has a key. But Joshua has to be picked up by five-thirty at the preschool." Edie gave her an address about halfway between the store and Marty's home. "I'll call to let them know what's happened and to clear your picking up Josh." There was a pause while Edie drew breath. "Miss Carlisle, thank you so much. I don't know what I'd have done if you weren't able to help. I'll leave my extra key for you in the mailbox, and I won't stay away a minute longer than necessary."

"Don't worry about anything but your grandchild," Shannon advised, already making notes to herself on the unprinted side of a Hale's bag. "I should be able to hold out until Mr. Hale comes home on Monday."

Shannon hung up the phone and glanced at her watch— 2:00 p.m. Finding Gale in the training room, she beckoned to her to explain the crisis. Gale looked worried. "*You're* going to spend a whole weekend with four children?"

"Yes," Shannon said firmly, her resolve slightly shaken by her friend's reaction. "And it would help if you showed some faith in me."

Gale nodded bracingly. "Right. It's not as hard as it sounds. And if you need help, I'm only a phone call away."

"Can you work tomorrow? I know you hate Saturdays. And you'll have to cover for me Sunday."

"Sure. Anything else I can do?"

"What do kids eat?"

"Bring home a pizza. They'll love you for it."

SHANNON WAS TEARING lettuce for salad, with Tulip leaning against her leg, when the older boys trooped into the house. Evan stopped in surprise at the kitchen doorway, Jarrod and Grady piling into his back.

She smiled confidently and explained the problem. "So you're stuck with me for the weekend. Salad and pizza for dinner all right?"

Grady came near her to look into the big stainless-steel bowl. "Don't put sprouts in it, okay?"

"Okay. What kind of pizza? I thought I'd pick it up when I get Josh."

"The Mama Mia combination," Evan and Jarrod said simultaneously. Then Evan opened the refrigerator door and Jarrod delved into a cupboard, lost to all communication as they followed a primal need for sustenance.

"It has everything on it," Grady said with a grimace of distaste. "They're animals. Josh and I like Canadian bacon and pineapple."

"Sounds good to me, too. I have to pick up a few things at the Willamette Mall tomorrow. Do you guys skate?" The mall had an authentic Parker carousel she and Joshua could visit while the older boys occupied themselves at the ice rink.

Evan and Jarrod looked at each other. "If we're forced," Evan replied, his tone less rude than reluctant. "Skating's kind of..."

"Nerdy," Jarrod supplied. "Being new here, we're trying hard to fight that image. Course Evan has to fight harder than I do."

The telephone rang, and Grady snatched it before either of the other two boys could reach it. "Hi, Amy," he said enthusiastically. "No, this is Grady. Yeah, he's—" Before he could finish the sentence, Evan had pulled the receiver from him. He walked into the pantry with it and closed the door on the cord.

Shannon turned to Jarrod in surprise. "His new woman," he explained, popping a cracker into his mouth.

It seemed to disappear without his chewing or swallowing it.

"New woman," Shannon repeated, waiting for further explanation.

"Girlfriend," Grady interpreted. "You're pretty, but you don't know much, do ya?"

Thinking that about summed her up, Shannon returned to the salad while Jarrod and Grady went upstairs, sounding remarkably like the Fifth Army on the march. Evan was still in the pantry when she left to pick up Josh.

Josh's delight at her presence served to bolster her flagging confidence. They picked up the two pizzas, and she hurried back to Marty's, prepared to set the table, pour drinks and scour the neighborhood for the older boys.

To her surprise, Evan was setting the table and Jarrod pouring the soft drinks she'd brought home into glasses with the NFL logo on them. With salad tongs in hand, Grady looked through the salad greens for any sign of something foreign.

"Thanks, guys." As she shrugged out of her coat, Grady took the pizzas to the table. "You're certainly well organized."

"Setting up is our job when Dad's cooking on Edie's day off." Evan squatted down to help Josh with the stuck zipper on his jacket. He worked with a gentleness that softened her impression of the cool intellectual.

"We're supposed to clean up, too," Jarrod said, "but if you'd like to win us over by doing it for us, we'll understand."

Shannon looked at his irrepressible grin and had to laugh. "I think we should work together and win each other over."

And that was pretty much how the weekend went. On Saturday Evan and Jarrod watched while Shannon skated with Grady and Josh. Grady's sunny disposition helped him absorb all his awkward moves and falls with laughter. Josh squealed with delight while Shannon skated him slowly around the circle. When Grady tried to catch her free hand, they went down in an awkward tangle of arms and legs, laughing hysterically.

Seduced by the fun, Jarrod soon appeared, inching his way awkwardly toward them, his feet moving alarmingly in opposite directions until he landed on his backside with a thump. He grinned at Shannon and his brothers as they tried to help him up. "I don't think it's scientifically feasible to expect to support 160 pounds on two slivers of metal fourteen inches..." His treatise went unfinished when he suddenly discovered himself upright. "Oh!" he said in surprise.

Shannon propelled herself slowly forward, holding his arm so that he came with her. His grin broadened. "Hey, this isn't so bad."

"Concentrate on gliding," she encouraged, picking up their pace. "Pick a spot in the distance and head for it."

Shannon was never entirely sure what happened next. Gaining confidence, Jarrod took several steps on his own and began to laugh, delighted by his progress. Then suddenly his weight and speed pulled him away from her, and she watched helplessly as he veered to the right, obviously out of control. His eyes widening as he gained momentum, and flailing the air wildly, he headed straight for the sidelines. Two bystanders in conversation and one unsuspecting young woman tying on skates were felled like flies. He would have perpetrated further destruction if the bench he knocked over hadn't spun around and spitefully knocked him off his feet.

Assured that his victims weren't seriously hurt, Shannon skated to Jarrod, her runners spewing ice as she stopped.

"I told you this was nerdy," he accused, rising to his knees. "I think I'm done."

Grady coasted to a stop beside them, holding Josh by the hand. Jarrod glowered at him. "How'd you do that?"

But Grady was laughing too hard to answer.

"Ready?" Shannon asked, tugging at Jarrod's arm.

"Isn't it time for lunch?"

"Come on," she prodded. "Don't be a sissy."

"I'd rather be a sissy than look like a nerd."

"Come on, I'll help you." Evan reached a hand down to pull his brother to his feet.

All the others turned to him in surprise. He stood with relative ease and yanked Jarrod to a standing position.

"I thought you couldn't skate," Shannon said.

With a glance, he indicated his free hand holding on to the railing. "I can't. But I figured you'd need help getting Brian Boitano here to his feet."

"Oh sure! Laugh!" Jarrod gestured indignantly and lost his balance. Only quick reactions by Shannon and Evan saved him.

"Try to remain calm," Shannon suggested, readjusting the cap that had slipped to Jarrod's ears. "Grady and Josh are doing fine. Why don't I get between the two of you, and we'll see if we can get around the rink without maiming the spectators."

Jarrod looked at the considerable distance and expelled a heartfelt sigh. "Then can we have lunch?"

"If you're still alive, yes," she promised.

Jarrod looked at Evan. "Dad sent her to pay us back for all the times we've blown the rules."

Positioning herself between them, Shannon held out both hands. "Your father's innocent. He doesn't even know I'm here." Jarrod gave her his hand, and she closed hers over it. "He was at your grandfather's place in the mountains when Edie tried to call. I'm only helping out in a crisis. Honest."

Evan looked at her hand, then at her. He was easing up toward her—she could see it in his eyes. He gave her his hand. "When Jarrod and I were little, we tied a baby-sitter to the water heater. It's important to me," he said significantly, "that you don't let me fall and look like a nerd."

She smiled and tightened her grip on him. "There's nothing that'll make anyone look more nerdy than an unwillingness to laugh at himself. Hold on."

At four in the afternoon Shannon literally had to drag them off the ice. Each boy, including Jarrod, had acquired a basic ability to move around on his own. Once that goal was achieved, however, it proved less fun than trying complicated moves for which they were unprepared and which inevitably led to dramatic pileups. Evan had loosened up considerably and was shouting and laughing with the rest of them by the time Shannon insisted they head home. It was after dinner before she remembered she'd never made it to the carousel.

"IT'S GOOD TO BE BACK in civilization. Want to go for a drink? Maybe pick up some girls?" Henry Hale stood up from the table where he and Marty had spent the past three hours going over figures and glanced at his watch. "It's only midnight."

"*Only* midnight," Marty repeated, raising his arms to stretch as his brain reeled from the onslaught of numbers. "How old are you, anyway?"

"Younger than you, apparently." Henry grinned and began to gather up the pages of his report. "I suppose you'll want to call home first."

"Edie'll still be up watching old movies. Dad?" When Henry stopped in the act of crossing to the hall closet for his coat, Marty pushed his chair in and, leaning on the back of it, looked at him. "What would you do if one of the women you're always chasing responded to you?"

Henry looked alarmed for a moment then, drawing a shade against any revelation of honesty, winked as he opened the closet door. "You think none of them has?"

"No, I don't," he said evenly. "I think you're just playing a role. Like this afternoon—" he paused, hoping to see a guilty look on his father's face "—with the temp who took minutes for our meeting."

Henry tossed Marty his leather jacket, completely impenitent. "She was a pretty little thing. I hope they don't bring the curtain down for a good long time. Make your call. I'll get the car out of the garage."

On the fourth ring Marty began to think Edie had changed her Saturday night routine of tea, popcorn and vintage movies until 2:00 a.m. Then a voice that was familiar despite the sleepy grogginess in it said, "Hale's, Portland." There was a pause, a yawn, then a small gasp. "I mean . . . hello?"

Marty asked hesitantly. "Shannon?"

He heard a rustling in the background. "Yes. Hi, Marty." She sounded more alert, though her voice was still thick with sleep. "How's the meeting going?"

"What are you doing there?" he asked, ignoring her question. "I did call home and not the store?"

She laughed softly. "Edie's daughter-in-law had to have labor induced and had a little girl by Cesarean section early this morning. Edie's son was a little panicky because his wife's family is so far away. Edie asked if I'd stay with the boys for a few days so she could be there. Don't worry," she added hastily. "Edie called tonight and everybody's fine. She'll be home Monday afternoon in time to put dinner on."

Marty glanced at his watch. "Look . . . I can be home in a couple of hours."

"We're doing fine." She sounded genuinely firm. "The boys might be getting more junk food than you'd like, but I thought the important thing was to keep them happy while you're gone."

He could imagine his raucous, rowdy boys making her life difficult. "Shannon, I'm sorry . . ."

"Why?" she demanded in what sounded like real surprise.

"Well, I'm sure you had other things to do with your weekend."

"I'd have worked, but Gale went in for me. I've really had a lot of fun."

"'Thank you' hardly seems like enough..." he began.

She laughed and yawned. "Remember that the next time you threaten to transfer me north."

Marty suddenly found himself in desperate need of a mental image to go with her sleepy voice. "Where are you?" he asked.

There was an instant's pause. "What do you mean?"

"Where in the house are you?" he clarified.

"Oh." She sounded hesitant. "I slept on the sofa last night, but these guys have drained every ounce of my energy and I'm so bruised..."

Oh, God, he thought. "Bruised?"

"We went ice-skating at the Willamette Mall."

"Ah." He drew a relieved breath. "And you're not very good?"

"I'm passable, but Jarrod is hopeless. His clowning around had all of us landing on our... well, you can imagine. When it was time to leave, he had fallen and was laughing so hard I couldn't get him up. If it hadn't been for Evan helping me drag him to the bench, Jarrod would probably still be there."

"You got Evan on the ice?" he asked. He tried to imagine his eldest son tossing aside his self-possession as he surrendered to the fun of learning to skate. But the picture refused to form.

Shannon laughed. "He even enjoyed himself."

There was a pause while Marty wondered what had happened to the people he cared about while he was away. Shannon was having fun with his children? Evan was playing?

"So, what I was leading up to," Shannon said, "is that I'm in your bed. It's easier on my bruises."

Marty suddenly felt his heart beating. He put a hand over it and rubbed, but it didn't seem to quiet. "In my bed," he repeated softly. His mind conjured up the image of auburn hair against his pillows, brown eyes closing sleepily, a pink mouth against the phone only a breath away from his. "That's an image I'll enjoy falling asleep on. Good night, Shannon."

"ARE YOU GETTING UP?"

Shannon opened one eye and saw Tulip sitting beside her, tongue lolling in quiet contentment. Concluding sleepily that it probably wasn't Tulip who had spoken, she opened her other eye. Josh sat at her left side eating cold pizza. Breakfast!

She sat up in alarm, and Tulip leaned over to wash her face. She put an arm around the dog and leaned into its sturdy form, closing her eyes. "What time is it, Josh?"

"Sunday," he replied.

Right. She gently shoved the dog off the bed, swung her legs over the side and stuffed her feet into her slippers. "Put that pizza back and I'll make you some breakfast."

"I'm full," he said. She looked up at him to see that the pizza had disappeared. "Evan and Jarrod are eating Doritos, and Grady had a hot dog."

With a groan Shannon headed for the shower to fortify herself for her last day of child care. Prompted by guilt, she made bacon and eggs and toast for lunch and was pleased when it was greeted with considerable enthusiasm.

During the quiet afternoon, while Evan and Jarrod labored over homework at the dining room table and Grady lay on the living room floor with Tulip and the Sunday comics, Shannon and Josh prepared to bake cookies. Finding jam and walnuts, she mixed the dough for a double batch of thumbprints.

By the time Shannon had removed the first cookie sheet from the oven, Grady and Jarrod had come into the kitchen to investigate the source of the aroma filling the house.

"Cookies!" Grady breathed, his eyes brightening with anticipation. "Edie always *buys* cookies."

"She has a lot of work to do," Shannon said, rolling a small ball of dough between her palms. "Cookies take a lot of time. You can have one in a few minutes. I have to spoon jam into them first."

"Don't put your hands on them." Josh stood beside Shannon on a kitchen chair, and Jarrod caught his small hand as it reached toward the tray of cookie dough balls.

"That's his job," Shannon said, gently disengaging Josh's hand. "He presses the thumbprint in so that I have a place to put the jam."

"Oh. Sorry, Josh. Where's the jam?"

Rolling another ball of dough, Shannon pointed to the other end of the counter. Jarrod took the jar in one hand and dug a teaspoon out of the utensil drawer, apparently determined to speed up the process.

"Just a little," Shannon cautioned.

Shannon pointed Grady to a cookie sheet of plain balls of dough. "Those have to be dipped in egg white and rolled in nuts, if you'd like to help."

Grady took one look at the bowl of egg white already messy with nuts and grimaced. He leaned back to shout into the living room, "Evan! Got a job for ya!"

Evan came to the doorway of the kitchen and Grady explained the problem. "We'll get to taste them faster if you can roll 'em in that junk."

Pushing up the sleeves of his sweatshirt, Evan washed his hands, elbowed Grady aside and, after brief instructions from Shannon, set to work.

"Our mom has food catered," Grady said, leaning his elbows on the counter on the other side of Shannon. "She has a yacht and has lots of parties on it."

"She's in movies!" Josh said. "Oops!" His too enthusiastic thumb had destroyed the ball of cookie dough.
Shannon reformed it and put it back in place.

"I've read about her," she said casually. The boys seemed
very well adjusted to the loss, but Shannon was sure their
mother's defection must have hurt. She trod very carefully,
wary of saying the wrong thing. "She's very beautiful."

"She has three houses and three cars," Grady went on.
"She never comes to see us."

"Yes, she does," Evan corrected quietly.

"Three times in two years," Jarrod said, spooning jam.
"Big deal."

"She divorced Dad, you know," Grady informed Shannon.

Evan worked methodically. "He didn't love her anymore."

Jarrod's voice became defensive. "Yes, he did. She's the
one who was always running off to make a movie. She didn't
care about him!"

"I'm sure they both care about each other," Shannon
said quickly, afraid of allowing bitter feelings to erupt that
she wouldn't know how to handle. "After all, they were
married for quite a while and had four children together.
Just because a man and a woman can't live together anymore doesn't mean they don't still care about the love that
brought them together and the children they have."

The boys were distracted from the heavy conversation
when Tulip put her paws on the counter, investigating the
tempting aroma. Evan gave her a spoonful of cookie dough,
then they all went back to their duties, the issue of their
parents forgotten for the moment. Shannon watched the
lively intelligent faces at work, listened to their witty repar-
tee and their surprising observations, and wondered how
fame and possessions could ever replace their presence in
Monica Hale's life.

Later that evening Shannon considered it ironic that Monica Hale was interviewed on television on a segment of *Hollywood Inside*. Grady saw her image while he changed channels in search of *Monsters from the Forbidden Planet* and excitedly called his brothers.

Shannon joined the boys as they gathered around the television and watched a beautiful dark-haired woman talk about a role for which she was competing in a new Steven Spielberg movie.

"I'd love to work with Steven," she said in a husky voice. "I've done primarily glamour roles so far, but I'd love to do his Dark Queen with all her—" the lovely eyes glanced wickedly at the camera "—jealousies and complexities."

"When does it start filming?" the interviewer asked.

"Right before the holidays," she replied. "Or maybe after. Depends on how quickly they make their decision on the queen. It's the only role still uncast."

The interviewer thanked her for appearing, then listed the following week's guests as the credits began to roll.

Evan walked silently upstairs. Jarrod watched him while Grady continued his search for the movie. "Mom was supposed to pick us up for the holidays," Jarrod explained to Shannon. "If she gets the part, I guess we're out."

Shannon was at a loss for words. She should say something comforting, she knew, but as a child of a neglectful parent herself, she knew nothing would really ease the pain.

She was also unexpectedly overwhelmed by the knowledge that Marty had been married to that beautiful, sophisticated woman. Seeing Monica Hale on television sharply reminded Shannon of her inadequacies as the female half of a relationship.

Unable to think of any sage advice to console herself or the children, she went to make popcorn.

THE HOUSE WAS DARK, except for the thin glow of the nightlight in the upstairs hall. The 2:00 a.m. quiet made the house seem unnatural, as though his children and his dog had been kidnapped. Certainly nothing, even sleep, could make the house so still. Marty dropped his bag near the sofa, shed his raincoat and climbed the stairs.

He checked Evan's room first because it was nearest to the top of the stairs. The boy lay on his stomach, blankets down to his waist. Instinctively Marty moved to draw them higher. Evan shifted, turning his head, and Marty saw muscles move in his shoulders along the thickening breadth of his back. He's changing from boy to man, Marty thought, re-settling the blankets, and I still haven't made peace with him about his mother. I've got to do that before it's too late.

Across the hall Jarrod lay somewhere under a disorderly pile of blankets, snoring softly. Marty smiled and closed the door.

At the end of the hall on Jarrod's side, Grady and Josh slept in bunk beds. In the bottom bunk Josh was curled in the fetal position, the matted, battle-scarred stuffed monkey clutched in his arm. He was completely uncovered. Tulip lay on three-quarters of the narrow bunk, her muzzle pushed into the wadded blankets. The dog lifted her head in surprise, then flattened her ears and wagged her tail as though embarrassed to have been caught napping on the job. Marty ruffled her ears, then tugged on the covers until the dog shifted, allowing him to cover Josh. Marty took a moment to enjoy the miracle of his youngest son. Something good had come out of that year that he remembered as the darkest of his life.

Easing his head from under the top bunk to reach up and check on Grady, Marty found himself confronted by a pair of blue eyes that were bright even in the dark. Grady hung over the side and reached out for a hug. "Hi, Dad," he whispered. "I thought you weren't coming home till to-morrow."

"Hi." Marty held him an extra moment, grateful as al-ways for his sunny, loving warmth. "I called last night and talked to Shannon. She told me about the crisis with Edie. You guys doing okay?"

"Sure. We even made cookies."

"No kidding. Did you save me some?"

Grady reached under his pillow and pulled out a bag containing several now-unappealing samples. "I'm not sure, but you can have one of these."

Marty bit back a smile, holding his hand up in refusal. "Thanks, anyway. I'll check the cookie jar when I go downstairs. Go back to sleep, son."

Marty pushed the door to his room open and watched the weak ray of light from the hall pick out the soft shape of Shannon's body under the blankets. She lay on her back, her face turned away from him, one arm at her waist, the other flung out over the edge of the bed.

He approached quietly, taking her hand and folding it under the covers. With a muttered protest, she turned her head toward him and flung the arm out again. He smiled at the thought that even in sleep she couldn't be easily managed.

Shannon stirred, and he stiffened worriedly, afraid of how she would react if she awoke in the middle of the night in a strange bed and saw him standing there. But she opened her eyes slowly, took a moment to focus on him, then smiled and raised the wayward hand toward him. "Marty," she said sleepily, undisguised pleasure in her voice. "You're home."

Marty closed his hand around hers, sat on the edge of the bed and fell in love. He was home. He wondered how difficult it would be to convince her that she was home, too.

"I'm relieved to see you in one piece," he teased gently. "I'm sorry I woke you."

"It's okay," she said, letting her eyes fall closed again. "As long as it doesn't mean you want your bed back."

"No. I'll sleep on the sofa."

She made a small contented sound. "Good night, Marty."

Amusedly philosophical about her easy dismissal of him, Marty put her arm under the covers again and pulled the blankets up. He was comforted that she hadn't been frightened to find him in the room—better than that, she'd actually seemed pleased.

He was going to make something of this relationship, he resolved as he stood and crossed to the door. He was a past master at beginning again. He turned for a last glimpse of her and saw her slim white arm in the shadows. It had escaped the blanket again. He smiled and closed the door. So it wouldn't be easy. What was?

Chapter Ten

All was right in the world. Shannon had never awakened with that feeling before. The very instant she gained awareness her mind had always flooded with the myriad details that filled her working day—checking for lost shipments, arbitrating clerk/department head problems, keeping a close eye on the daily financial picture.

But this morning was different. She heard rain falling on the roof and beating against the windows with torrential force. She smelled coffee and bacon, heard young voices shouting and laughing. She stretched happily, luxuriously in her warm cocoon of blankets, no longer asleep but not quite awake. She'd dreamed this dream so many times, had truly believed in it for so many years that the vague impressions settled around her with comfortable familiarity. Cozy home, breakfast cooking, children laughing, a bed still warm from the body of the man with whom she'd shared it.

That thought brought her upright. She put a hand to her forehead, trying to sift reality from the dream. Rain was beating against the windows, and she did smell bacon and coffee, and heard the boys' voices. Cautiously she slipped a hand beyond the side of the bed in which she'd been curled. It was cold and unrumpled.

Relaxing, she remembered seeing Marty's face during the night, remembered holding his hand. He'd come home early, worried about how she and the boys were coping. He had touched her face. That had been real. She smiled wryly as she swung her legs over the side of the bed. Her subconscious had simply embellished that part a little.

The sense of rightness began to slip. What was she doing in Marty Hale's house with a small army of children? She was out of place. Glamorous Monica Hale belonged there. The feeling grew as she remembered the image of their beautiful mother and how helpless she'd felt in comforting them because they wouldn't see Monica for Christmas. Hurrying into yesterday's jeans and sweater, she ran downstairs, her brief experience fixing breakfast for Marty's boys leading her to believe that he might need help.

In the kitchen Evan sat at one end of the table, poring over a book and making notes while absently sipping at a glass of milk. In the middle of the table, Jarrod and Grady arm-wrestled raucously. Marty stood at the stove, turning eggs with remarkable equanimity while conducting a conversation with Joshua, who sat on the counter near him, clutching his monkey.

Toast popped, and Shannon took a plate from the cupboard and reached into the refrigerator for butter. Marty gave her a warm smile as she passed him. "Good morning."

"Hi, Shannon!" Still holding the monkey by a paw, Joshua stretched out both arms to her.

Though surprised by the gesture, she required only a moment to react. She put the plate and butter down and went to lift him off the counter. He wrapped his arms and legs around her, hugging her. Warmth filled her, and the feeling of being out of place lessened. At Marty's raised eyebrow, she grinned. "You're monopolizing my buddy," she said, and she carried Josh closer to the toaster.

Marty served Jarrod and Grady, effectively breaking up the bout of arm wrestling. "Mom was on TV last night," Evan said, glancing up from his book.

Breaking more eggs into the pan, Marty asked with interest, "Anything new?"

"She's up for the part of the Dark Queen in the new Spielberg movie."

"They're filming in Morocco," Jarrod put in, nibbling on a slice of bacon. "I guess that does it for her picking us up for the holidays like she promised."

Evan closed his book with a slam. "You don't know that. God, you're such a cynic!"

"I'm…" Jarrod began hotly, but Marty turned from the stove and said quietly, "You have different perspectives. Can't you just accept that about each other? Anyway, if she gets the part, she'll probably have too much to do to think about Christmas. You guys should prepare yourselves to spend it with me, just in case."

"Oh, no!" Grady put a hand to his forehead as though he were in great pain. "Someone should alert Santa! We should get bonuses for having to stay with Dad."

Nodding, Jarrod chewed and swallowed. "We'll call Spielberg. I'm sure when he realizes that we have to spend Christmas with Darth Va—" Marty turned from the stove, spatula twirling threateningly in his hands. "Actually, we've tolerated it every Christmas since we were born." Jarrod gave Marty a quick smile. "We can probably put up with it another year." He paused, then added when Marty turned back to the stove, "If we try hard."

His anger diverted by his brothers' comedic reactions, Evan sighed and leaned back as Marty put a plate of bacon and eggs in front of him. Marty clapped a hand on his shoulder in wordless consolation. Shannon saw Evan's gaze follow his father as he went back to the stove, his expression confused. She realized for the first time that he found his father's love and understanding difficult to comprehend in view of his own quarrelsome attitude.

Shannon put Josh on his feet, handed him the plate of toast and sent him toward the table. She wandered to the stove to look over Marty's shoulder.

"Up, over easy or over hard?" he asked, holding two eggs in his right hand. He looked disgustingly fresh, she thought, for a man who had come home in the middle of the night after a long weekend studying figures. He wore jeans and a dark blue sweatshirt that deepened his eyes several shades. She saw a softness in his gaze that was different from the teasing affection he had for his boys—and it was directed at her. The little pulse of warmth that had started in her chest with Josh's hug broadened its radius.

"Over easy, please. And just one. No bacon."

He nodded, replacing one egg. "You're sure about the bacon?"

"Positive."

By the time Marty served her breakfast, the three older boys gathered books and jackets and ran for the bus. Jarrod and Grady called a goodbye to Shannon before wrestling each other out the door, but Evan paused in the doorway. He smiled briefly. "Thanks, Shannon," he said, and followed his brothers.

"Enjoy," Marty said as he took Josh's hand and started for the stairs. "I'm going to get this guy ready for preschool."

"Aren't you eating?" she asked.

"Josh and I ate first," he said, looking down at his youngest with a smile that combined fondness and frustration. "He's usually up by six."

Dressed and combed, Josh insisted on hugging Shannon before going out to the car. "Will you come back tonight?" he asked, his blue eyes wide.

"Your dad's home now, sweetie," she said, helping him with the zipper on his jacket. "You don't need a baby-sitter anymore."

Josh looked plaintively at his father. "Tell her, Dad."

Marty took the chair beside Shannon's and sat down. "She's welcome to visit us anytime, Josh, but she has her own house to take care of. She just came for a couple of days to help us out."

"Can you come visit, then?" Josh insisted.

Shannon hugged him again. "I will. I promise."

"Tonight?"

"Maybe next week."

Josh looked disappointed but resigned. "I love you, Shannon," he said.

A little stitch of pain wrinkled Shannon's brow. "I love you, Josh," she replied.

Marty put a hand on her shoulder, then followed Josh out the door. She recognized it as the same gesture he'd given Evan, an offer of support despite his inability to offer a solution.

When Marty returned home twenty minutes later, the kitchen was clean and Shannon was enjoying a second cup of coffee. "How do you go through that every morning," she asked in wonder, "and still arrive at the store with a smile?"

He poured himself a cup. "When Edie's here, it goes more smoothly, although the noise level is about the same." He reached into the refrigerator for the milk and added a shot to his coffee. He grinned at her as he leaned back against the counter. "So, do you need a month in intensive care?"

She shook her head, laughing. "Your kids are great. They were very tolerant of me." With a small frown she admitted candidly, "Evan's not sure about me, though. Still, he's flawlessly polite. I give you credit."

"He loves his mother. I think he still clings to the hope that she's coming back." He glanced at Shannon for a moment, then said quietly, "He probably thinks you could get in the way of that happening."

His gaze pulled her in, wanting her to admit what she kept trying so hard to resist. Or did she? She'd never been so indecisive in her life—thinking one moment that a relationship with Marty could give her what she'd always dreamed of, but realizing the next that four other lives were dependent on him and would be on her, if she allowed anything to develop. One moment she thought she had the courage, the next she remembered the beautiful woman who had been Marty's wife and the boys' mother and knew she would fail.

Still unsure, she took a casual sip of her coffee and said evenly, "Perhaps you should explain to him that we're only business associates."

His eyes locked on her again, making mincemeat of her attempt at maintaining a distance. "I never lie to my kids," he said, straightening and heading for the stairs with his coffee. "Give me ten minutes to shower and change, then the bathroom's yours."

ARRIVING AT THE STORE ten minutes after opening on a Monday morning under the same umbrella, Marty and Shannon caused a minor sensation. They had come in separate cars, but had pulled into the parking lot side by side. What the employees would presume hadn't occurred to Marty, but he judged by the tension he sensed in Shannon that it had occurred to her.

Without her usual smiles and greetings for the staff, she headed for the elevator in a straight line, looking neither right nor left. Christmas music wafted cheerfully from Musak through the thick crowds of shoppers on the first floor.

"You've now convinced them that we've had a weekend of sin," Marty said, holding the elevator door for her.

She stepped into the car without looking at him. "I'll issue a memo," she said, glancing at him with a reluctant smile. "Did you notice that they looked more delighted than horrified? Aren't people unpredictable?"

"Most people are in favor of love."

Shannon stared at him as the car rocked to the fourth floor. "We're not in love."

He looked at her as though she were one of his children. "I've been trying to tell myself that, too."

"Listen to yourself," she said firmly. "You're right."

The doors parted and they stepped off the elevator.

"Shannon!" Gale called from the door of her office down the hall. "Can I talk to you for a minute?"

As Shannon detoured to speak with Gale, Marty walked into Shannon's office, gave a satisfied pat to the gift he'd dropped off during the night, then went into his office. A phone call claimed his attention.

Shannon didn't see it immediately. After her brief conversation with Gale, she was distracted by the news of a shortage the previous day in Sporting Goods' cash bag. She went straight to her desk, leaning over it to make a note to call the cashier. It was time to make a serious effort to get to the bottom of the mystery.

Then she turned, thinking how much she needed a cup of coffee, and saw it in the middle of the carpet—a full-size carousel horse on a stand. She stopped, blinked and approached it cautiously, afraid a sudden move would cause it to disappear. She walked around it, wondering what miracle had brought it to her office.

She recognized it as the work of the carvers, Stein and Goldstein, an example of the Coney Island style of carousel horse. She noted with the passion of possession she rarely felt about anything except the store itself that it probably still wore its original paint. It was a black-and-white pony with high-set eyes and an aggressive expression that were the hallmarks of the artists, Stein and Goldstein. With reverence she put her fingertips to the faded red and yellow flowers carved into its halter and the tassels on the blanket.

Shannon's fingers found a small card fastened with a fabric bow, and she leaned down to read the message. "Shannon, if it were up to me, I'd see that you had *every-*

thing. But for now, will you settle for this small token of my appreciation? Marty.''

Emotion rose in Shannon with an intensity she'd never felt before. She'd known pain and disappointment, been depressed and disillusioned, but she'd never been so touched, felt so understood or been made so happy. And the pricelessness of the gift went beyond its considerable monetary value. Marty had looked inside her heart and read one of her dearest wishes.

STANDING AT THE CORNER of his desk, Marty just had time to hang up the telephone before a pink silk, gray tweed missile launched itself into his arms. He turned to take the full impact of her leap, bracing his legs so that they didn't hurtle together over his desk and out the fourth-story window.

Her grip on his neck was strong enough to choke a wrestler, but he bore it silently, relishing the new sensation of having her eager to be in his arms. She leaned back to look at him, her eyes dewy with emotion, her lips unsteady with it. "Marty, she's so beautiful! How did you know? Where did you find her? It must have cost a fortune!"

"You told me," he replied, "and I found her in Bend on Sunday morning. The woman who owned the antique shop was a friend of my father's. She was happy to open the shop for me and to know that the horse was going to a good home."

She hugged him again, as fiercely as before. "God, I can't believe it. I own a Stein and Goldstein!"

"Think of it as a Christmas present delivered two weeks early."

As she literally hung from his neck, Marty closed his arms around her and held her firmly, preparing to sit on the edge of the desk. It was a moment before he became aware of the sudden change in her—the tension, the stiffening of her muscles. Before he could prepare himself for it, she braced her arms and pushed him away.

Her eyes wide and frightened, she took two steps back from him, her fists clenched at her sides.

Drained in an instant of the pleasure for which he'd waited so long and enjoyed so briefly, he slumped onto the edge of his desk, gathering every measure of his self-control to keep from shouting at her in frustration. "Shannon, I would never hurt you," he made himself say reasonably.

She swallowed and admitted quietly, "I know that. Marty, I'm sorry." She looked down at her fingers, embarrassed that she'd been unable to control her reactions, horrified that she'd hurt Marty. She glanced up at him, her eyes filled with regret. "It's a long story, and I don't want to ruin your beautiful gesture with it. Please know that you couldn't have done anything that would have made me happier."

She didn't look happy, Marty thought. For a moment she'd looked terrified, and now she looked miserable. He'd been gradually coming to the conclusion that someone in Shannon's past had abused her. Now he was sure of it.

He didn't know what to do for her, except dismiss the subject with which she seemed so uncomfortable. He stood up and walked around to his chair, pretending to look busy. "I'm glad you like it. I'll help you take it home tonight. I'll follow you in my car and get it on the elevator for you."

She smiled gratefully and backed away toward her office. "Thanks, Marty."

"HOLD THE DOOR. Hold the door!" In the doorway of the miniscule elevator at Shannon's building, Marty, the wooden horse under his arm, was sandwiched between the rubber bumper closures on the doors.

"Libby!" Shannon patted the horse's head consolingly. "Marty, you're going to decapitate her!"

"Then hold the doors," he repeated patiently.

Shannon reached around him to hold the door away, but it continued to bump against her hand while the other door continued to beat at its victim's shoulder. Marty turned the horse sideways and set it down, discovering it took up the entire front of the small car. Standing in what little room was left in the back, Shannon patted its head again. "Just relax, Libby," she said. "It's just a short six flights up."

Holding the doors open, like Samson supporting the columns of the temple, Marty asked, "Libby?"

"For 'Liberty,'" she replied, a slight defensive quality in her tone. "She's carved in the Coney Island style, very all-American. It seems appropriate."

Marty studied her for a moment, then nodded. "While you're riding up, I'll be running up in all-American style to meet you on six and carry her off for you. If you can't reach around her to hold the doors open, lean on the Door Open button."

"Right," she said. "Don't be too long."

In the process of turning away, he looked over his shoulder in time to see the doors close on her teasing wave. Running up six flights, Marty thought it strange that she seemed to have successfully suppressed whatever had frightened her this morning. He tried not to think about how unhealthy that was for her.

"Careful. Careful! Watch out for the table. Marty, her ear!" Shannon said, directing Marty's delivery of Liberty through the doorway of her apartment, across the living room, past the bookcase and to a spot near the window beyond which was darkness and the lights on the river.

Shannon tossed off her coat, stood back and stared at the carved horse, beside herself with delight. Marty absorbed the pleasure of seeing her so pleased.

She turned to him, her eyes and her smile softening. "Thanks again, Marty."

He put his hands in the pockets of his cashmere overcoat. "I'm glad you like it. I wanted you to know how much I appreciated your stepping in for Edie like that."

She moved toward him, her arms folded. "I didn't mean for the horse, though I love it. I meant for not getting angry about this morning."

He sighed. "It's hard to get angry about something you don't understand." He shifted his weight and added gravely, "And I seldom get angry, anyway, if that's been a problem for you with other men." He waited for her to admit or deny that it had been. When she didn't, he went on, refusing to let her shut him out. "I don't shout much, except at football games, and I don't throttle, hit or even intimidate. Ask my kids."

Shannon laughed, looping her arm in his as she walked him to the door.

"But you'll never learn that about me," he said, "until you let me a little closer. Think about that."

He opened the door, and she put a hand on it to prevent it from opening all the way. Then she put her hands on his shoulders and stood on tiptoe to kiss his cheek.

Marty leaned down to make it easier for her, careful to keep his hands in his pockets. Her hands were cool on his face and a little shaky. Her eyes were filled with affection.

"I will," she promised. "See you tomorrow."

Shannon leaned against the door after he'd gone, tears welling in her eyes. She'd be a fool to let him get away, she thought. A complete fool.

As Marty walked across the dark parking lot to his car, he tried to analyze what had happened today and found it impossible. He couldn't make sense of Shannon's reactions because he didn't have all the facts. And he couldn't decide whether she'd ever trust him enough to share them with him.

"WHY ISN'T MAINTENANCE doing that?" Henry asked, watching Shannon as she clung to the top of a fifteen-foot ladder. She was checking the lights on a Christmas tree suspended from the ceiling. The troublesome bulb went on, suddenly wrapping the dark tree in a shawl of brilliant color once again. The employees on the floor applauded and Shannon squealed, throwing her arms out in delight.

Marty closed his eyes as though summoning patience as she backed down the ladder. "Because our normally be-everywhere, do-everything assistant manager suddenly has even more energy to burn."

Henry frowned up at him. "Why?"

Marty sighed. Relieved that she was down safely, he put an arm around his father's shoulders and continued their progress toward Sporting Goods. "I don't know. It has something to do with me. I think she's working up to letting me into her life. When she's planning something, she's always indefatigable."

Henry stopped in his tracks, smiling. "You two are in love?"

"I am," Marty replied. "I'm not sure about her."

"Pardon me?"

"I'll explain later. So you're staying through Christmas?"

Henry shrugged. "It's only another ten days, and I thought I could give you two a hand." A woman with two little boys and an armload of bags passed between them. "And I was lonesome," he added when their paths meshed again. "You don't mind, do you?"

"Of course not." The look in his father's eye concerned him a little. It reminded him of the look that had been there the first few months after Marty's mother had died.

Then Henry nudged him in the ribs. "Maybe you could find me a job in Cosmetics with that little Hilary."

"She's young enough to be your granddaughter," Marty said. "I've got just the spot for you in Sporting Goods."

This was going to be quite a Christmas, Marty thought later, after introducing his father to the Sporting Goods staff. Henry was already winking across the aisle at a pretty young woman in Furniture and Appliances. With his father trying to hide his loneliness under the facade of a geriatric Don Juan, and Shannon hanging from the ceilings, he had his work cut out for him. Things were going relatively well at home, except that the nearer it got to Christmas without word from Monica, the more morose Evan became. The boy had been so sure she'd fulfill her promise to pick him and his brothers up to spend the holiday with her. Marty was sure there were times she forgot she even had children, much less had made them a promise.

"I DON'T KNOW WHAT to do!" Kathy Baker cried. It was closing time, two days before Christmas, and the young cashier's eyes reflected her frustration as she looked at Shannon and Marty from inside her wire cubicle. "This time it's Shoes and Luggage's bag that's short. It's not happening back here. There's only me and Laurie Marsh, and she's been here as long as I have. It's got to be one of our clerks, going around to busy departments and pilfering. Maybe one of the new people. God knows at this time of year, with three and four clerks on a register, it's impossible to guess where it's happening. But we've lost a hundred dollars since this started."

Shannon looked at Marty. "Any ideas?"

"Nothing brilliant," he said. "Maybe if we issue a memo to buyers that there's been a recurring problem with the cash bags and ask them to be more careful and more vigilant, whoever's doing it will stop, or get nervous and trip him or herself up."

Shannon nodded. "Sounds good to me. Thanks, Kathy. Keep us posted." Shannon looped her arm in Marty's and walked with him to the elevator. He noted with a private smile that she no longer concerned herself with the dangers to employee morale because of fraternization.

Since the day he'd given her the carousel horse over a week ago, they'd hardly had a moment alone. Work hours had been long and hectic, and lunch breaks too rushed and public to allow personal conversation. They walked out to the parking lot hand in hand every night, and she always kissed his cheek before getting into her car and driving off. He wanted more.

"You want to tell me again why you won't come over tomorrow night?" Marty asked as they walked down the long, empty corridor to the administrative side of the floor.

"Because it's a special time for families," she said. "I don't want to mess that up for your kids."

"My kids like you."

"They're expecting their mother."

Marty sighed. "Only Evan seriously expects her, and I think even he's losing hope."

"Well, if she does show up, my being there could be a problem."

Marty caught her arm and pulled her to a stop. "A problem for you, or a problem for the kids?"

"For everyone," Shannon replied patiently. "Christmas isn't a time for confrontations."

"What confrontation?" Marty demanded. "She doesn't stand in your way." He narrowed his gaze and asked quietly, "Why are you afraid of her?"

Shannon rolled her eyes at his obtuseness. "She's a world-famous actress and one of the most beautiful women in America. Do you think that could have something to do with it?"

"There's nothing left inside," Marty insisted.

"There has to be. The boys love her."

"They love the mother ideal, and they're fascinated by her wealth and prestige."

Shannon pulled her arm away and walked on. "So am I. Don't argue with me, Marty. My mind's made up. Anyway, your father made me promise I'd come for dinner Christmas day. That's more open to friends and outsiders. I wouldn't feel so guilty about that.''

In Shannon's office Marty followed her to the coat tree, took the garment for her and helped her into it. ''I don't want you to be alone Christmas Eve.'' He turned her and framed her face in his hands. ''Please come.''

''Marty, I've been alone on Christmas Eve for ages,'' she said reasonably.

He sighed impatiently. ''There's no reason for that anymore. Come and be with us.''

''No,'' she said with quiet firmness. ''You can comfort yourself with the knowledge that I'll spend the time wrapping your present.''

Marty rolled his eyes and went into his office for his coat. ''Now I know why I had only boys!'' he shouted from beyond the half-open door. ''Girls are impossible to deal with.'' He reappeared, pulling his collar up. Outside, rain fell in buckets.

JOSH OPENED THE DOOR at Shannon's knock, then ran back into the house to report loudly, ''Shannon's here and she's got *presents*!''

The three older boys and Henry, gathered around a board game on the floor, came to relieve her of her packages. She handed her car keys to Evan. ''There are two more big ones in the trunk.''

Marty came out of the kitchen to trade her coat for a glass of hot apple cider. They'd been casually affectionate with each other since the day they'd talked, but she wasn't sure what the protocol would be in front of his children. When he leaned down to kiss her lightly on the mouth, she was pleasantly surprised.

Joshua immediately took her hand and pulled her to the tree to show her everyone's gifts. When she wrapped her blue wool circle skirt around her legs to sit beside him on the floor, Tulip took it as an invitation to share her gift, as well.

A soggy rawhide bone a foot long landed in Shannon's lap. "Thank you, Tulip," she said feebly, holding it between thumb and forefinger.

Apparently thinking it had been sufficiently admired, Tulip reclaimed it and galloped back to the kitchen. Edie stuck her head out to wave a wooden spoon at Shannon.

By the time Evan reappeared with the boxes, Josh was beside himself with excitement. The other boys were also clustered around her, unashamedly interested in what she'd brought. She distributed the gifts, called Marty and Henry over and sent Grady to the kitchen for Edie.

"Can I get her present, Dad?" Josh crawled under the tree, apparently not expecting to be denied. He emerged a moment later, bright-eyed and disheveled, with a long, slender box covered in bright paper with colorful elves on it, and a frayed, lopsided bow that looked as though it had been handled many times until the desired effect had been achieved. He handed it to her proudly. "I wrapped it."

She hugged him to her, touched by the effort and affection apparent in the work. "It's beautiful, Josh."

Everyone now seated on the floor, Josh got comfortable in front of his package and looked hopefully at his father. "Now?" he asked.

Marty looked at the other boys, pretending indecision. "I don't know. Does anybody really want to open presents?"

The boys attacked their gifts in a collective rush that made the adults laugh.

"All right! Jeans!" Jarrod held up stone-washed denims, a broad smile on his face. Evan, also looking pleased, held up a black pair.

"I guessed on sizes," she said, preparing to explain that they could be exchanged. But the boys were already racing upstairs to try them on.

"Porsche Pit Crew," Grady said, reading the lettering on a hooded, long-sleeved red sweatshirt. Then he laughed, pulling it on. "Look, Dad! I'm official."

"Dad! Dad!" Josh stumbled blindly toward his father, a sweatshirt over his head, the bright Batman emblem emblazoned on the front.

Shannon reached for him and slid her hands up under the shirt to widen the turtleneck by spreading her fingers. When his face finally emerged, his eyes and his face glowed. "How do I look?" he demanded.

"Very handsome," Shannon assured him.

He looked disappointed. "I want to look scary."

"You would look scary to bad guys," she said, adjusting the hem of the shirt and cuffing back the sleeves. "To me you look handsome."

Josh threw his arms around her. "I love you, Shannon."

She hugged him hard. "I love you, too, Josh."

Marty watched the exchange with a pressure in his chest that was part pleasure and part pain. She belonged in his house. But she was blinded by something in her past that left her feeling inadequate and lacking in the basic ability to love and to be loved. He'd once been so certain he could draw her out of that past, but he was only now beginning to realize what a formidable enemy it was.

Edie's squeal of delight brought him back to awareness. She held up a bright pink velour sweat suit. "I'll probably be kidnapped by a sheikh at the grocery store and you'll never see me again."

Marty, sitting behind Shannon, his knee propped up to support her back, leaned forward to say softly in her ear, "There's that sheikh again."

Shannon leaned back with a laugh. "Told you. He's every woman's dream."

"Deerskin gloves!" Henry pulled his gift out of the box and slipped a hand into one of them. "Perfect fit," he said. "Thank you, Shannon." He reached across the mound of discarded wrapping paper that separated them and squeezed her hand.

Josh pointed to his father, directing operations. "Now it's your turn, Dad."

Marty pulled the shiny leather briefcase out of its nest of tissue with a whistle of approval. Henry leaned closer to admire it. "It's about time you had a new one," he said. "Your other one was always so full it looked like it was filled with helium."

"It was crushing my morning croissant," Shannon explained with a laugh. "This pocket—" she pointed to a roomy, gusseted pocket in the front "—is for our doughnuts."

He caught her chin and quickly kissed her. "Thank you," he said.

"Now it's Shannon's turn. Open it, Shannon," Josh encouraged. "You're going to *love* it."

Grady elbowed him. "Sssh! You'll give it away."

Evan and Jarrod returned, wearing the jeans that were a perfect fit. Shannon would have paused to admire them, but Josh was bursting with impatience. She pulled off paper and ribbon and lifted the lid of the box. On a bed of velvet was a tiny gold carousel horse on a delicate gold chain. She pulled it out of the box and held it against the palm of her hand, speechless. The boys crowded closer to admire it.

"It's beautiful," she breathed finally, looking into Marty's eyes. Then she smiled at the boys. "Thank you, all of you."

Edie and Henry herded the boys into the kitchen to set the table for dinner. Resisters were dragged away, and it was obvious to Shannon that she was being awarded a moment alone with Marty.

Shyly Shannon placed the pendant around her neck, and Marty took the ends of the chain to clasp it, then turned her toward him to evaluate the result. The gold horse lay against her small breast in its green wool sweater, looking somehow more precious than it had in the jeweler's locked case.

He looked at her to share that thought, then was surprised into silence when she leaned forward and kissed him. She did it lightly, gently. As she drew back, he quelled a flare of desire, a need to pull her back and kiss her as he'd wanted to for weeks.

Shannon's lips tingled with that brief touch of his mouth. She was filled with the sweetness of his gift, with the warmth of his family, and a desire that matched what she saw in his eyes.

As though by mutual agreement, he opened his arms and she went into them, her lips parting as his opened over hers. His tongue teased cautiously, and she opened eagerly to its invasion, losing herself in the discovery of a kiss that gave as well as took, pleased as well as plundered. She wound her fingers in his hair and felt him take a handful of hers. She lost all sense of time and place, awake only to the delicious demands of his artful mouth.

He finally pulled away with a small laugh, resting his forehead against hers as he gasped for breath. "Merry Christmas, Shannon," he said.

She could no longer deny the love growing inside her. Against the background of her life, it was the most beautiful gift ever offered or received. She acknowledged that fact in wonder. "Merry Christmas, Marty," she whispered.

EARLY IN THE EVENING a knock on the door brought Evan's head up from the cards in his hand. He, Jarrod, Grady and Henry were playing poker at the dining table. The other three were laughing over a bad play on Grady's part and hadn't noticed the knock. Evan's head swung to Marty, who sat on the sofa with Shannon, Josh between them.

Shannon saw Marty's eyes close for a moment, and suddenly she knew who stood on the other side of the door as well as he and Evan did. "Go ahead, Evan," Marty said.

Evan began a cool stroll to the door that ended in a run in the last few steps. Shannon heard the door open, then Evan's delighted shout of "Mom!"

That brought all heads up from the table, and the other boys ran for the door, Josh scrambling off the sofa to join them. Shannon looked at Marty in alarm. He squeezed her knee and gave her a resigned smile. "Brace yourself. Monica is an experience."

As Marty stood and helped Shannon to her feet, the boys returned, leading a tall, dark-haired woman in a full-length red fox coat. Shannon was stunned by her beauty and elegance as the boys pulled the woman to a stop several feet away from her. Television hadn't done her justice. Her complexion was dewy, her hair lustrous, her eyes large and hazel.

"Hello, Marty," Monica said, putting both arms up.

Marty leaned down to slip into her embrace, wrapping his arms around her for a moment, then drew away. "Merry Christmas," he said. "We thought you might be too busy getting ready for your new movie to visit."

She tossed back that luxurious head of hair and shrugged under the elegant fox. "Susan Sarandon got it." Her beautiful red mouth took on a wry slant. "Can't win 'em all."

Shannon saw something in Monica's eyes when she said that, some quick flash of pain or regret that was gone so quickly she might have imagined it. Then the large eyes focused on Shannon, and she could think about nothing else for a moment.

She had expected Monica to dislike her, to resent her presence among her husband and children on Christmas Day. But she merely studied her with a strangely clinical detachment, then sighed, nodding slowly. She extended her hand. "Monica Hale," she said. "Ex-wife, bad mother."

"Mom," Evan scolded quietly.

Shannon took her hand. "Shannon Carlisle. Friend of the family."

Monica glanced up at Marty. "That true?"

"For the moment," Marty replied.

Shannon saw that quick flash of regret again. Then Monica turned toward Henry, who stood at the dining room table. She went to him and put her arms around him. Shannon knew that only good manners made him respond, and only with a decided lack of enthusiasm. "How are you, Henry?"

"I'm well," he replied, his usually lively eyes cool. "I'm sure I needn't ask about you. You always take care of yourself."

Smiling despite the insinuation, Monica patted his cheek. "That's what life's all about, darling."

"No," Henry said quietly. "It's not."

"Mom, I want to show you my stuff," Grady said, pulling irreverently on the sleeve of her coat.

"I want to see it, love, but first I want to ask your father if I can take the four of you away with me for a week."

The boys' enthusiastic response was loud and immediate. Even Jarrod, who claimed to understand and accept his mother's foibles, grinned from ear to ear.

"At Cannon Beach?" Grady asked.

Monica put her free arm around him. "Yes."

"You still got the yacht moored in Hammond?"

"Yes."

"All *right*!"

Marty quietly groaned, knowing the juggernaut of mother love was rolling, and he could do nothing to stop it and would hurt all those involved, the boys particularly, if he tried. Even Josh, who hardly recognized her, was caught up in his brothers' enthusiasm.

"School starts a week from Monday morning," Marty said to Monica.

"I'll have them back Sunday afternoon."

"All right."

Henry stormed into the kitchen from which Edie had never emerged, and Shannon remained with Marty while the boys pulled Monica upstairs to help them pack.

Shannon wrapped her arms around Marty's waist and looked up into his eyes, offering comfort. "I'm sorry," she said.

He drew her head to his shoulder. "Why?"

"Because they're so fascinated with her and willing to leave you at a moment's notice on Christmas."

He shrugged. "They love her. They'll grow up more sound and stable that way."

"It isn't fair."

He kissed her forehead. "I don't require justice, just well-adjusted kids."

An hour later Monica left in a flurry of fox and perfume, her boys trailing after her. Josh stopped to hug his father. "Evan says you can't come."

Marty snapped the top of Josh's jacket. "That's right. I have to stay and watch the store."

Josh leaned against Marty's leg. "I'll miss you."

Marty picked him up and walked to the door where the other boys had stopped. "I'll miss you, too. Be good for your mom, okay?"

Grady looked up at Marty as Monica took Josh to the limousine and driver that waited at the curb. "You going to be okay, Dad, all alone?"

Marty hugged him. "I'm not alone. I've got Grandpa and Shannon and Edie."

"But they're kind of quiet, you know? You won't get bored without us?"

Jarrod rolled his eyes and pushed Grady aside, awkwardly putting an arm around Marty's shoulder. "He's probably glad to be without us for a week. Aren't you, Dad?"

"Yes," Marty replied, catching him in a neck hold. "I was going to sell you into slavery for a week if your mother didn't come through."

"Nice guy." Smiling, Evan reached out to shake Marty's hand.

Marty suddenly remembered Evan as an eight-year-old, bright-eyed and loving, proud that his father played professional football. They'd been so close before the divorce. He understood that their relationship had to change as Evan matured, but he longed for the simplicity of emotion, the warmth they'd shared. He extended his hand. "Have a great time."

"Sure." Evan took two steps down, then turned to look back at Marty in the glow of the porch light. "Thanks for letting us go."

Marty looked back at his firstborn, wondering if the boy would ever understand that it would never occur to him to prevent them from seeing their mother—that it just didn't occur to her often enough to visit. This was always the way she did it, with a splash of limousine and liveried driver and the promise of luxuries even his relatively wealthy father could only imagine. It made Marty's day-to-day routine look like cough medicine in comparison.

Marty put an arm around Evan's shoulder and walked with him to the car. "Have fun. And keep your eye on the other guys, all right?"

"Right. Bye, Dad." Evan got into the back of the limo with his brothers, and everyone waved as the driver, with Monica beside him, drove off into the night.

Chapter Eleven

"I'm sending the two of you home for a week." Sitting at the dining room table with Edie, they shared a last cup of coffee before Shannon left. Henry spoke with a frown of concentration. "Call it vacation, earned leave, whatever..."

Marty and Shannon looked at each other in perplexity. "Home?" Marty asked.

"To Bend. Home. The ten acres where you grew up." Henry seemed to come out of his preoccupation in a grim mood. "You need a rest."

Marty looked from Shannon to Edie. "Do I look pale? Have I started babbling?"

Edie shrugged. "You always babble." She turned with a frown to her employer's father. "What are you talking about, Mr. Henry?"

"Justice, damn it!" Henry slammed a hand on the table, making Edie and Shannon jump.

Marty reached across the table and anchored his father's fist. "Dad, what's the matter?" he asked quietly.

"You!" Henry shouted at him, his face reddening. He yanked his hand away and took another sip of coffee. "She sashays in here like she's some gift to those kids when you're the one—"

"She's their mother, Dad," Marty said reasonably. "She has a right to see them and they have a right to love her. I can deal with it."

"You deal with too damn much!" Henry bellowed, pushing away from the table. "I'm giving you a week off— you and Shannon. You're going to Bend and relax and I'll stay here to keep an eye on the store. But I want you back on Saturday. I'm not going to be here alone when the little beasties get back."

Edie frowned at him again. "What am I? Invisible?"

Henry turned to her. They'd developed a sparring relationship in the ten days he'd stayed with Marty. "We should be so lucky. They're going to drop you off at your son's."

Edie looked hopefully at Marty. "Mr. Hale...?"

Marty turned to Shannon, the prospect of a week alone with her drawing him like a beacon. "How do you feel about a week off?"

She smiled at him, excitement lighting her eyes. She looked at Henry. "With or without pay?"

"IT'S A MANSION!" Shannon exclaimed, staring up at the square, two-story white house with black shutters, fluted columns and stairways descending from both sides of a broad front porch. Holding the collar of her red wool coat closed against the lightly falling snow, she thought the house looked gracious and charmingly pompous. Her father's antebellum home had appeared cold, despite its beautiful lines, even from the outside.

"It must have been wonderful to grow up here."

"It was." Marty pulled up the collar of his overcoat. His blond hair was already dusted with snow. "There's a grape arbor in the back, and a rose garden, and a path that leads to a beautiful woods with a stream. If you help me get all your bags into the house, we can change our clothes and I'll show it to you. Unless you're hungry."

Shannon shook her head, blinking her eyes against the falling flakes. "I'm still stuffed from the lunch Edie's daughter-in-law fixed when we dropped Edie off. I vote we have a late dinner."

"All right. You take your stuff. I'll take mine."

Shannon stood surrounded by four bags while Marty prepared to start up the steps with his one suitcase. "Very funny," she said with a gloved hand at her hip. "I happen to know you're more of a gentleman than that."

Marty paused, his hand on the railing, his expression deadpan. "That's only in Portland where I have to set an example for my sons and a store full of employees. I'm home now. This is where I was raised and formed. I can be myself."

Shannon folded her arms. "Well, if we're reverting to type, I'm at heart a spoiled little rich girl who's accustomed to service and attention—from staff, anyway."

Marty's eyes darkened as snow began to build on his shoulders. He smiled wickedly. "I intend to see that you have a lot of attention this week."

Shannon understood the implication and accepted it. Her mind, her soul were ready for it. She simply wasn't sure what her body would do. She smiled, hoping he wouldn't see uncertainty in her eyes. "I'd be more amenable to...receiving attention from the man who carried my bags."

Marty saw the flash of emotion and noted with relief that it wasn't fear. A certain dubiousness in light of what she'd been through was understandable. He went back to her to take a bag under the arm that carried his own case and pick up another in his free hand. His eyes teased her as she picked up the other two and followed him. "I'll bet Elizabeth Taylor doesn't travel with this much stuff."

"I'll bet Richard Burton never complained about helping her carry it, either."

"But he's no longer with us, is he?" Marty waited at the top of the steps while Shannon struggled up. She dropped both cases at the top and frowned teasingly at him.

"Are you going to be like this all week? I kind of like the other guy you left in Portland."

"I'll teach you to like this one," he said with a grin. "Trust me. Key's in my back pocket. My hands are kind of full."

Giving him a moue of disapproval, Shannon unbuttoned his topcoat and reached inside it and around to the back pocket of his brown slacks. Slipping her fingers inside, she felt the warm, taut curve of his hip. Warmth rose in her like the effects of a neat brandy. She stood so close to him that when she looked up his eyes were only inches away and looking into hers. Their message was an unrepentant challenge. She let her hand linger for a moment, and he noted her acceptance of the challenge with a lift of his eyebrow. Then she clutched the keys and removed her hand. "I suppose you expect me to open the door, as well."

He smiled, but not his usually warm and open smile. There was something dangerous in it, something that made that imagined brandy seem like a double. "If you would please."

A long black and white tiled corridor separated two banks of rooms and ended in a staircase that curved up to a gallery and the second floor. "That's why you thought of putting a gallery in Books and Stationery," Shannon exclaimed, forgetting the burden of her suitcases. She looked up at the paintings visible above the oak railing.

"That's right, but the store and our families are taboo subjects while we're here." Marty started up the stairs, then called down to her. "Hustle up, Carlisle, or it'll be too dark to see the creek." At the west end of the gallery, Marty turned down a short corridor with a bedroom opening on either side. He indicated the room on the right with a jut of his chin. "Think you can be comfortable there?"

Shannon stepped into a wide room decorated in yellow with blue and brown accents. French doors opened onto a porch beyond which snow fell more swiftly than before. She caught a glimpse of a dormant garden and white-capped woods. Marty pushed open wide wardrobe doors and indicated a full-size dresser. "If you need more room," he said dryly as he dropped her cases on the bed, "I'll store a few things for you. You've got twenty minutes to change."

Shannon hurriedly removed the blue pants and sweater in which she'd traveled and replaced them with jeans and a thick white turtleneck. She kicked off low-heeled black shoes, pulled off knee-highs and yanked up woolly white socks and cuffed flat-heeled boots. She put on a blue-green down jacket and ran out into the hall, stuffing her hair into a white knit hat trimmed in fake fur. She banged on Marty's door. "Your twenty minutes are up!" she called.

"I've been waiting for you for fifteen."

Shannon spun around at the sound of Marty's voice. He stood at the end of the hall near the gallery, his ankles crossed and his arms folded in an attitude of long-suffering patience. He wore jeans and a beige down jacket, which he zipped up over a natural-colored fisherman's knit sweater as she walked toward him. Warmth and gladness, both only vaguely familiar to Shannon until Marty had come into her life, bubbled up from the depths of her cautious nature.

"Too bad," she said, racing past him. Then she added over her shoulder as she ran, "You should have used it for a head start!"

Shannon hit the black-and-white tile, her boots clicking loudly on them as she ran into a wide, airy kitchen, searching for the back door. Following a hall off the side of it, she found double doors that opened onto a wide back porch.

"Stop!" Marty's voice called from behind her. "The steps'll be slippery!"

Shannon quickly assessed the stone steps with their coating of new snow and guessed that he was probably right. She began to pull on her gloves as he burst through the double doors, stopping in relief at the sight of her. "I didn't expect you to listen to me," he admitted in mild surprise. "Is it part of some new campaign to keep me off balance?"

She took his arm and began to pick her way carefully down the steps. "You already are unbalanced," she said cheerfully.

He sighed, resigning himself to this heretofore hidden and taxing side of her. "There's a subtle difference between off balance and unbalanced."

"I know, but this isn't an evening for subtleties," she said, gesturing with a gloved hand at the cloudy sky darkening in brooding, dramatic blues, at the defoliated forest ahead of them, looking like an intricate pattern of lace against the encroaching darkness. "It's a time for emotions you can understand, laughter, tears, jealousy, rage."

Shannon tucked her other hand around him so that she held his arm in her two hands, and he made an effort not to react to the gesture, though it made him weak with wanting her. It was so important not to frighten her. "Rage?" he asked. "I don't know anything about rage."

"Me, neither. What about jealousy?"

"No, I haven't had a lot of experience with that, either."

"Hmm." Shannon muttered a small, thoughtful sound, then moved ahead of Marty as the path narrowed through the naked trees. That had sounded to Marty like something of an admission.

After fifty yards they reached the snowy, grassy banks of a narrow, roiling stream. Shannon got close to the edge to look down the six or so feet into the water. Marty pulled her back, knowing the rounded edge of the bank was slippery.

"Who are you jealous of?" he asked, holding her to his side with an arm around her shoulders.

"Well, that's a bald question," she accused, softening the scolding quality of the statement by wrapping her arms around his waist.

"You said it wasn't an evening for subtleties."

"Monica." She said it quickly, suddenly, and the sound of it rang around them over the rushing of the water and the silent, drifting snow. An icy wind whipped along the creek, and Marty turned slightly to shield Shannon from it.

"Why?" he asked, tilting her face up with his free hand. Her dark eyes were vaguely troubled. "You saw for yourself that it's over."

"She knows what she gave up," Shannon said quietly. "She regrets it."

Marty was so startled by the conviction in her voice that for a moment he didn't know what to say. Then he shook his head. "Not enough to come back. She's built another life without me. I've rebuilt mine without her. We cross in and out of each other's only for the boys to see her, and that's very seldom."

He didn't understand the problem, Shannon thought, because he was secure enough in himself as a parent that it wasn't a cause for concern. But for her, involvement with him meant involvement with his boys, and they loved their mother. She leaned her head on his shoulder. "Sorry. I think we've wandered into one of your taboo subjects."

"No." He laid his cheek on the top of her hat. "Monica's no longer my family."

"She's part of your life."

"She's part of my children's life, and one day soon they'll wise up to her."

Shannon accepted that in silence, then pulled away from him and looked down into the stream. "Are there fish in there?"

Marty bit down on his lip in frustration. He was torn between feeling helpless to convince her that Monica was history and being delighted that Shannon cared enough to be jealous and felt that it was important enough to admit.

He moved to look over her shoulder and hold her back from the edge. "There are rainbow trout in it in spring and summer."

"Then we can't have any for dinner."

"True, but I'm sure there'll be something in the freezer. Want to look?"

Shannon leaned her head back against his shoulder. "You can look and I'll sit in front of a fire, preferably with a glass of mulled wine or a hot buttered rum."

Marty turned her around and rested his forearms on her shoulders, leaning down to look into her eyes. "I'm surprised to discover this demanding, sluggardly side of you."

She shrugged, his arms a delicious yoke around her neck. "I've never been able to indulge it before."

"It might be a mistake," he warned, "to indulge it now."

"I'm your guest."

He shook his head. "I don't live here anymore. We're both my father's guests."

"Doesn't he have a cook or a housekeeper?"

"He gave them the holidays off, knowing he'd be with me and the kids."

"All right, I can be reasonable." Shannon wrapped her arms around his again and started back up the path. "I could toss a salad, or chop vegetables, if you find steaks or fish fillets. Then I can sit by the fire while you take care of the dishes."

"We'll discuss doing the dishes when the time comes."

"Maybe we can find paper plates."

"ACTUALLY," Marty said lazily, shifting the plump pillow under his head, "I think I could develop a sluggardly side, too." He lay on his back on the thick burgundy-colored carpet in front of a stone fireplace where a perfect fire leaped and crackled. Beside him, Shannon sat with her knees drawn up, leaning against the patterned chintz sofa.

Shannon sighed contentedly. "Your father knew I'd have things to teach you. You did a good job with the steaks, Hale."

"Your spinach vinaigrette was excellent."

"So you're doing dishes?"

"Guess again."

In a move so sudden Marty never saw it coming, Shannon flung herself astride his waist, her hands pinning his wrists to the floor beside his pillow. Her eyes full of firelight and laughter, she said menacingly, "Perhaps you'd like to reconsider."

Just as swiftly, caught up in her playfulness, Marty turned her onto her back, pinning her hands over her head with one hand while laughingly threatening to tickle her into submission with the other.

He saw the panic rise in her eyes at the same moment it occurred to him that, in view of her strange sensitivity to being touched, it had probably not been a wise move. He moved immediately, angry with himself for forgetting, angry with her for making spontaneity impossible. He sat up stiffly against the cushions, reaching for his wineglass on the end table. "You started it," he accused mildly, looking into the fire as he sipped. "If you don't want a man to touch you, you shouldn't leap on top of him."

Shannon sat back on her heels, covering her face with both hands. She tried to make sense of her reactions when she'd deliberately instigated the contact, but she couldn't think. She looked into Marty's face, saw hurt and disappointment, then shook her head. "I'm sorry," she said. "It's better if I'm alone."

He knew she didn't mean at this moment; she meant forever. "It's not better," he said firmly as she tried to get to her feet. He tried not to sound desperate, to remain calm. "It's familiar, but it isn't better. You know I'm not like your husband, or whoever did this to you. It isn't fair to me to believe that I'd hurt you, too."

Her eyes were filled with shame as she tried to warn him off. "I'm messed up, Marty."

He absorbed that admission, then sighed and shook his head. "Who in hell isn't? I know you've kind of...secluded yourself with this pain, so you don't see that everybody else is carrying around his own burden. You're not unique, Shannon."

She shook her head, impatient with his willingness to understand. "You're the kindest man I've ever known, and I can't let you hold me. That's not weird?"

He shrugged. "Depends. You haven't told me why."

She sat down, leaving a space of several feet between them. Her brow pleated and her lips tensed. "If I get in there and dig it all out..." She drew a deep breath as though the prospect required fortification. She looked up at him, and he saw how much she wanted to—needed to. "I'll lose everything I've gained in two years."

"What have you gained?" he asked quietly. "Quiet solitude in your condo, a reputation as a good businesswoman and a fine boss who keeps a polite distance between herself and everyone else, the exquisite loneliness of perpetual control? That isn't freedom from the pain, Shannon. That's imprisonment of another kind."

She stared at him and, in her eyes, he saw her resentment at his discovering the truth.

"I know about loneliness," he said.

She gazed into the fire, but he saw the mocking tilt of her mouth. "Your house is like Los Angeles International Airport."

He laughed softly. "I know. The kids brought me back from the edge more than once, but many of the things I lost when Monica left, they can't replace for me. I'm probably as frightened of failing again as you are of...whatever haunts you."

Shannon looked at him again, her expression doubtful.

"Do you think you're the only insecure person in this world?" he asked. "I blew a marriage of thirteen years, and I'm still not sure what happened. Monica loved me once. I've pretty much resigned myself to the fact that she just saw something more appealing and grabbed it. I imagine life as a pampered star beats cooking, quarrels and car pools."

Her doubtful look turned to a frown. "I don't."

He drew a knee up and rested his wrist on it, his wineglass dangling from his fingers and catching the firelight. "The point is, she did. And sometimes at night I stare at the ceiling and know that I had to have failed her for her to have found it so easy to walk away from us. I left football because I was starting to feel the aches and pains, and I quit modeling because I hated it. I had good excuses for quitting every time, excuses that made me sound responsible, even heroic. The truth was, I didn't want to do those things anymore. I quit."

He sipped his wine, understanding why she was reluctant to dredge up old pain she had dealt with, however inadequately, so she could go on. All the woolly fears he usually faced in the middle of the night now stared him down.

He turned to her, letting the fears show. "So here I am, with an administrative job given to me by my father, in a business in which I have insufficient experience to be effective, trying to hold together three teenagers and a little boy who need a lot more than I can give them by myself. And there's only one reason I didn't run away at the end of my first week at the Portland Hale's."

Shannon gave him a fragile smile. "Because the only other place to go was Myrtle, Montana?"

He didn't smile. "No. You were there. You prodded me and teased me, but every time I needed an answer, you had it. Every time I didn't know which way to turn, you explained my alternatives. Whenever I felt out of my depth, you came into my office looking bright and competent and helped me through."

He waited for the point to hit her, but she simply listened, then looked at the dancing fire.

"Don't you get it?" he asked.

She turned to him with a shallow sigh. "You're telling me I'm really not a bad person."

He closed his eyes for a moment, then shook his head. "No. I'm telling you that every day, in a hundred little ways, you do for me what you won't let me do for you. You help me."

Shannon pulled both knees up and wrapped her arms around them. "I'm sure a lack of business experience in an intelligent, hardworking man is easier to deal with than frigidity in a woman." She glanced at him, her expression filled with regret. "Particularly when what you need now in your life is a warm and caring helpmate."

"Shannon, you're not frigid," he said calmly.

"Not clinically, no." She sighed wearily and rested her head on her knees. "But it amounts to the same thing. I don't like to be touched."

"That isn't true anymore," he observed quietly. "Remember Palm Springs? Remember last night when we exchanged gifts? Remember just a few minutes ago?"

Tears welled in her eyes. "I thought I was over it. But a few minutes ago," she reminded him, "I panicked."

"I...probably got too rough." He saw her tears and lowered his voice, reaching a hand to her. "I'm sorry."

She gave him a scolding look for assuming the blame. "No, you didn't."

He took hold of her hand and resisted her effort to pull away. "Then what was it? Don't you want to find out?"

She let him draw her toward him, but her breath was quickening, her agitation rising. "I'll only hurt you, Marty," she pleaded, "and embarrass myself."

"I'll live," he said implacably, "and you will, too. Finally." He pulled her between his knees, looping his arm loosely around her body. "Shannon, if you don't get rid o this, you'll spend the rest of your life this way. Do you really want that?''

Faced with the alternative, she almost found it tempting, but she finally dropped her head and shook it. "No."

"Then tell me what frightened you." he insisted.

She tried to think. She had sat astride him, teasing him, then he had rolled her onto her back, pinning her hands over her head. That image was a familiar nightmare, though the man in it had been Keith, not Marty. She pushed at his hands, tears falling freely down her cheeks. "You held me too tightly," she cried. "Keith...he always held me too tightly!"

Hearing the name, Marty locked his fingers together, holding firm against her attempts to escape. Her hair flayed his face as she struggled. "I'm not Keith, Shannon. Whatever happened after Keith held you too tightly won't happen now."

Her tears and struggling were now frantic. "I can't get away," she said desperately. "I can never get away!"

Marty opened his arms. "Yes, you can," he said quietly. "If that's what you want."

In the throes of the old horror, it took Shannon a moment to realize she was free. She prepared to stand, to run away, her instinct to seek escape stronger than intelligence or common sense. Then, as she pulled away, the movement itself helped her see that she had no reason to escape. She had nothing to run *from*—she was free.

After a lifetime of emotional captivity, she found herself reaching for a lifeline. Instinct took over once more, and she reached in the one direction where the complexities of fear and harsh memories told her she would be safe. She went back into Marty's open arms.

For the first time that she could remember, arms closed around her to offer comfort. Then tears she'd held back almost as long as she'd yearned for comfort sprang from a deep well of heartache. She cried until her eyes burned and her throat ached, and the muscles in her arms quaked from her grip on Marty.

She finally pulled away, rubbing the heels of both hands across her eyes. "If you want to hear it," she said, "I'll tell you everything."

She looked pale and shaken. The anger Marty always felt when he guessed at what had brought her to this rose in him. But she needed quiet now and time to tell her story. "Whenever you're ready," he said.

She took another moment to collect herself, then began, her voice husky with emotion but steady. "A lot of it you know already. I explained about my mother leaving and my father being resentful and undemonstrative." Marty nodded. "Well...when I was little, I knew my father didn't like me. I guess it was natural in my child's mind to presume it was my fault. Then my mother left, and I was sure I had to be pretty terrible if she chose not to take me with her and he couldn't spare the time to speak to me."

She swallowed, the tone of her voice deepening in remembered anguish. "Other kids talked about things their families did together, about being tucked in at night, being hugged, or spoiled, or scolded. At the park with my grandmother I saw other children sitting in their parents' laps, being carried on their shoulders, holding their hands. I wanted that so badly."

She sobbed a little and he rubbed her back, waiting for her to go on. "Except for those Saturday afternoons with my grandmother, life was so bleak. No matter how good I tried to be, how good my grades were, how artfully I approached him, my father wanted nothing to do with me. After a time I came to accept that." She heaved a ragged sigh, reliving the grim truth. "With that acceptance came the understanding that I was probably seriously flawed. I was a teenager by then and working at the store. My co-workers didn't seem to notice anything wrong with me, and neither did the kids at school, but I tried to keep my distance from them so they wouldn't see it, whatever it was."

Her voice began to sound more normal, and she appeared to relax. Marty couldn't. She looked up at him, and he could see in her eyes that there was more.

"I planned my life around the store. I took business management classes in college with a minor in merchandising. My father didn't want to hear any of my ideas, and gave me only the jobs he hated, but I knew I was good at the work and that others in the store respected me for it. Somehow that imaginary ugly part of me didn't affect my work at Carlisle's. Then, three years ago, my father died, and despite all that he withheld from me, I grieved as though we'd been important to each other, because the fact that we hadn't been seemed almost worse than his death. Anyway..."

She sat a little straighter, as though bracing herself. Her voice remained calm. "I went into his office the day after he was buried and decided I finally had the chance to do what I'd always wanted to do—to run Carlisle's. I was going to put all the old miseries behind me." She gave him a grim little smile. "I guess I was like you starting over. This was a new chance. The staff liked me, I had confidence in my ability to do the job, and I was free of my father's dislike. I felt as though the world had opened a new door for me."

And then, on what seemed such a positive note, her tone changed and the haunted look returned to her eyes. Her brows drew together, and she warned with an apologetic glance and a catch in her voice, "We're...getting to the hard part."

Marty kissed her temple. "When you say it out loud, you'll be rid of it."

Shannon hoped he was right. Weekly visits to a therapist for months hadn't gotten rid of it. But there was no turning back now, no keeping it to herself. She no longer had control of it. It was no longer inside her; it seemed to sit on her like a heavy burden. She knew no other way to shake it off but to keep talking.

Chapter Twelve

"I hired Keith Barron to work with Gale shortly after my father's death," Shannon said, struggling to remain calm, to make sense. "He was intelligent, charming and had considerable experience in retail. Gale was already my right hand, but I thought a man in administration would give us a perspective we were lacking. I was right. He was very good. When he began to notice me, I ignored him. When he persisted, I was surprised. No young man had ever breached the wall I put up." She drew an unsteady breath. " 'But this is a new me,' I reminded myself. 'Whatever had been wrong with you—whatever your mother couldn't live with and your father couldn't like—you must have fixed.' "

A solitary tear slid down her cheek, and Marty took the handkerchief from his pocket and wiped it away. She didn't seem to notice, but continued with her story. "I think I fell in love with him because he made me forget I had that other, faulty side. He made me feel beautiful and desirable and whole." Another tear fell as she focused on Marty. "He was warm and sexy, always hugging me, telling me how much he loved me and needed me. We were married that fall."

She paused, wiping her eyes and clinging to what was left of her self-control. Trying to ease the burden for her, Marty guessed gently, "He beat you, didn't he?"

She shook her head, surprising him. "No. He never struck me, but—" Her mouth trembled with tears, but she swallowed and went on. "By Christmas I was living in a nightmare. The touch I thought would finally vindicate me as a person, as a woman, became something I dreaded. He could never touch me in simple affection or kindness without having to make love to me. I . . . I couldn't go to him for comfort or consolation without Keith considering it a sexual invitation. Can you imagine what it's like not to be able to touch someone you need and love because you know all you'll get from them is—" She shook her head, as though to dispel the memory. "It got to where I couldn't hug him or snuggle in bed or touch him to share a laugh. He wasn't rough or cruel. He simply couldn't see me in a way that wasn't physical."

She sobbed and Marty held her, filled with helpless anger. "I stayed with him for a while," she went on, "agonizing over why this man I thought I'd loved had become repulsive to me. I craved touch, didn't I? Didn't I want to be held and cuddled and loved? Why was it making my skin crawl and my mind writhe? Was there truth to my childhood belief that I was flawed?"

"God, Shannon." Marty leaned his cheek on her hair and closed his eyes, feeling her pain. "He was the one who was flawed."

"Even though I came to accept that and left Keith..." She sighed against Marty and settled herself more comfortably. "That year killed the brave little effort I'd made to be a whole person, to prove to myself that there wasn't something ugly in me that everyone could see but me. I was back to square one, or, rather, farther back than that. Emotionally I was afraid to make another attempt to go after what I'd wanted all my life, and physically I couldn't tolerate the contact I would need to find it. I settled for the only thing I thought I could have in my life—the store."

Shannon heaved a sigh and closed her eyes, finally purged of the burden she'd carried so long. Slowly she felt the darkness inside her diminish. Absorbing the comfort of Marty's protective embrace, she lay still. Ugly memories seemed to fade with the undefined anxieties that had been a part of her for as long as she could remember. She was tired and felt strangely out of tune.

"Oh, Marty." Her face still buried in his shoulder, Shannon put a hand to his face. "Aren't I pathetic?"

He held her hand to his mouth and kissed her palm. Then he enfolded it in his and brought it down between them. "No, I think you're heroic. Just try to remember it's behind you now."

She sat up, pale and rumpled, and made a halfhearted effort to smooth her hair. She saw the empathetic pain in his eyes, and reacting to an instinct she didn't question, she put her arms around his neck and put her cheek to his. "Thank you, Marty. That must have been as hard for you as it was for me."

He ran a hand lightly down her spine. "Only because I care so much about you."

Shannon leaned back to look at him, her arms still encircling his neck. "I've wanted to be rid of that for so long. But nothing, or no one ever mattered enough before for me to dredge it all up and face it." Then, suddenly more weary than she ever remembered being, she dropped her head to his shoulder. "God, I'm tired."

He held her close for a moment, placed a light kiss at her neck, then stood and pulled her to her feet. "Come on. I'll take you upstairs."

"I can—" she began to protest, but he had already lifted her in his arms and was striding toward the stairs. "Just like a sheikh," she teased, surprised she was able to. "You'd look charming with a tea towel on your head."

He slanted her a disapproving glance as he cleared the top of the steps and turned down the hall. "Behave yourself,"

he warned, "or I'll sell you to the first caravan we come to."
He gave her unlocked door a light kick and walked into the
dark room.

It was cool compared to the cozy downstairs, and Shannon shivered as he stood her on her feet. Marty turned on
the small lamp near the bed, tossed the spread and blankets
back and sat her down on the edge of the mattress. He
pulled her boots off and eased her back against the pillow,
swinging her legs up and covering her with the blankets. He
sat beside her, combing her hair back from her face with his
fingers.

"Are you all right?" he asked softly.

She was a little surprised to discover that she was. She was
confused and disoriented—but free.

"Yes, I'm fine." She sighed sleepily. "I can't quite believe I told you all that."

"Now it's over," he said, tucking the blankets under her
chin. "Tomorrow we're going to make a grocery list, go
shopping, then I'm going to bore you with old family albums."

Shannon snuggled into her pillow, pleased at the prospect. Her eyes closed. "Would you really sell me to a caravan?"

He leaned down to kiss her forehead. "Of course not. I'm
saving you for myself."

Shannon fell asleep, smiling.

"WHO'S THIS DEVILISH-LOOKING little boy?" Shannon had
been through three fat photo albums and now looked
through a shoe box filled with loose photos. Beyond the
kitchen window, a bleak, wintry dusk made the warm, easy
atmosphere inside seem even cozier. Marty stood at the
counter, scooping mocha fudge nut ice cream into parfait
glasses.

In a bulky yellow sweater over black tights, Shannon took
the photo to him. He slapped the lid on the tub of ice cream

and wiped his hands as he leaned down to examine the photo of two little boys arm in arm.

"Me," he said. "You've been looking through that stuff for hours. Don't you recognize me?"

She made a face at him. "Of course I did. I meant the other boy."

"That's Bobby Berger." Marty put the ice cream tub in the freezer. "We were best friends until we figured out how to make gunpowder. Then our parents wouldn't let us play together anymore."

Shannon laughed. "That was narrow-minded of them."

"Who can figure parents." He put a spoon into each glass and handed her one. "You're sure this is all you want for dinner?"

She groaned in anticipation. "We can have chips and dips for dessert and popcorn while we watch television."

That morning, when she'd made hamburgers for breakfast and watched cartoons while they ate, Marty had been concerned about her. When she'd filled their grocery cart with junk food and eaten two tacos, a burrito and a paper bowl of nachos at Taco Terrific for lunch, he'd become really worried. But after watching her bright eyes and hearing her laughter all afternoon, he began to understand. She was relieved—recklessly happy. Here was the little girl and the giddy teenager there had never been time for. T. Shannon Carlisle had found herself.

Marty took the photo from her, dropped it into the box and pushed her toward the living room. "If you insist on eating ice cream in the dead of winter, let's do it by the fire."

"It doesn't feel dead to me." She sat on the floor in front of the sofa where they'd talked the night before. "It feels very much alive. *I* feel very much alive."

Marty sat beside her, stretching his woolen-slippered feet toward the fire. He leaned over to kiss her cheek. "I know. Any minute now you're going to blow up and shower good cheer and old photos all over eastern Oregon."

Shannon laughed at the thought. "I have been kind of obnoxious, haven't I?"

"No," he replied seriously. "It's nice to know that silly little kid lives inside you."

Shannon put her ice cream aside as though she'd suddenly lost interest in it. She pulled Marty's arm around her and leaned into his shoulder. "I've had such a wonderful time today, Marty. I woke up feeling so free and so alive. Like a child—only a child from someone else's life."

Marty put his parfait glass on the end table and wrapped both arms around her. "It's *your* life, Shannon. You exorcised your ghosts and took charge. That's why you feel so good."

"I feel so good because I'm with you." She pulled back to look at him, her eyes dark and clear. "I'm always happy with you. Even when the situation is impossible and everything's going wrong, being with you feels right."

Marty had to concentrate on remaining calm. She looked very young, and the newness of personal peace shone in her eyes. He was afraid to wonder if she was finally going to see things his way. He tried to act casual. "I hate to say 'I told you so,' but I did, so I will. It feels so right because you love me just as I love you."

She smiled, and there was something of the temptress in it. "You're sure?"

He nodded confidently. "Absolutely."

Looking into the silent invitation in her eyes, Marty felt his pulse thrum, his blood move. He freed her hands and leaned down to capture her mouth. It opened under his, and her tongue met his gently, tentatively.

Marty leaned back against the sofa, drawing her between his knees to take her weight. She leaned into him with an eagerness that delighted and frustrated him.

Shannon felt the first unrestricted stirrings of passion she'd known since the very early days with Keith. She'd been so sure she'd never yearn for a man again, never want to share herself with him, never want to know him in the most profound sense of the word. But the need was building in her now as Marty's body cushioned hers and enveloped her with arms she knew were straining to be gentle and patient.

Marty's hands roamed down her back, up her fragile ribs, then gently, cautiously, over her breast. It was the first physical intimacy in a relationship in which each knew the scarred and still-bruised depths of the other. It seemed to bring renewal to the foreground, relegating heartbreak and regrets to the past. This was new and had startling, astounding potential. Part of her wanted to race toward where this would lead, but another part of her wanted to withdraw.

Shannon shifted under his hand, not because she felt any trace of fear, but because she remembered so clearly how she had reacted in bed toward the end of her marriage. Her mind knew the difference between Keith and Marty, but she couldn't be sure what her body would do, and she wouldn't hurt Marty in that way for anything.

She felt Marty's shuddered sigh as his hand fell away. He wrapped both arms around her and dropped his head to her shoulder, kissing the sensitive spot behind her ear. "Tired?" he asked.

She nuzzled his cheek, feeling the beginnings of a bristly beard. "No," she replied.

Marty remained still, surprised she hadn't snatched at the excuse. He had thought some of the old fear had returned when he touched her breast, had even expected that it might. He was determined to give her time, promised himself that at her smallest hesitation he would draw back. But now that he'd given her the opportunity to retreat from his lovemaking and she'd refused it, he wasn't sure how to proceed.

Shannon had never imagined that a man could be so still. Her father had always been tense and nervous; Keith had hurried from one point to another. Most of the men she worked with swaggered, laughed loudly, fidgeted and swore.

But for all his wry amusement, Marty could be so serene. More than once she had seen him in the midst of a crisis or a dilemma, stop still, gather quiet around him and use it to restore order or gain understanding. It was that serenity, that willingness to search for the cause behind the problem, that brought the smile back to her lips and allowed her to be honest. Sitting in the circle of his arms, she suddenly wanted this more than anything. "I want you to make love to me," she said softly, "I'm just not sure how I'll react."

He ran a hand gently up and down her arm. "You're afraid."

"No," she denied instantly. "I want to make love with you. My mind knows that. I'm just not sure what my body will do. It's been turned off for so long, and I'm afraid it might have a memory." She put a hand on the one that stroked her arm. "Do we want to put you through that when what you need in your life is a warm, responsive woman?"

He enveloped her in his arms, then held her tightly, possessively. "You have a responsibility to be what you are," he said gently, "not what I need. I want to make love to you, not because I need comfort and coddling, and sexual gratification, but because I want to know you, the woman who came through all that deprivation and careless sexual attention and remained bright, funny and giving, the woman who warmed and lit my life at a gloomy, frightening time."

He combed his fingers through her hair and gently pulled her head back. He grinned. "If you think your body will resist letting her out, if you think you might scream or want to run or hit me with a fireplace poker—" she laughed softly at the picture "—I think I can handle it. I'm hardly delicate. On the other hand..." He grew serious. "If you think you're rushing it, that you're not ready, I can handle that, too."

Shannon realized there was no decision to be made. Such generosity made choice unnecessary. She looked around the dark, fire-lit room, remembering how he'd teased about the poker. "Here?" she asked. "In front of the fire."

He nodded. "There are a couple of quilts in that trunk we pushed aside to lie here. We should be very comfortable. If you want to get them, I'll put more wood on the fire."

Within moments the fire roared, spreading its warmth and glow to the space where Marty had opened one of the quilts. He tossed the other one nearby for later. Besides the anticipation of making love to Shannon, and the awe he felt at her willingness to make love with him, he felt a suddenly alarming sense of responsibility. He was tight with longing yet he would have to move carefully, slowly, considerately, no matter what he felt. He would have to forget himself and remain aware of her.

Sitting in the middle of the quilt, Shannon reached up to take his hand and pulled him down beside her. Reading his eyes, she smoothed a finger over the frown between his brows. "You aren't required to read my mind or second-guess my every need," she said, leaning forward to touch his lips with hers. "Just be Marty. That's what I want. That's what I need."

Bending his knee up behind her to support her back, Marty pulled Shannon into his arms and kissed her. She'd freed him of the responsibility for her pleasure, but that only made him feel it more keenly. And as her mouth moved receptively, eagerly over his, he gave to her, drew from her, feeling all the desire that had lain dormant in him for so long awaken. The intensity of it was no surprise, but his willingness to control it was. Despite Shannon's caution, his every thought at this moment was for her.

Reaching under her sweater, he bracketed her warm, slender waist with his hands. Slowly they rose upward, his thumbs stroking over the delicate jut of her ribs, then the small swelling of her breasts, working easily, attentively over her beaded nipples. He felt her stiffen, but heard the little intake of breath that indicated pleasure rather than fear.

The front of his sweatshirt clutched in her hands, Shannon remained still, inclining her head and closing her eyes under the sweet tyranny of his touch. Her body was coming alive. After years of sleep, every nerve ending Marty touched seemed to spark into alertness. Shannon felt the tick of her pulse, the rise and fall of her lungs, the warm, languid movement of her blood. She knew with sudden certainty that the reaction she feared would never come. In this instance at least her body was wiser than her brain. Though deprived of it for a lifetime, it recognized love in an instant and seemed eager to let it have its way.

As Marty lifted the fabric of her sweater, Shannon obligingly raised her arms to allow its removal. She emerged from the tight turtleneck with a smile and a toss of her head to try to smooth her hair. But Marty took a handful of it and eased her back onto the quilt. Warm from the fire, it felt like silk under her shoulder blades and smelled faintly of lavender.

Leaning over her on an elbow, Marty looked into her eyes, watching for a trace of reluctance or hesitation. He saw only happiness and a flare of excitement. He stroked her bright hair away from her face. "All right?"

She smiled and reached under his sweatshirt, her fingers probing fascinatedly over warm flesh covering a sturdy structure of bone and muscle. "Yes," she said. She worked her hands up until he pushed to a sitting position and pulled the shirt and his T-shirt off.

Shannon sat up to meet him as he came down again, and he held her to him with a strong hand at her back. The sudden flesh to flesh touch of her small, silky breasts and his broad, muscular chest elicited a faint groan from both of them.

"Shannon," he murmured in her ear, unable to form a thought to follow her name.

She let him place her back on the quilt, too overwhelmed by her feelings to do anything but exclaim on a whisper, "Oh, Marty."

Kneeling over her, Marty kissed a trail from her clavicle to the waistband of her jeans. Then he parted the snap and drew the zipper down. Slipping his fingers into the waistband of her panties, he tugged gently, and she lifted up until both garments were down her legs and tossed aside.

In a gesture that was almost worshipful, Marty ran a tender hand over her stomach and down the length of her leg. "You're beautiful," he said.

She smiled and reached for the snap of his jeans. "I'm in love. Or you are. I'm not sure which accounts for your thinking I'm beautiful."

Marty lay back, and she knelt over him, easing his snug jeans and briefs down. Unconsciously she repeated his gesture of reverence, running her small hand across the flat plane of his stomach, over the protuberance of his hipbone, then down the muscular length of his thigh and calf. He needed no more arousal, which she noted with a sense of power she'd never known in her life. But she felt humility rather than arrogance.

She reached out to touch him, but he intercepted her hand and pulled her down beside him. At her expression of surprise, he cradled her head on his arm and laughed softly. "I'll lose my mind," he explained, his free hand tracing along her hip, inside her thigh. She bent her knee to allow him access and let herself relax against him at the first gentle touch of his fingers. "There are things I want you to know first."

The revelation came upon her as gradually, as inevitably as the climax. Unfocused tension began to build inside her, pleasure that brought with it an almost painful lack of something unexplained, that built and grew until she was forced to focus on it, to pinpoint it in her mind in the vain hope that it would relieve her body. But the concentration seemed only to increase the disquiet until what she chased suddenly turned to strike her without warning, shaking her with pleasure she'd never imagined in her moments of deepest longing. She shuddered for moments, lost in the power of the first real lovemaking of her life.

Finally surfacing with some measure of coherence, Shannon reached for Marty, needing to repay, to share. He gasped at the first touch of her hands, thinking desperately about remaining in control, holding on to awareness of Shannon and... But he was lost within seconds as she touched and stroked him with the new confidence and the passion to please of a woman who has been cherished.

When he rose over her, she took him in eagerly, anxious to satisfy him, sure she had experienced all there could be of pleasure. Marty entered her, delighted with what she'd given him, but trying to recapture control so that he could give her more.

With their bodies entwined, their passions meeting, their love giving, and giving again, Marty lost all sense of awareness and slipped over the edge, a victim of Shannon's eagerness to share what she felt. And as Marty held Shannon close, determined not to lose her in the throes of his own pleasure, her world flew apart again, bombarding her with hot sensation. They clung together until what each felt privately communicated itself to the other and became a profound sharing of something both thought had been lost to them forever.

After long moments Marty tried to shift his weight from Shannon, but she tightened her grip on his back. "No, stay." Shannon sighed and kissed his shoulder, unable to understand the depth of what she felt, much less explain it. "I have no words, Marty."

Bracing himself on his forearms, he kissed her long and lingeringly, too filled with emotion himself to find words for her. "I don't think there are any." He felt dampness against his shoulder and saw a tear slide down her cheek.

"I wish I could tell you what you've made me feel," she said, emotion brimming in her eyes, then overflowing.

"Shannon." Marty rolled onto his back and pulled her with him, still locked in his embrace. "You don't have to. I felt it all." He reached beside him for the second quilt and tossed it over them. Securing it around her with his arms, he kissed her damp forehead. Worried by her tears, he teased. "And you never even tried to reach for the poker."

She sighed and relaxed her weight against him. "I think fear has given up on me forever."

"I'm going to hold you to that," he whispered.

"THAT'S ENOUGH. It's perfect." Marty leaned against the large ball of snow they'd spent considerable time forming and wiped a gloved hand across his brow. Then he patted the white globe. "This is good."

"No, it has to be bigger!" Shannon put both her mittens flat against it and tried to push.

Marty brushed her hands away. "If we make it any bigger, the middle of the snowman will be bigger than the bottom.

She smiled, sincere delight behind the gesture. "It'll be a genuine reflection of our week here, a monument to all the wonderful food we've eaten."

It was already Wednesday, but Marty had tried not to count the days. "That I've cooked," he said.

Shannon rolled her eyes. "Let's not start that. I faithfully provided moral support, encouragement and empathy when the goulash went wrong."

"Who insisted that it didn't have enough hot paprika?"

Shannon put her hands on his shoulders, her eyes wide with sincerity, backlit with laughter. "That doesn't matter. When it came out like those thready things in a car wash and hot enough to ignite asbestos, I was there for you. I reassured you that you shouldn't blame yourself."

"That's because it was your fault."

Shannon withdrew her hands and folded her arms, assuming a sort of dignified pout. But Marty saw the change take place in her eyes, the softness of laughter, the beginnings of desire. "Well, if that's your attitude, I'm tempted to go back inside and let you finish this project by yourself."

Distracted by the subtle change in her, Marty watched her eyes and said absently, "The snowman . . . was your idea."

Her eyes roved over his face, lingering with a slow caress on his lips. After three days of making almost constant love to her, he felt the imprint of her mouth as though she had actually kissed him. "If you're going to criticize my efforts to help you, and refuse to let me build my first snowman my way . . ." She sighed, giving him a pouty glance before turning away to start back toward the house, "I'm going back to bed."

"All right, look." Marty pulled her to a stop. Taking hold of her shoulders, he sighed as though the concession he was about to make was costing him a great deal. "Maybe we need to step back from this and put a little more planning into it."

"Planning?" She was trying hard not to smile, and that made the banked desire in her eyes hotter than their goulash.

"Yeah." Marty leaned down to taste her mouth. Cold and dry, it warmed to him instantly, holding on, drawing out the easy, playful kiss. "I think we should find a comfortable spot and really talk about this. Explore in depth . . . what we're really after here."

Her voice softened, becoming husky. "Find an activity that will stimulate our creativity, help us achieve a certain level of excellence . . ."

Marty turned her toward the house and started walking, holding her close. "I'm beginning to see it now. A tribute to what this week has meant to us."

"Something we'll remember forever."

"But I can't quite get it into focus."

Shannon stopped, hooked an arm around his neck and stood on tiptoe to reach his mouth. This time her lips opened over his, her tongue darted into his mouth in search of his, and she drank from him like someone dying of thirst. Crushing her to him, Marty felt his body ignite, then swept her into his arms and hurried for the stairs.

SHANNON WAS ACCUSTOMED to bouts of insomnia. They usually accompanied periods of low sales at the store, or lost shipments. She'd never been kept awake because she was too happy to sleep. But that was the case as she wandered around the kitchen at five in the morning the day she and Marty had to leave for Portland, making certain everything in the house was as they'd found it.

A week had passed too quickly, yet in those few days her entire life had changed. The troubled woman who couldn't give and couldn't take was gone forever. Marty's kindness and sensitivity had helped her face the past and put it away. The imprint of his body had turned a grim future into something she awaited with hope and anticipation.

Shannon gathered the albums she'd enjoyed perusing all week and took them to the deep drawer of the hutch from which Marty had taken them. She replaced them, then noticed one album in the corner of the drawer that had never been removed. She pulled it out and sat back on her heels to look through it, a smile on her face.

The eight-by-ten on the first page was a wedding photo. A beautiful, laughing, dark-haired woman looked up at a handsome young man—Marty. Shannon turned the page and saw snapshots of what was probably a honeymoon in some tropical location. Then there were baby pictures of Evan; the infant's serious expression left little doubt who the subject was. There were more babies, little stair-step boys in matching outfits, their mother herding them together, their little faces filled with love and adoration as they looked at her. There was a malamute puppy.

Shannon replaced the album in the drawer and closed it firmly. Marty had probably deliberately left that album in the drawer. Knowing her insecurities about replacing Monica in his and the children's lives, he chose to show her only the photos of his childhood.

Her sudden freedom from the burden of her past, and her happy foray into lovemaking, had made her believe she could step right in where Monica had been. "Fool," she whispered.

She went into the kitchen and poured herself a cup of coffee, feeling the newly discovered zest for life drain out of her. She would never fit into Marty's family. His children liked her, but they'd never look at her as they'd looked at Monica. She hadn't the maternal skills to inspire their adoration. After all they'd lost, they deserved a woman who could offer warmth and ready affection, and she was too new at it.

She heard Marty stirring upstairs and began to set the table, an artificial smile on her face.

"WE COULD SAY we had car trouble." In jeans and Marty's blue sweatshirt that fell to her knees, Shannon stirred a fragrant pot of stew. They were packed and ready to leave after lunch.

"No good." Marty put a hand at her hip and pushed her gently aside to reach into the oven. "Every hung over employee uses that one." He pulled out a pan of golden biscuits and placed it on a trivet. "My father would never believe it."

"We got lost?" she suggested, pulling bowls out of the cupboard.

Turning the pan of rolls over into a napkin-lined basket, Marty shook his head. "We got here all right. It would be hard to sell anyone on the notion that we got lost going back."

Shannon ladled stew into the bowls and frowned thoughtfully. She carried the bowls to the table, then looked up at Marty as he put the basket of rolls in the middle. "I've got it!" Rare winter sunlight poured through the small-paned windows that surrounded the kitchen, burnishing her hair, finding something in her eyes Marty didn't under-stand and didn't want to see. "Hostile aliens from a blue star were on a raid to replenish their breeding stock for colonial expansion. Since you and I were—" she bobbed her head from side to side in affected embarrassment "—well, in conjugation at the time..."

"Amo, amas, amat?"

"They snatched us up into their spaceship," she contin-ued, ignoring him, "truly impressed with our prowess."

Marty pulled her chair out and pushed her into it. "Pre-sumably they left a blue starian behind to explain this to Dad and Edie and Gale."

Shannon shook her head at him impatiently as he sat across from her. "Marty, don't you know anything about this stuff? At this very moment a dauntless news reporter is tracking the ship and will arrive here in time to see us beamed aboard. It'll be in all the papers. He'll keep our memories alive for years until our son comes down to earth to prevent World War III."

He might have sustained the game if she hadn't men-tioned their child. He knew he'd been foolish, that it was presuming a lot, but even before they'd made love on the quilt in front of the fire, he'd wondered what a child of theirs would be like, look like.

He was asking for trouble, he knew, but he'd seen some-thing hiding in her eyes since he'd looked into them upon awakening that morning, and it scared him. He passed her the basket of rolls. "Actually," he said with careful non-chalance, "I was hoping we'd have a girl. Women have come into their own. *She* could prevent World War III. Particularly if she got help from her brothers."

Shannon looked at him over the proffered basket of rolls. Her eyes grew wide and dark, that little pinpoint of misery hiding there all morning finally coming forward. She selected a roll and lowered her eyes, making a production of tearing it in two and buttering it. "I suppose it'd be easier to stop whining and go home."

Certain now that something serious troubled her, Marty dipped a spoon into his stew and tried to think logically. "Oh, I don't know. That was beginning to sound like an excuse we could sell. What didn't you like about it?"

Shannon sighed and looked up at him, knowing he'd seen inside her and wouldn't let it rest. She decided it was probably time to deal with it, anyway. She smiled, wanting him to know how much she loved him, how much this week would always mean to her. "I didn't like us teasing about having a daughter. It's . . . well." She hunched up a shoulder, as though shielding herself. "It hurts, that's all."

"Why, Shannon?"

She looked at him, apparently surprised that he didn't see it. "Because it's impossible, that's why. You have four young boys who need you. I can't just walk into that and mess it all up."

He tried hard to see beyond what she was saying, but for the life of him it didn't make sense. "How would you do that?" he asked.

Shannon dropped her spoon with a clatter. "They love their mother, for one thing."

He nodded. "True. But they see her once, maybe twice a year. They need someone for the other ninety-nine percent of their lives."

"They have you."

Marty pushed his untouched bowl away and leaned toward her. "True, again. They are most of my reason for being and I'd die for them without question, but I am physically and psychologically unequipped to be everything they need. They need softness, sweetness and understanding that can look beyond their bad behavior and have compassion for the developing man, instead of the impatience I feel when they make a decision that compromises all I've tried to teach them. They need mother love, Shannon."

This time Shannon nodded sadly, fatalistically. "And can you think of anyone less prepared to give it to them? You've helped me come a long way as a woman, Marty, but a mother has to have a generosity and a responsiveness that died in me long ago. I can now respond to a man, thanks to you, but I'll never have the hugs and smiles and the unrestrained warmth kids need from a mother. I lived without it. I'd never knowingly inflict that lack on other children."

Marty pushed away from the table, needing room to move. He got to his feet and strode across the kitchen, then back again. He couldn't accept that all he had discovered would be taken from him. "Where is this coming from?" he asked, stopping to lean against the counter right behind her. "I don't know what you're talking about. The kids insist that they had a great time when you stayed with them. And how can you have hugs and smiles for me and not for them? That doesn't even make sense."

Shannon pushed her bowl away but remained seated, putting a cold hand to her forehead. "It does, Marty. Loving you and feeling warmly toward you is easy. You know how to reach it in me, where to find it when I don't even think it's there. But to be a good mother to your children, I'd have to be experienced in warmth and patience." She turned in her chair to look at him, willing him to understand. "Marty, Evan doesn't like me, and I've seen Jarrod and Grady look at each other as though wondering what planet I've come from. Josh gives me love unconditionally, but pretty soon he'll need more of a reason to like me. He'll need to know that I can give *him* something."

Marty pulled the chair from the end of the table and placed it beside Shannon's. He sat a few inches away from her, looking into her eyes. "Kids will love you with the least encouragement. If you care about them and you're honest with them, they'll give you all kinds of latitude to make mistakes, and that's all they want back—that when they've blown it, they know it hasn't changed the way you feel about them." Shannon opened her mouth to speak, but he caught her hand and held it, going on. "I didn't realize how generous my kids were until Monica left and I had to deal with them by myself. I was scared, but I was there and she wasn't, and I think they gave me credit for that, even though they didn't understand it."

Shannon shook her head helplessly. "Marty, the store is really all I know...."

"The question is," he said evenly, "is it all you ever want to know?"

"I don't want to make an ugly mistake we'll both regret."

Marty sighed and dropped her hand, leaning against the back of his chair. "I don't think that's it. I think you're drunk on the love and warmth you and I've built together. After a lifetime without it, you have it at last. You're not afraid you won't have it to give my kids. You're afraid you'll give it and they'll ignore it, preferring what they get from Monica."

Shannon got to her feet defensively because that explained so clearly what she'd spent the morning trying to sift through. Buried inside her, it had been a serious, genuine concern. Spoken aloud, it sounded cowardly. Hurt, she turned on him. Walking around the table, she stopped at the chair he had first occupied and leaned her hands on the back of it. "You're forcing this because you don't want to fail at anything else. You want to hammer me into place in your family because it fell apart on you once and you're not going to let it happen again."

Marty unfolded to his feet with slow deliberation. Anger billowed inside him along with pain and the grim acknowledgment that she was at least partly right. He didn't want to lose her, but whose welfare did he have in mind? Hers or his? He admitted to himself that he had forced this showdown because he had hoped to ward off failure.

With the table between them, they looked at each other grimly. "You might be right about that," he said quietly. "So I'm faced with failure, and you're faced with nothing more than you had before, except that now you can make love without fear. You're settling for the short stick again, Shannon, because sex is the only facet of love you've conquered."

"Unlike you," she said stiffly, "I don't expect to be able to have everything."

"That's a good thing." He replaced the chair with methodical care, then looked at her, his blue eyes calm but accusing. "To have everything, you have to give everything, risk everything. You're still not woman enough to do that. And you told me fear had given up on you."

She sighed wearily. "I was wrong."

THROUGH THE GENTLY rolling hills of the Warm Springs Indian Reservation, Shannon sang along with the voice of Roberta Flack. She was trying to show Marty that he was wrong. And she was trying to prove it to herself. Her mind and spirit were free of their burden now. She couldn't have Marty and didn't want anyone else. But certainly there would be a future for her, even though her heart was trapped.

She could see now that they'd been foolish, even reckless, not to look ahead. How could two people who worked so well and happily together with a strong friendship between them ever think that that friendship could be easily converted to love, particularly when four children and an ex-wife were involved. This wasn't a television serial drama, after all; this was life with all its practical problems and nitty-gritty demands. And, despite all of Marty's claims to the contrary, it wasn't realistic to assume that one could have everything.

Shannon leaned over her seat to pull a can of Pepsi out of the cooler in the back. Sitting forward and rebuckling her belt, she snapped off the pull-top and offered the can to Marty. He'd kept his eyes diligently on the road for the past thirty miles. "I'm the one who warned you against fraternization, if you'll recall."

Still staring at the road, he took a slow sip from the can, then said calmly, "If you want to act detached from the problem and in control of this mess, you can get out and walk."

"It might be more entertaining than driving to Portland beside a mannequin with a face from Mount Rushmore."

Marty gave her a quick, cool glance. "What I wouldn't give for James Bond's ejector seat."

Shannon turned slightly toward him, trying to hold on to reason. "Marty, I know that I don't have it in me to be a mother to four boys. Would you rather I took on the job and failed? What kind of a mess would we have then?"

"You thought you could never stand being touched," he reminded her reasonably, "and learned differently. You thought you'd never be able to let a man make love to you, and we've done little else for five days. Fear has kept you all locked up for years. And now you're going to slip back behind bars because you're afraid of four kids."

"Marty, any woman would think twice about taking on four children, and I'll wager eighty percent of them would walk away."

"You're not any woman," he replied mercilessly. "You're very intelligent, remarkably strong, wickedly clever, and have the survival instincts of an endangered species. You could do it. I know you'd even come to love it. But you'll never know."

"That's better than trying, then learning for certain that I *couldn't* do it."

Marty had no arguments left. He was tired, hurt, angry and dispirited. He didn't deal very well with failure himself, so he didn't have to stretch the limits of his understanding to grasp her unwillingness to take such a major step and find out she'd overestimated herself. The problem was that in order to let her step away from failure he had to accept failure himself, to acknowledge that somehow he'd been less than she needed.

Edie had so much to report on the five days spent with her grandson that Shannon and Marty were spared further conversation until he pulled up in front of Shannon's condo. It was raining.

"You don't even have to get out of the car," she said briskly, giving Marty a smile for Edie's benefit. "Once I get my bags on the elevator..."

But Marty was already out of the car and pulling her bags from the trunk. Shannon smiled at Edie and wished her a happy new year.

In the middle of the living room, Shannon turned to Marty to tell him to leave the bags there, but he walked past her to the bedroom and placed them on the old steamer trunk at the foot of her brass bed.

"Grady's got a doctor's appointment Monday morning," he said, "so I'll be about an hour late coming in."

"No problem. I'm always early." She followed him back out to the living room, wanting to stop him, to hold him back, to rekindle the warmth and fun of their days in Bend. But that was over and they both knew it. She realized bleakly that she was going to have to put distance between them if either of them was to face the future with any peace of mind. But they could talk about that later. "Thanks for helping me with the bags."

"Sure." He opened the door and held it for a moment as he turned to look at her, all her feelings of an instant ago reflected in his eyes. Then he closed them a moment, as though to dismiss what he felt. "See you Monday, then."

MARTY PULLED into his driveway, relieved to see that his father's Jaguar was absent. Henry was probably with some nubile young thing from the Junior Shop or Cosmetics. He knew some of the staff was meeting at Freddy's tonight to see the new year in. Marty shook his head wryly as he handed Edie her smaller bag and carried her larger one and his own to the porch. He shouldn't demean his father's conquests. As a septuagenarian, Henry was far more successful with women than he was.

Edie put on a pot of coffee, then went to her room to unpack. Marty carried his bags upstairs, noticing how eerily quiet the house was. The nights had been still in Bend, but he'd had Shannon in his arms then and the sounds of their midnight whispers and their mingled heartbeats. Their lazy caressing movements had had the stuff of life about them. He sat on the edge of the bed for a moment, letting the debilitating pain flow over him.

Losing Monica had hurt like hell because they'd been comfortable together for a long time. But he'd finally gotten over her. He suspected that the pain of losing Shannon would last a lifetime. Their relationship had the potential for so much more than comfort. He'd only glimpsed the vital warmth, the pervading humor, the passion that had helped each of them, if only for a few days, put the past aside and enjoy the moment.

Impatient with his maudlin thoughts, Marty pulled things out of his suitcase and put them away. As satisfying as it was to grab the present, he'd watched his children grow up long enough to know that one's only stock in life was a willingness, even an eagerness to face the future, and at the moment Shannon couldn't do that. At least she couldn't do it with him.

It wouldn't kill him, he thought as he went downstairs in response to the smell of coffee. He'd started over too many times for that, but it sure as hell took the light out of everything.

Edie was already pouring two cups of coffee. Dressed in a long light blue velour robe, she handed him a cup. "Is it anything you want to talk about?" she asked.

He shook his head, accepting the coffee. "Thanks, but I don't think so. How's your grandson?"

"Beautiful, smiling, pointing toward the encyclopedia." She raised an eyebrow at Marty. "But I told you all that on the way home. You weren't listening, were you?"

He winced penitently. "Sorry."

She shrugged. "Forget it. It's hard to notice things when you're lovestruck. Harder still when something gets in the way of that love." She patted his shoulder consolingly. "I wouldn't give up on it. Well, I'm off to bed. No seeing the new year in for me. I'm exhausted."

"Good night, Edie." Marty settled in front of the television, rejecting all the musical New Year's Eve programming for an old Jimmy Cagney movie. The character's pugnacious attitude was more in keeping with his present mood.

It was after one o'clock when he heard the commotion on the porch. He pulled the door open as a tall young man reached out to knock on it. Leaning heavily on the young man, an arm draped around his shoulders, his left eye black and blue and his jaw dark red and swollen, was Henry.

"Dad!" Marty reached out to relieve the young man of his father's weight. Together they supported Henry as far as the living room sofa.

The older man fell into it gratefully, smiling vacantly at Marty. "Nishe party," he said with a slur. Then he put a limp hand to his chin. "But the confetti hurts."

"Mr. Hale, we're so sorry!"

For the first time since he'd answered the door, Marty noticed Hilary from Cosmetics. She stood beside the young man, her face pale, her eyes distressed. "Glenn didn't know he was my boss. I mean, Mr. Henry always acts like that, and we all just sort of..." She hunched a shoulder, obviously wishing she hadn't begun an explanation.

"He had her in a corner and was trying to kiss her," Glenn said, his expression regretful as he tried to explain his actions. "She came to the party with me, and all I saw was the back of this guy who was trying to force her into something she didn't want. I turned him around and slugged him before I realized how old he was."

Marty looked down at his father, feeling less annoyance over his romantic pursuits at the moment than compassion. Suddenly alone and lonely himself, he saw Henry's behavior in a new light.

Glenn shook his head. "I'm really sorry. Do you think we should take him to a doctor?"

Marty leaned down to study his father's injuries more closely. The eye itself wasn't damaged, though it and the cheekbone would be purple for several days. His jaw was bruised, but his teeth looked fine. He straightened and put a hand on Hilary's shoulder. "I'm sorry, Hilary. I'm sure he wouldn't hurt you for anything."

"Oh, I know that." She smiled shyly. "All the girls on the floor know that. I'm just so sorry this happened."

"You won't hold this against her, will you?" Glenn looked mildly belligerent. "I did it, not her."

Marty shook his head. "Of course not. Why don't you two go back to the party and I'll take care of him."

"You're sure there's nothing we can do?" Hilary asked.

Marty led them to the door. "I'm sure." He put his hand out to the young man. "Nice to meet you, Glenn...?"

"Stapleton," the young man supplied, finally relaxing, smiling. "Nice to meet you."

Marty smiled at Hilary. "See you Monday."

"Right." Obviously relieved, the couple turned away into the darkness.

By the time Marty had removed Henry's coat, stretched him out on the sofa, bathed his bruises and forced a cup of coffee down him, Henry was almost coherent. Marty, sitting opposite the sofa on a matching chair, coaxed him into sipping a second cup. Propped in a corner of the sofa, his head lolling limply against the back, Henry groaned. "I kissed who?"

"Hilary Noble."

"Hilary Noble." Henry repeated the name thickly.

"The little blonde in Cosmetics."

"Oh . . . yeah." Henry raised his head and held the warm coffee cup to his chin. "She packs a punch."

"Her boyfriend hit you."

"She seeing Mike Tyson?"

"Glenn Stapleton. Nice kid. Said he wouldn't have hit you if he'd seen how old you were first."

Slowly Henry lowered the cup to his lap, then focused with difficulty on Marty. "I've embarrassed you."

Marty shook his head, catching the ottoman with the heel of his running shoe and pulling it closer. He crossed his ankles on it and sipped at his cup. "Hardly. But you have caused me some concern. I wonder if you'll ever get over Mom enough to enjoy life again. This experiment with women you're conducting becomes more dangerous the older you get."

Henry propped his elbow on the arm of the sofa and leaned his forehead in his hand. "I've always had so much to do, so many plans, and your mother was always as enthused about them as I was." He dropped his hand, a small reflective smile curving his mouth. "I thought we had forever." The smile faded, and Henry stared into nothingness. "And then, after thirty-eight years that seemed like about two and a half, she was gone and there I was, still full of

plans and dreams that lost their substance because I had n⟨
one I could share them with.''

Marty's heart ached for him, not simply because he'⟨
loved his mother, too, and knew what a special woman she'⟨
been, but because he understood the loss of a love, the fu
tility of trying to grasp at what was no longer there. ''An⟨
looking for a younger woman makes you feel youn⟨
again?''

Henry raised an eyebrow in thought for a moment, the⟨
nodded grimly. ''Simple and sad, isn't it? I hear the foot
steps behind me, Marty. I'm next, and being with a youn
ger woman helps dull the sound, I guess. God!'' He covere⟨
his eyes again, his mouth pinching closed in emotion. ''You⟨
mother must be turning in her grave.''

His throat constricting, Marty moved to sit beside Henry
Leaning against the back of the sofa, he dropped a hand o⟨
his father's shoulder. ''I doubt it, Dad. She understood yo⟨
so well. I'm sure she knows how much you loved her an⟨
that you're having trouble dealing with things without her
But, the truth is, you're going to have to.''

''The truth is,'' Henry said vacantly, ''I don't want to
I've tried and it doesn't work. It was better when you an⟨
the boys were nearby, but now that you're almost tw⟨
hundred miles away, I can only deal with the loneliness b⟨
pointing the Jag in the direction of Portland. You can't liv⟨
your life with me hanging on to the fringe of it.''

Marty shook the shoulder he held. ''Dad, you can han⟨
on to the fringe of my life as long as you want to. Hell, yo⟨
can jump into the middle of it, but you're only seventy an⟨
a strong, youthful man. You need your own life, your ow⟨
pleasures, your own satisfactions. I think you should loo⟨
for a woman your own age.''

Henry cast Marty a dry side-glance. ''Women my age ar⟨
old.''

''Dad, *you're* old.''

''You just said I was youthful.''

Marty grinned. "You're a youthful old man."

Henry sighed and frowned. "What kind of a prospect does that leave me?"

Marty patted his shoulder. "With a youthful, older woman, the possibilities are limitless. You could travel, take up archaeology, oil painting."

"Mud wrestling."

"That, too. But you've got to buff up your attitude. You feel lonely and alone because you're looking for comfort and companionship in the wrong places among women who have nothing in common with you. You can't have Mom back, but I'm sure there's a wonderful lady out there somewhere who'd like to get to know you, to share things with you."

Henry sighed again and downed the rest of his coffee. "Was Hilary very upset?" he asked moodily.

"Because you'd been hurt, yes. But I assured her she still had a job."

Henry nodded and leaned forward to put his cup on the coffee table. Then he turned to look at Marty. "You and Shannon have a good time in Bend?"

Marty was sure it all showed in his eyes, the love, the fun, the grief, but he tried to bluff, anyway. "Great. Shannon loved the snow."

"So where is she?"

"At her place. We were both very tired."

Henry looked at him until he was forced to look back. "It's not working out, is it?" Henry asked.

Marty said nothing for a moment, finding it difficult to admit it aloud. He finally decided he was being cowardly. He gave his father a wry grin. "If you think it's hard attracting women at seventy, you should try doing it with four kids."

Henry frowned. "I thought she liked them. They sure seem to like her."

"She had a rough childhood and a rotten marriage. She doesn't think she has anything to give them."

Henry's frown deepened. "She doesn't seem short of anything important to me."

"She isn't," Marty said. "But unless she believes that there isn't much I can do."

Henry reached back to put a hand on Marty's shoulder. "Maybe you need a steady older woman, too, son. Maybe we could find some lusty spinster sisters with a lot of money."

Suddenly the picture of himself and his father arm in arm with two bony-kneed old ladies in hats formed clearly in Marty's mind. He began to laugh and was still laughing when he helped his father up to bed.

THE BOYS WERE BESIDE themselves with excitement. "We rode on the yacht!"

"Now her pool's enclosed!"

"We had caviar and pâté and oysters!"

"Mom wants Evan to come and live with her!"

Delighted to have them back again, grateful for the noise of their presence, Marty absorbed only the sound and not the substance of the last statement. Then suddenly the words registered and he turned to Grady, who had spoken them. "What do you mean?"

The boy was dragging a camouflage duffel bag toward the stairs. "She wants Evan to live with her. She thinks she can get him into movies."

Anger and panic rose in Marty. How like Monica to make a suggestion Evan was bound to leap at without discussing it with Marty first. How like her not to consider that Evan had one more year of high school, that he could be too dazzled by her life-style to finish. How like her not to consider what she would do with him when she had to be away.

"Is your mom outside?" Marty asked as Jarrod walked past him, suitcase in one hand, the skeleton of something small with long yellow teeth in the other.

"No, her driver brought us home. Look at this rad beaver skeleton, Dad. I found it on the beach. Mr. Grover in biology is going to have apoplexy!"

Josh, looking as though he'd just been aroused from a nap, raised his arms to Marty. "Hi, Dad." He fastened his arms tightly around Marty's neck and went right to sleep.

Evan came in carrying his bag and everyone else's odds and ends. He closed the door behind him and gave Marty a tentative smile, dropping everything in the middle of the floor. There was a mild arrogance about him, a satisfaction with himself that was usually foreign to Evan's nature. He put his hand out to Marty and Marty took it, thinking it felt like the touch of gloves before two boxers went to their corners to wait for the bell.

"Have a good time?" Marty asked.

Evan nodded slowly, as though unable to put it into words. "Bill Kemper from the Visible Wind came to visit while we were there." At Marty's blank look he explained tolerantly, "It's a rock group, Dad. He's the lead singer. And Mom's agent spent a couple of days with us. He thinks he can get me into commercials."

Marty nodded, handing Josh to Jarrod as he and Grady returned to reclaim the rest of their things. "Is that something that appeals to you?"

"Well, yeah. I mean, you did it." Evan seemed to draw himself up to his full height, not that much shorter than his own, Marty noticed. "Mom's going back to L.A. in February, and she wants me to come live with her."

Marty grabbed a jacket, a scarf and a soccer ball from the pile and started for the stairs. "Come on. We'll talk upstairs."

"You're going to say no, aren't you?" They had reached Evan's room, and Marty stood at the foot of the bed while

Evan dropped the things he carried onto it. The boy looked up at him as though he murdered babies.

"I'm not going to say anything for a while." Marty replied calmly, though anger, resentment and confusion roiled inside him. This father/son antagonism was natural, healthy. All the books said so. But how could the kid so easily turn him aside when he'd virtually forsaken all hope of a personal life to keep the family together, and Monica had simply walked away? He knew kids didn't think that deeply, but it hurt all the same. "You and I both could use some time to think about it."

"I don't need time," Evan said, walking to the post at the other end of the foot of the bed. "You took me away from my mother, and now I have a chance to spend some time with her. I want it."

"Evan, you're old enough to remember who left whom." Marty knew a psychologist wouldn't have approved of that response, but he'd been pulled in too many directions lately. Selflessness was getting a little old.

"She left you because you wanted her to be stuck in the house."

"She tell you that?"

"I figured it out."

It was on the tip of Marty's tongue to tell him the truth about his conclusion, but years of shielding his children from pain prevented him from doing it.

"You have another year of high school, Evan," Marty said reasonably instead. "Then what about college? What about your novel?"

Evan shrugged, dismissing with youthful blindness the building blocks of the life he had planned. "I'll finish high school in L.A. and I'll get around to college and my book. Right now I've got the chance to work in commercials, maybe even in movies, to meet famous people and do important things. And to be with Mom."

Marty nodded. "I know it seems very clear in your mind, but I want to make sure you make the right move, Evan. Mom's life is full of pressures and—"

"Just because you couldn't handle it doesn't mean I won't be able to."

Marty looked into Evan's eyes and saw nothing there with which he could connect. The boy had made up his mind. Marty turned and opened the door. "We'll talk about it again when we're both feeling fresher."

Marty went back downstairs and found Jarrod and Grady making sandwiches. "Edie's putting Josh to bed," Jarrod said when Marty looked over his shoulder at the variety of sandwich makings spread out on the counter. "White or wheat?"

At the other end of the assembly line, Grady asked, "Ham and cheddar or corned beef and Swiss?"

"Wheat," Marty replied, "ham and Swiss, and hold the jalapeños on mine."

Grady leaned confidentially toward Jarrod and said under his breath. "He's getting old."

Marty rapped his knuckles on Grady's head before putting one arm around his shoulder and the other around Jarrod's. "So, did you all have a good time?"

"Her yacht's radical," Grady said, piling meat and cheese on the plate Jarrod passed him. "And we met Bill Kemper."

Jarrod glanced over his shoulder to explain, "He's the lead—"

"Lead singer with the Visible Wind," Marty filled in with a superior lift of his eyebrow. "I knew that."

His eyes wide, Jarrod put a hand to Marty's forehead. "Dad! You just identified a musical group that became popular *after* 1970!"

"Evan told him," Grady said. "I heard him."

"Thank God!" Jarrod put a hand to his heart as though recovering from a great shock. "I thought our father had been kidnapped while we were gone and replaced with a pod person.''

Marty throttled the back of his neck with one hand.

"Mom was nice to all of us," Grady said, slapping a slice of whole wheat on top of a sandwich already six inches high and handing the plate to Marty. "But she's more like a baby-sitter, you know. I mean, she doesn't really know what we like anymore. She tried to give us Cocoa Puffs for breakfast."

Plates in hand, they moved to the table, Jarrod retrieving the carton of milk from the refrigerator on the way by. "We had fun," he said, dropping his plate and the milk on the table then going back into the kitchen for glasses. "'Cause there were all kinds of people coming and going, and her house is like great!" He passed glasses around and poured.

"She likes Evan better than us," Grady observed without any apparent concern over the fact.

"I'm sure that isn't true," Marty said. "It's just that he's always been . . . closer."

"It doesn't hurt our feelings," Jarrod said with such matter-of-factness that Marty was startled. "Grady and I were talking about it just before we left. Because it's like…it's not real love, just sort of a…a fuss. I mean, she introduced Evan to her agent and everybody else who came over and she said—" Jarrod assumed a husky falsetto that made it difficult for Marty to keep a straight face "—'Do you believe that this gorgeous young man is my son? I was a precocious child, of course.'"

"That means she was young when she had him," Grady explained.

Marty nodded gravely, "Thank you, Grady."

Jarrod shrugged, the conclusion obvious. "She likes him better than us because he's good-looking and older, so he makes her look young for her age. Anyway, I wouldn't want to live with her. Her friends are really nerdy." He attacked his sandwich with sincere enthusiasm.

Marty turned to Grady, who sat beside him. "How do you feel about that?"

Grady sighed and rolled his eyes. "I'm glad to be home. All that stuff's fun for a while, but it starts to get to you. It's sort of like Mom's just acting in another movie." He picked up one of the five peppers lined up on his plate. "Sure you don't want a jalapeño?"

Chapter Thirteen

Marty walked the length of the Books and Stationery gallery before the store opened, thinking moodily that some good had come out of his presence at the Portland Hale's. The gallery looked classy and solved an old problem. Poole was thrilled. His father had gone back to Bend on January 2, pleased with what had been accomplished.

Now it was the end of January. Sales figures were dismal, and the new cash registers for the expanded inventory system were causing chaos everywhere. Evan wasn't speaking to him, and Shannon was all sweetness and civility. In the three weeks since their return from Bend, he and Shannon had relied on their earlier friendship to carry them through the day-to-day business of the store. Their dead romantic love lay between them, and they stepped over it daily in the interest of their work. It didn't affect their performance, except to take every iota of pleasure out of it. He wasn't sure how much longer he could stand it. Despite all his efforts, the threat of failure seemed to loom over every facet of his life.

"You done good, Hale." A hand touched his back, and Marty turned to face Shannon. She wore white today, a soft sweater patterned with silk leaves outlined in pearls. Her hair was like a dark flame. He was reminded suddenly, painfully, of snow and firelight and Bend. He had to swallow to speak. "Good morning," he said quietly.

Shannon saw their week together reflected in his eyes and knew instantly that she wouldn't be able to talk about what she wanted to discuss. Resigning herself to it had been painful enough; explaining it to Marty would be self-inflicted torture. She turned away from him and looked out over the gallery. "Surveying your domain?" she asked. Ten minutes before opening the store was quiet, clerks opening their registers, preparing for another day.

"While it's still here," Marty replied with a lightness he was far from feeling. "Have you looked at the dailies lately?"

"Don't worry about them," she said calmly. "Houdini couldn't make them look any better. It's a fact of life in retail—you coast from January to March." Knowing he'd been seriously concerned about the not-unusual dip in sales, Shannon went on gently. "You spent your first two years in the family business in promotion and acquisition, so this probably looks awful to you, but it happens every year." She bumped a shoulder against him, needing to touch him, but afraid to test their cautious restraint too strongly. "And, anyway, I made a special point of checking the figures in the departments to which you've paid special attention."

Marty looked down at her, his personal and professional attention snared. "Books and Stationery and its nifty gallery did twenty-two percent over last year in the last two weeks before Christmas, and the trend continues into January. Sporting Goods, where you removed weapons and added more fitness equipment, is up seventeen. Your Dapper Shop in Men's is up ten and the Rogue Shop is up twelve."

A small sense of satisfaction crowded into the grimness that pervaded his mood. "Thanks for checking that," he said, wanting to touch her, but afraid to. He'd had such a tight cap on his emotions since Bend that he didn't want to risk explosion. "I've been meaning to do it, but the inventory setup has had all my attention."

"You're a good manager, Marty," she said gravely, sensitive to his concerns. "You're doing a good job. The staff thinks you're fair and honest. You've taken over, Marty. The Portland Hale's is yours."

Marty heard something in that statement he didn't like, something that sounded like goodbye. Before he could analyze it completely, Shannon distracted him by staring across the floor, a frown between her eyes. He followed her gaze and saw a solitary female figure walking down the aisle between Shoes and Luggage and Women's Accessories.

"Who?" he began to ask quietly.

"Laurie Marsh," she whispered. "Assistant cashier."

Together they watched her turn into Women's Accessories. Shannon had noticed the clerk scheduled to open that department leave it with an empty cup, intending, she was fairly sure, to spend five minutes having coffee before picking up the cash bag that contained her register's daily advance from the cashier. That was a routine followed by most of the staff. "But why would she be heading for an *empty* register?" Shannon asked softly.

Marty watched the woman glance furtively right, then left. "Maybe she doesn't know it's empty," he speculated.

Shannon and Marty stood in silence while Laurie Marsh stopped directly in front of the register, hidden from sight on her own level by a tall rack of hats. From their aerial view, they watched her look quickly around again, then reach into the purse slung over her shoulder and...put something *into* the register that was always left open at night.

Shannon turned to Marty. "I did see her put something *into* the register?"

"Maybe we're both hallucinating. Come on." Before they could move away from the railing, Laurie ran out of the department and up the aisle toward the elevator, darting a glance upward as she passed the gallery. She stopped dead at the sight of Shannon and Marty looking down at her, apparently certain she'd been seen. She paled, then her face crumpled and she ran.

Shannon followed Marty down the gallery stairs and across the floor to the Women's Accessories department. He pulled open the register drawer and found it empty of change and containing only five crisp twenties. Shannon stared at them, then looked at Marty, asking in confusion, "What?"

He took the bills and tucked them into his breast pocket. "A thief with a conscience, maybe? Let's go to my office and ask Kathy to come talk to us."

When they opened the administrative office door, Laurie was already sitting in the chair facing Shannon's desk, sobbing. Kathy was kneeling beside her.

"She came here when she realized you saw her," Kathy explained, her eyes dark with sympathy. "She called me."

"Laurie?" Shannon asked. When the other woman looked up, her face red and swollen from crying, Shannon couldn't resist the impulse to lean down and put an arm around her. "Laurie, why?"

Laurie continued to sob, then straightened and seemed to pull herself together. Anger appeared in her eyes with the obvious shame and regret. "Because I can live without ever having an extra dime, but it was Christmas! Sara wanted a doll and Robbie wanted a dump truck. That was all." She shrugged, a weary sadness now slumping her shoulders. "Such small requests, really. It isn't their fault Bob never sends me money for their support. It isn't their fault my check has to stretch so many ways that I can't even get a credit card. They never complain that I'm too tired to play with them when I get home, that there's seldom money left for the movies or new clothes."

Her resolve returned suddenly. "They weren't even asking for the expensive, sophisticated toys everyone else was buying for their kids. I thought they should have the doll and the truck. It was easy to short the change rounds I distributed during the holiday rush. The clerks were too busy to count what I gave them and usually asked me to put it in the register.''

Tears stormed suddenly out of her small burst of defiance. ''I knew it was wrong, but I also knew no one would suspect me. I felt guilty, but when I thought about my children and how happy they'd be, I did it, anyway.'' She looked into Shannon's face, her eyes filled with misery. ''But my conscience was killing me. Then my brother sent me a hundred dollars for Christmas and I saw a way to put it back. But there have been so many people around doing inventory and putting in the new registers that I couldn't replace it until this morning.''

Shannon looked at Marty, knowing how she would have handled the situation, understanding that she would have to bow to his wishes. He took her arm and headed for his office. ''Excuse us for a few minutes.''

They faced each other near his desk. ''What are your thoughts?'' Marty asked.

''She represents a majority of women in a position so grim they no longer think straight. I feel sorry for her, and I'd like to do something for her. She's been a good employee for a long time.'' She sighed, then added in an even tone, ''But store policy has been to dismiss any employee caught stealing money or goods.''

He nodded, a thin smile barely curving his lips. ''I wonder if there's a precedent for an employee trying to put the money back?''

Shannon had to smile back. ''None that I've ever heard of.''

''All right, let's set one.'' Marty sobered. ''Let's let her return the hundred and call it square. She can stay on. If anything like that happens again, she's fired and we prosecute.''

Shannon was pleased by his compassion, though not entirely surprised. She knew firsthand the infinite tenderness of the man inside Martin Hale, and even wondered for a moment why she could have decided so calmly to walk away from him. Then she remembered the four young boys who depended on him, how much they would need from the woman who married their father and how ill-equipped she was to fulfill that need.

She put a hand on his arm, unable to hold back the gesture. "I think that's very generous."

He covered it with his, the grim mood that had been on him all morning lightening a little. "Generosity's not that difficult. It's really very easy to give when you realize that you lose nothing by doing it."

She gave him a chiding look. "Is there a subtle message there?"

He widened his eyes innocently. "If you hear one, you must be listening for it." He opened the connecting door and ushered Shannon back into her office.

Kindly but gravely, Marty informed Laurie Marsh of their decision. Her shock at being allowed to stay on released another torrent of tears. Marty repeated the final stipulation to the agreement, and Laurie agreed, throwing her arms around him and then Shannon before hurrying off to the employees' lounge to freshen up and get back to work.

Kathy smiled at Marty and Shannon as she walked to the door. "I'm proud to work for the two of you. I hope this regime lasts a good long time."

Kathy's parting words silenced both of them as Shannon followed Marty into his office with two cups of coffee. She was relieved to see that among the things dropped on his desk this morning before he'd toured the gallery was the usual white bakery bag. Out of necessity the ritual of meeting every morning had been maintained; out of deference to their respect for each other, the civil touch of coffee and doughnuts had remained also.

The predictability of his guilelessness touched her, and she put aside again the subject she'd intended to bring up. "Something bothering you this morning besides the dailies?" she asked as she took the chair facing his desk.

He glanced at her as he sat, holding his tie away from the coffee cup. His look was filled with irony and a gentle censure.

"Besides that, too," she said.

He sighed and leaned back in his chair. "I had an argument with Evan this morning. It's become a daily routine with us. His mother wants him to come and live with her." He explained about the potential career in commercials and Evan's determination to put his writing plans aside to be with his mother. "Maybe he'd be happier with her, but I don't want his whole life messed up because I wasn't strong enough to say no."

"I doubt it would affect his whole life," Shannon said quietly, "at least not in terms of damaging it. Maybe it would be good for him to spend nonvacation time with his mother and see what the hectic life of a movie star is really like. Maybe he'll hate it."

"Maybe he'll love it," Marty said gloomily, propping his feet on the corner of his desk in a gesture that reminded her of his first few days on the job. He'd grown more responsible since then, more serious. "Then I'll have lost my firstborn for good."

Shannon moved her coffee to safety several inches away from his feet. "Seems to me you once explained that you must sometimes risk everything to gain everything." She smiled sympathetically. "I don't have the guts for that kind of heroism, but you do."

Marty looked at her for a long moment, then folded his hands across his flat stomach. "And something's been on your mind for a couple of days. I can see it in your eyes right now. What is it?"

Shannon steeled herself. She would have to ask him sooner or later. Now was as good a time as any.

"I've been thinking about Myrtle, Montana," she said.

Marty concentrated on holding back the flinch. Knowing their relationship was over was one thing, putting five hundred miles between them was something else. "Dad called from there last night. They've had thirteen inches of snow."

Shannon sat up straight and reached for her coffee cup. "Now that I know how to make a snowman that shouldn't be a problem for me if you'd consider transferring me."

"You never finished it," he said quietly. She looked up at him, uncertain what he meant. "The snowman," he clarified. "You never finished it."

Shannon got a clear picture of the two of them under the pile of blankets, warming each other from the inside out. Longing, hot and immediate, swept over her.

"Well." She looked into her cup and thought the unfathomable blackness a perfect reflection of her feelings. "There are probably some things some of us aren't meant to master."

Marty lowered his feet, pushed his chair up to the desk and leaned toward her on his forearms. "You're settling for the dregs again, Shannon, when you could have everything."

Unconsciously Shannon leaned her upper body toward him. "And you're trying to ward off what you consider failure by molding me to fit where I don't belong. It isn't failure, Marty. It just wasn't meant to be."

"You can't know you won't fit if you're unwilling to try."

"I won't use your kids as test cases."

Marty shook his head impatiently. "My kids all have a firm grip on reality, except for Evan, and he isn't misreading the truth. He just doesn't want to face it. They would help you, Shannon. I would help you. You'd have so much love you wouldn't know what to do with the extra."

Shannon reached across the desk toward Marty at the same moment that his hand went in search of hers. They laced fingers on top of the manila folder. "Marty," she said desperately, "that's how it would work for *you*. You were conceived in love, grew up loved, and though it's fallen apart now, you loved and were loved by Monica. You have kids who are crazy about you. You know love inside and out."

Marty tightened his fingers. "Shannon, love doesn't come to you as something small that has to reach a certain age and attain a certain growth before it's any good to you, before you can use it. You don't have to be experienced with it for it to work for you. It's powerful stuff immediately, and it's bottomless, boundless. But you have to give it to activate it. You can't just hold it. That renders it useless."

Shannon reached her other hand across the desk, and Marty took it without pause. "What you gave me," she said, "literally brought me to life again. But my ego is so fragile that one small rejection and I could be useless again. Your children will need a woman who is strong enough to help them adjust to sharing you, to doing without their natural mother most of the time, and to being able to deal with her when she walks back into their lives. I would like nothing more than to promise you at this moment that I could be that woman, but I don't know for certain that I can. Please don't hate me for being honest."

He couldn't, of course. Marty dropped one of her hands then, still holding the other, stood and walked around to the side of the desk where he pulled her into his arms. She went into them, choked with pain and emotion, racked with longing and remorse. "I don't know what I'll do without you," she whispered.

Marty held her close, rocking her gently from side to side. His throat felt as though he'd swallowed fire, but inside he felt icy, empty. "You'll meet some freewheeling bachelor who'll snap you up and make you happy as hell. Damn it."

Shannon held him as though this were endless love they were pledging rather than a truce for parting. "Then you'll ask Henry about sending me to Myrtle?"

"I'll call him tomorrow. When do you want to go?"

The silence felt eternal. Then Shannon sighed and pulled away. "I'll stay a few more weeks until the kinks in the inventory system are ironed out. But I'd like to leave as soon as possible after that. It won't get easier."

"Right." Marty caught her face in his hands and kissed her, hungrily first, to satisfy the need for her, then sweetly to let her know he understood. "I'll never get over you, you know."

Shannon reached up to hold his wrists, dropping her lashes because looking into the love in his eyes was too painful. "You'll meet some Suzy Sunshine who'll be everything you need."

"You're everything I need."

"Who'll be everything you and the kids need," she amended.

He sighed and dropped his hands. "Let's not argue that again. Sit down and let's see if we can figure out why National Mills shipped us seven gross of horse blankets."

"Horse blankets?" Shannon had to smile as she sat. "That should distract us from personal problems."

A FEW DAYS LATER, when Shannon returned to her office after taking a break with Gale in the afternoon, the last person she expected to see occupying the chair that faced her desk was Evan. In jeans and a jean jacket with a backpack at his feet, he looked very much like his father might have at sixteen. A melancholy little pain burned in her chest as she smiled and closed the door. He stood and returned the smile.

"Do you have a few minutes to talk?"

Surprised further by that suggestion, Shannon darted a glance toward Marty's office, then remembered that he'd had an afternoon appointment out of the store.

"He's at Kiwanis this afternoon, isn't he?" Evan asked.

Puzzled, Shannon nodded and took her chair behind the desk. "Yes. Sit down, Evan. What is it?"

"I...ah..." Evan straightened the sides of his jacket and cleared his throat. His blue eyes focused on hers, but she could tell that it required effort. "I wondered if you'd talk to Dad about letting me live with my mother. He's probably told you we've been arguing about it."

Shannon nodded. "He's been upset because you can't see his side of it."

Evan expelled a half sigh of exasperation. "He doesn't see my side, either. The divorce wasn't all her fault. I should have a right to be with her."

Shannon asked quietly, "Evan, didn't she leave your father? Doesn't she stay away for long periods when you never even hear from her?"

"She's a star!" he explained, the desperation in his tone sounding like an attempt to convince himself as well as her. "Her life's so different. Important people don't live by the same rules."

"Evan, if people, important or not, have children, they have to be there for them. You're at a crucial point in your life. It's critical that you finish school and be prepared for college." Shannon groped for reason and diplomacy. "I think your father's concerned that the demands of your mother's career might keep her too busy to consider the things *you* need."

"I'll finish high school," Evan said, his eyes flashing excitement, "but Mom's agent thinks he can get me into commercials. I'll be able to take care of myself."

Shannon nodded again. "That does sound exciting, but your father went that route and he knows how hard it is. And once you get a little older, you can't get by on your looks and your body. You might find yourself with children to look after one day and needing a job that allows you time with them. You'll have to have an education for that, Evan.''

Rationally defeated, Evan took on an expression that was younger than the cool maturity he usually projected. There was a certain insolence in it, thinly covering a fragile vulnerability. "If I went to live with my mother," he suggested softly, "I could be out of your hair."

Shannon looked at him, understanding for the first time that Marty's oldest son was every bit as afraid of her as she had been of him. Apparently Marty had said nothing at home about her impending transfer. Evan knew she and his father were in love and probably sensed that she felt inadequate around him and his brothers. He hoped to get what he wanted by offering her what he presumed would make her life easier.

She stared at him for a long moment, letting him become uncomfortable before she replied. Then she dropped the air of helpful friend and became the adult. "Don't try to blackmail me, Evan," she said. "I know you dislike me, and I hate to disillusion you, but *I* like *you*, and I'm not anxious to get rid of you. The decision about where you should live is one that should be made between your parents and you, but if I had anything to say about it, I wouldn't make a casual decision about your life in the interest of making mine easier." He didn't have to know she'd chosen an even easier way out. She stood and went to the coat tree for her suit jacket. "If you want to be considered an adult, that's something you should learn. Come on, I'll take you home." As Evan followed Shannon to the elevator, she was pleased to see that he had the grace to look ashamed.

FEBRUARY ARRIVED with predictable grimness. The weather was wet, the sky was an unrelieved pewter color and tempers were thin throughout the Portland Hale's. Now that inventory was completed and the new inventory system was in place, the extra Christmas help was laid off and full-time clerks' hours were cut back.

Marty looked over January's figures on the third day in February, their grimness relieved only by the bright spots of increased sales in Books and Stationery, Sporting Goods and Men's Wear. They afforded Marty little consolation, however. Tomorrow was Shannon's last day at the Portland Hale's. He tossed his pen onto the desk and leaned back in his chair, letting the pain roll over him.

As though he were deliberately prodding an open wound, he let his mind conjure up her image—bright hair, sparkling eyes, a body that would live forever in his mind's eye and in the sensory memory of his fingertips. He remembered her at her desk, all perceptive clarity and remarkable stamina, sitting on the floor with him and the boys on Christmas Day, laughing and teasing, lying beneath him on a quilt before a fire in Bend, her body warm and giving, her eyes wide and dark and filled with wonder.

Restlessly he pushed away from his desk and the depressing sales figures to stand at the window and look out at the rainy cityscape. It was gray and gloomy, like his mood. He knew he'd come through this. For all the failures of his fresh starts, he seemed to have enough resilience to jut his chin out one more time. He had his children—well, most of them. He had his father, Edie and the respect of employees who were becoming friends. That was an abundance of blessings.

If he'd had Shannon, too, he'd have considered that he had everything. He hated to give credence to her theory that some people simply had to settle for less, but if he was to go on, that was what he'd have to do.

The phone rang shrilly and he reached for it, almost resigned to his fate.

SHANNON DID A SLOW CIRCUIT of the store, trying to look as though it were her customary, detail-checking walk-through. But it wasn't. It was a memory-gathering tour, an attempt to record all the sensory impressions in this store that had been her salvation as a young person and her whole reason for being as an adult. Until Martin Hale.

Her eyes ran over the patina of old wood, the gleam of the chandeliers. She touched silk and fur, sniffed the musky elegance of good perfume, returned the smiles that greeted her and felt for the final time the overall oneness she shared with the establishment that had been her only legacy. She'd once thought that nothing could ever make her leave this place, but she hadn't known then what it was to love and be loved by a man she couldn't have.

Shannon stood at the railing of the mezzanine and looked down on the winter quiet of the departments on the first floor. She contemplated the enormity of a love that hurt so much she had to leave the store to find relief from it. Despite her resolve to free herself and Marty of each other, her mind was always filled with him, her heart remembering, her body wanting. She only hoped that the snowy wilds of Montana would soothe the feverish pain.

With a despondency she'd never known in her years of solitude, Shannon headed for the elevators. She'd been putting off going back to the office for an hour now. Marty had transfer forms for her to sign, and she hated to accept the finality of it. But long respect for the paperwork that kept a business rolling made her walk into the office with a forced smile.

Marty was walking out, shrugging into his overcoat. "Sorry to abandon you," he said hurriedly as she turned and walked him back to the elevator. "I just talked to Jarrod. He said the preschool called. Josh seems to have a bad case of the flu. Edie can't pick him up because she's in bed with it, too. Josh is too uncomfortable to stay until I get off."

"Marty, I'm sorry," she said as the elevator doors parted and Marty stepped in.

He shrugged. "Don't be," he said. "It's just another family crisis. And it's not your problem."

The doors closed between them before Shannon could determine whether that had been a subtle barb.

As Shannon wandered into Marty's office, wondering if the forms had been left out for her to sign, Gale appeared, waving a slip of paper. Her eyes were wide, her cheeks flushed. "I talked to Monica Hale!" She handed Shannon the note. "You were both away from your desks. She says she'll be by for Evan early Monday morning."

So Marty had agreed to let him go. Shannon wasn't sure whether it was the right course of action, but she felt reasonably sure that prolonged exposure to his mother would help Evan see her and his father differently. She dismissed the tiny pang of hurt she felt that Marty hadn't mentioned it to her. As he'd said just a moment ago, it wasn't her problem.

"So." Gale's dark eyes lost their excitement and became sad. A forced smile didn't delude Shannon. "You ready for our girls' night on the town tonight? Fortify yourself. Poole's been crying for days."

Shannon nodded and pulled Gale into her arms. "That's why I haven't been down to see her in the past few days. I think I'd fall apart. Look..." She held her friend at arm's length and said firmly, "I'm depending on you to look after everybody. Marty, Mr. Hale does a great job, but he's got a lot of responsibilities at home, you know. It'd help him a lot if you could second-guess some of his needs around here and relieve him of the small stuff."

"Shannon," Gale said with a tilt of her chin, indicating, Shannon guessed, that she was about to offer an opinion where she suspected she hadn't the right. "Are you sure things couldn't work out between you two?"

Shannon shook her head. "Gale, I'm not mother material. You know that."

"What is mother material?" Gale asked. "You love, you comfort, you scold, you hug. Big deal. That's just being a good friend, only you do it with a kid instead of another adult. I happen to have firsthand knowledge that you're well equipped in that area."

Shannon hugged her again. "Thanks, but there's more to it than that, and Marty works so hard at keeping his family together. I wouldn't want to mess that up." Patting Gale's back, she pulled her away. "Go close the doors against all late comers so we can get this farewell do on the road. I need to party."

Chapter Fourteen

Shannon awoke chilled and stiff, her arm wrapped around Libby's foreleg, the side of her head permanently dented, she was sure, from leaning against the carousel horse's flank.

"Ohhh." Groaning aloud, she held on to the horse and tried to pull herself to her feet. Every muscle in every limb and every other place that had a muscle cried out in protest. Finally standing upright, Shannon tried to remember why she had fallen asleep sitting on the floor, fully dressed.

The effort to recall hurt her head. It felt like someone else's this morning, fuzzy, achy, heavy. She had a vague memory of Japanese food and Emelienne taking the cleaver from the chef and showing him the proper technique for chopping. Another image flashed in her mind of Poole reading a tedious list of accomplishments during Shannon's tenure as proprietress of Carlisle's. It had ended in tears and another round of champagne. Then...she winced against the pain in her head as she chased the memory...there had been a foray into a male strippers' establishment, a conga line down Burnside and a Chinese fire drill near the Morrison Bridge.

She patted Libby's head and realized that the fact that she was home safe and sound was nothing short of miraculous. As Shannon's fingers made contact with the carved flowers in Libby's halter, all the grief of leaving Carlisle's and Marty that the playful, rowdy evening had pushed aside came flooding back. Shannon clung to the one item in her condominium except for a few items of clothing that remained unpacked. She intended to wrap Libby in a blanket and put her in the back of the car. The horse was a link to Marty that would help her recall him in an instant during the lonely days and nights in Montana.

Shuffling toward the bathroom, Shannon put a hand to her throbbing head, thinking that remembering Marty would never be a problem.

"YOU'RE LOOKING a little rough this morning." Shannon was cleaning out her desk when Marty arrived with the white bakery bag sticking out of the pocket of his briefcase. Shannon glanced at it and felt her stomach roll.

"Maybe we could have only coffee this morning," she suggested, setting a box of tissue, a bottle of aspirin and a fistful of pens and pencils with more care than was necessary in one corner of a cardboard box. They seemed to clatter resonantly, anyway.

Marty walked through to his office, trying not to notice the bruised look in her eyes. "Poole says you danced with Tom the Tiger at the Rascals Club," he called from beyond the door, "and that *he* tipped *you*."

"That was Gale," she called back, then put both hands to her forehead as it vibrated. Unfortunately the vibration stimulated her memory, and she suddenly knew that it hadn't been Gale. "Oh, God." She folded her arms on the corner of the box and rested her head on them. At least she could take comfort in the fact that the worst had already happened. She was leaving Marty and his boys, she was leaving Carlisle's, her reputation was in ruins, and her head would probably never work again. There was something settling about understanding where you stood, even when it was hip-deep in—

"Hi!" Gale burst in, a long tubular package under her arm. She looked disgustingly fresh—true evidence, Shannon thought, of who had danced with Tom the Tiger. "Here's the poster. It was worth my life getting it back from the girls in Alterations."

Shannon frowned. "I thought Hilary had made you the best offer."

"Alterations upped it by five."

"You didn't tell them—"

Gale sat on the corner of Shannon's desk and looked into her face. "If you think you've kept how you two feel about each other a secret, you're crazy. I didn't even have to buy it back. It's their gift to you. I'll stop by this afternoon to see if you have time for one more coffee break." She got to her feet and smiled at Shannon, then her gaze shifted to somewhere behind her friend and her cheeks flushed. Shannon didn't have to turn to know that Marty stood in the doorway.

"Well. Bye." Gale left hurriedly, and Marty took the place she'd vacated on the corner of Shannon's desk. He picked up the poster and looked at Shannon. She would have called what was on his lips a smile if it hadn't been so full of sadness.

She snatched the tube back from him. "I'm going to throw darts at it on cold, lonely nights. You're sitting on my blotter, and I was going to pack it."

Marty put a hand to Shannon's head, gently cupping it until she looked up at him. "You're sure you're right about this?" he asked.

She had been a week ago, but now it hurt too much to be right. And she was hung over. She couldn't trust her judgment. "Of course I am. There's no other way. I can't marry you, and I can't stand to see you every day."

"Then why the poster?"

"I can't stand to see your three-dimensional person. A picture I can live with."

"You're settling again."

Shannon sighed. The action made her temples pulsate. "You must have something else to do," she said. The phone rang, eliciting a gasp from her as she covered both ears. Marty reached over the box to pick up the receiver. "Hale speaking. Hi, Margaret."

Margaret, Shannon knew, was Henry's secretary. Standing cautiously, Shannon tugged at the blotter on which Marty sat. He shot to his feet. "What?" he demanded. "When? Where is he?" He listened a moment, frowning darkly. "Is he going to be all right?"

Shannon stopped, her hands gripping the sides of the box, concern beginning to clear her brain. Had something happened to Henry?

"I'll be there tonight. Don't let him worry. Tell him I'll take care of things when I get there." Marty hung up and turned to Shannon, his eyes dark with concern. "Dad fell on the ice in the parking lot and broke his hip. Can you get me a flight to Bend tonight?"

"Why don't you go now?" Shannon asked, reaching for the Rolodex. Because I'll be gone when you get back, she thought frantically. Because we won't have time to say goodbye.

"I'll wait until Evan gets home from school. He leaves for L.A. with Monica Monday morning, and I want to be able to see him off." Marty walked toward his office as he spoke, then stopped in his tracks, muttering an expletive.

Picking up the phone to dial, Shannon turned. "What?" she asked.

"Nothing," he said, walking on. "I just remembered another hitch."

Preparing to punch out the travel agent's number, Shannon suddenly remembered why Marty had left in a hurry the previous afternoon. Edie and Josh were ill. He couldn't leave three teenage boys unsupervised while he went to see about his father. Dropping the receiver, not giving herself sufficient time to think about it, she went to the door of his office. "I'll stay with the kids until you get back," she said, "and I'll see that Evan gets off okay."

He looked up from his calendar. She couldn't read his expression, but she took an educated guess at what he was thinking.

"If you tell me it's not my concern, I'll beat you with your own poster." She turned back to her desk, then remembered a small detail and faced him again. "But you'll have to call Myrtle and tell them not to expect me on Monday. It might take you a few days to satisfy Henry that everything's under control and find him a nurse or whatever."

He came toward her as she spoke, his expression very clear now. It was filled with the love she always saw there, and a strange determination she didn't quite understand, but which unsettled her. "Stop right there," she said, taking a step backward. "Don't make this hard for us. It's a simple offer from one friend to—"

Ignoring her order, Marty grabbed her shoulders and kissed her, quickly but thoroughly. Then he held her away from him and looked into her eyes. "It was an offer from a woman with a generous nature. That's all it takes to be a wife. That's all it takes to be a mother."

She swallowed, wishing she could be convinced. "We don't have time to argue that now."

He nodded, dropping his hands, but his eyes, warm and stormy, still pinned her. "You're right. We'll argue it when I get back." He caught her face in his hands and kissed her gently. "Thanks, Shannon."

"Sure." Eager to be out of his reach, Shannon went to her desk to call the travel agent. This was no time for second thoughts. She mustn't be carried away by emotionalism. Though his touch and the look in his eyes reminded her of how much she was giving up, it would be cowardly to reach for those things if there was a chance the children would be shortchanged.

THE HALE RESIDENCE was pandemonium. Though obviously upset over the news about their grandfather, Jarrod and Grady greeted Shannon with enthusiasm, and Josh, sharing Edie's room while they were both "quarantined," shouted raspily for her to come and say hello. Edie tried to get out of bed to lend a hand but was so pale and weak that Shannon forced her back.

"I'll bring you both some soup," Shannon promised, pulling Edie's blankets up and hugging Josh when he reached out for her.

"But I should help Mr. Hale pack," the housekeeper insisted hoarsely, "and I thought I'd get Evan's clothes washed so he could pack, but I never put them in the dryer. I fell asleep...and then..." She winced. "I think I forgot."

"Well, don't worry about it," Shannon insisted, tucking Josh under the covers. "I have all day tomorrow to work on it. Just relax, and I'll bring you something to eat in a few minutes."

His bag packed and waiting by the front door, Marty said goodbye to the invalids, hugged Jarrod and Grady, then put an arm around Evan, bringing him to the car. "I hate to leave you just before you go," he said.

"I understand, Dad."

Evan looked more subdued than usual, Marty thought, as though he found the impending fact of his move sobering. The boy had always been so calm, so dependable. Marty remembered that in the early days of his single parenthood when life had been one crisis after another, he'd always been able to depend upon Evan to do what he asked, to look after his brothers, to help keep things together. The antagonism between them had been a later development, and one neither of them had completely understood or known how to handle. For the first time Marty could remember, Evan looked as regretful of that fact as Marty had always been.

"I want you to know that I love you," Marty said, "even though it doesn't always seem that way to you. And if you need me for any reason, I'll be there in a minute."

"I know, Dad." Evan's bottom lip gave one involuntary quiver, then he bit down on it. "Thanks for letting me go."

The night wind was cold and the boy was without a jacket. Marty knew he shouldn't keep him much longer.

"Be careful," he said. "Hollywood doesn't offer a very healthy life-style in a lot of ways, and your mom's liable to be pretty busy. I trust you to look out for yourself."

Evan nodded. "I will."

"Then take care, son." Marty wrapped him in his arms, unable to forget the small, sober child who had once loved him in the almost-man he now held. "And call us when you can."

"I will, Dad." Evan's voice sounded shaky in the darkness.

Marty opened the car door, tossed his briefcase and bag inside and got behind the wheel. Evan closed the door. Marty put the key in the ignition but was prevented from turning it by a rap on his window. He lowered it. "Yeah?"

Evan ducked his head down, his eyes looking into Marty's. "I love you, too, Dad."

Marty swallowed a burning lump in his throat. "I'm glad to know that, Evan." He reached a hand out, and Evan clasped it firmly, then let it go. "Bye."

Marty pulled out of the driveway, his vision blurred, his throat choked with emotion. He wasn't usually prone to bouts of self-pity, but damn it, did he always have to lose?

"I WANT A TELEPHONE I can dial out on!" the voice roared down the pristine, antiseptic-smelling hospital corridor as Marty headed for his father's room. Identifying the voice instantly, Marty was both horrified by Henry's behavior and relieved to hear him sounding so alive.

Marty rounded the corner of the room in time to see a sturdy older nurse push his father back against the pillows with one hand. "You're supposed to be resting."

"I have business to conduct," Henry insisted.

"Not at ten o'clock at night, you don't. Be quiet, Mr. Hale. You're keeping the whole floor awake." She picked up a syringe and reached for Henry's hip. Her broad form blocked Marty's view, but his father's lusty epithet left little doubt about what she'd done with the needle.

"You wouldn't work for *me* for a minute!" Henry yelled at her.

The nurse picked up her tray and turned to the door. "You've got that right," she replied with real feeling.

Marty intercepted her exit. "I'm his son," he said quietly. "I know it's late, but I've just flown in from Portland."

The nurse shrugged and rolled her eyes. "You can see him, although why anyone would want to is beyond me. Don't get too close. I think he's rabid."

Henry grabbed the bar above his head and pulled himself partially off the pillow. "Hitler!" he shouted after the nurse. "Ayatollah! Margaret Thatcher!"

"Dad!" Marty whispered sharply, approaching his father's bedside and pushing him gently back against the pillow. "What's the matter with you? You're keeping all the sick people awake."

Henry folded his arms and glowered at the ceiling. "They won't let me have a telephone."

"You've just done serious damage to your body," Marty said reasonably, pulling his blankets up. "You need rest and quiet for a few days."

Henry pushed the blankets down to his waist. "If you're going to take *their* side, I don't want to talk to you."

"Too bad," Marty said, pulling up a chair. "I've inconvenienced a lot of people to be here and I'd be careful how you treat me. I have access to a telephone. If you speak civilly to me, I might be tempted to make your calls for you.''

Henry sighed heavily, still glowering at the ceiling. ''I broke my hip,'' he said quietly. ''Only old men do that.''

So that was it. Marty pulled off his coat and sat down. ''A young man could break a hip falling on ice.''

''A young man wouldn't have fallen.''

''You're feeling sorry for yourself,'' Marty said brutally. ''I just talked to your doctor. If you remain quiet for a few days, we can get you home, hire you a private nurse, and you can be on the phone day and night if you want.''

Henry rolled his head to look at Marty. ''Who's been inconvenienced?''

''Nobody, really,'' Marty replied. ''I wanted you to feel guilty.''

Henry pointed at the plastic tumbler of water on the stand by his bed. ''Would you reach that for me?''

Marty stood and leaned over the bed, holding the flexible straw so Henry could drink. His father looked frail and old amidst the white linen of the adjustable bed. He guessed that his frustration at being unable to work was worsened by the fact that work was all he had left in life. There were himself and the boys, of course, but they were now miles away.

Henry sipped, then pushed Marty's hand away. ''Thanks. Evan's leaving this weekend, isn't he?''

Marty replaced the cup and sat down again. ''Monday morning.''

Henry nodded. ''I wouldn't have let Monica have him, but I suppose you know what you're doing. How's Shannon?''

''She's watching the kids for me. Edie's got the flu.''

''She's supposed to be in Myrtle on Monday.''

''She's going to be late.''

Henry turned his head to look at Marty, and Marty tried to take all concern out of his expression, to suppress the grief that overrode everything since Shannon had first asked him to arrange her transfer. "She's still convinced she's not cut out to be a mother."

"Yeah."

"Well, don't give up. She's a frighteningly smart woman. Maybe she had to leave you to see that struggling to make an effort is better than having no reason to make one."

Marty shook his head. "If she were reluctant to take on my kids because of the effort she'd have to put out, I wouldn't even want her. But she's reluctant because she's thinking of them. It's hard to watch that kind of woman walk away from you."

Henry narrowed his gaze on him. "You aren't considering this a failure, are you?"

Marty leaned back in his chair. "Well, it couldn't be considered a success by any stretch. But I'm coming to the conclusion that all nonsuccesses aren't necessarily failures." He smiled wryly. "In football, wins were a lot easier to determine. In life, they're hidden in the stuff you don't even see. I think I learned that from Shannon. She's had to work so hard, to be so brave, just to have the little things I've always taken for granted."

Henry nodded, then reached a hand out to Marty. Marty took it and pressed. "You'll get her back. I feel it in my bones."

Marty laughed softly. "Your bones are broken."

Henry laughed, too, then his eyelids slowly closed and he went to sleep, muttering, "Damn...that...nurse..."

SHANNON COOKED and did laundry most of Saturday with help from Jarrod and Grady. If they helped her keep the invalids comfortable and do Evan's laundry, she'd help them the following day with math homework Grady didn't understand and a science project for which Jarrod needed batteries and wire.

Evan packed up personal possessions to be shipped after he left. Shannon brought him milk and brownies in the middle of the afternoon. The state of his room reminded her of her own packing and the utter sadness it meant to her.

"Thanks, Shannon." Evan stepped over a box to take the things from her and stood for a moment, trying to find a bare spot on which to place them. He finally settled on the windowsill.

"You doing okay?" she asked.

He grinned, indicating the mess. "I guess so." He took a pair of sunglasses from his dresser and put them on. "Do I look like a Southern Californian?"

Shannon laughed. "A surfboard would finish the look nicely."

"Mom's going to buy me one," he said, taking off the glasses. "We're going to spend a lot of time at the beach."

Unwilling to upset the cautious friendliness between them, she smiled and nodded. "I'm jealous. I'm going to be snowbound in Montana while you're riding the curl."

He looked down at the glasses in his hands. "Dad told us you were leaving. I'm sorry it didn't ... I mean, I know you and Dad ... Well, Jarrod was taking bets that you were getting married. Grady thought ..." Evan stopped himself, apparently thinking better of what he'd been about to say. "I'm sorry."

Shannon sighed and reached out to touch his arm. "Sometimes things go the way you want them to, and sometimes they don't. I'll call you for dinner."

Shannon made scrambled eggs and toast for Edie and Josh, then called the boys to dinner. After devouring enough spaghetti to sink Sicily, Evan went back to his room. Jarrod and Grady helped Shannon clean up.

"Thanks for all your help today, guys." Shannon rinsed off silverware while Jarrod loaded the dishwasher. Grady put the milk away.

"We thought—" Jarrod said, working busily, keeping his eyes on the task "—this might become something regular around here."

Grady closed the refrigerator door and came to lean on the dishwasher. "But you're going away."

Shannon was surprised to find both boys looking disappointed. Guilt rose inside her with painful force. "I've been transferred to the Hale's store in Myrtle," she explained.

A look passed between Jarrod and Grady. Shannon saw it and stopped what she was doing to turn around and face them.

"It's us, isn't it?" Grady asked, his eyes accusing yet confused.

"Grady..." Jarrod warned under his breath.

It took Shannon a moment to absorb the shock of their shrewd perception. She was now sure this was something Jarrod and Grady had discussed, but she could see they'd put the wrong interpretation on it, and drew a breath, praying for the wisdom to explain.

"Yes, it is you," she replied, "but not in the way you think. Jarrod, stop messing with that and let me explain."

With a glare at his brother, Jarrod slid the rack in and closed the dishwasher door. Then he turned around, leaned against it and gave Shannon his attention.

"I love your father very much," she said, feeling the sweetness of it even as she said it. "But you guys deserve a wonderful mother. I mean...not that your mother isn't..."

Jarrod nodded, derailing her attempt to explain. "Yeah. Go ahead."

"Well, I had a mother like yours," she said, smiling to remove any sting the words might carry. "Kind of more interested in other things than in me. But I didn't have a great father like you've got. My father didn't like me, so I didn't grow up..." She paused to grope for words. "I don't know...warm and sweet and full of happiness like all of you are. I get grumpy and withdrawn and depressed. I don't think that would make me a very good mother.''

Jarrod nodded again. "It'd make you a good Evan."

Grady laughed, and Shannon gave them both a scolding look, barely suppressing a grin herself. "He remembers life with your mom more than the two of you do, so her being gone hurts him more. The point is, I just . . .'' Wishing she had never started this, Shannon tried to put the concept at its most basic and prayed they would understand. "I don't have enough to give you . . . good stuff of myself. Do you understand what I'm saying?"

Jarrod frowned. "Yeah, but it doesn't seem like that when you're here.''

"I love being here," she admitted quickly, "but day after day I might mess up, and I wouldn't want to do that to you.''

"You mean, you might get sick of us like Mom did." The words came from Grady, so directly, so sincerely, that she knew he hadn't chosen them for effect. They were heartfelt.

"No!" she said firmly, and a little too loudly. "It's because I love you and I want you to have a mother who would be better than me.''

Grady shook his head, still confused. "But right now," he said, frowning, "we don't have a mother at all. At least one who's here. Why would that be better?"

At a loss for words, Shannon was grateful when Jarrod grabbed his brother by the arm and headed for the stairs, pulling him along. "I'll explain it to him," he told Shannon over his shoulder. "He's a little slow sometimes."

ON SUNDAY MORNING Shannon awoke to the ring of the telephone. It was Marty. "Hi," he said, "are you in my bed?"

The teasing note in his voice was so heartwarmingly familiar that she had to give herself a moment before she an-

wered. She'd missed him so much in just one day. How was
he going to cope without him for a lifetime?

"Yes," she said. "Me and Tulip."

The large dog, nestled against Shannon's back, looked up
at the sound of her name. When Shannon patted her head,
she swung her giant tail, then settled down again.

Marty sighed. "I wish I was there."

Shannon allowed herself a swift mental picture of what
that would be like, then dismissed it to deal with reality.
"Tulip likes to lie diagonally," she said lightly. "I don't
think there's room for you. How's Henry?"

"Crotchety, in pain, generally impossible. But I think I've
found him a nurse so that he can go home. She's coming to
the hospital this afternoon so they can interview each other.
Pray that she's tolerant of crabby eccentrics."

"Poor Henry. Is there anything I can do?"

"No, everything's under control. I'm having a meeting
with the board this afternoon. They're perfectly able to
function on their own, but Dad would feel better if I met
with them and reported to him afterward."

"They've agreed to meet on Sunday?"

"They understand my situation. If all goes well, I should
be home tomorrow night." There was a brief, deliberate
pause. "I'm sure you'd like to be on your way as soon as
possible."

"Yeah." The reply was quiet, halfhearted.

"Tell the boys their grandfather is doing well," Marty
said with sudden briskness, "and I'll be home soon. Give
Evan an extra hug for me."

"I will. Marty?"

"Yes?"

Shannon held the receiver tightly, sure she'd have been
unable to say this if they'd been face-to-face. The long-
distance connection lessened the risk that she would fall
apart. "I love you."

There was silence for a moment, then Marty said unsteadily, "I love you, too, Shannon."

GRADY'S MATH WORKBOOK made as much sense to Shannon as everything else in her life did. Still, she had promised to help. Josh, bored with being in bed but ill enough to be clingy, sat in her lap, lolling against her while she tried to understand the book's instructions.

"Let's give it up and go skating," Grady suggested, hanging over her shoulder.

Shannon punched him playfully. "Pay attention. Let's try this problem and see if we've finally got a handle on it."

When their results matched the answers in the back of the book, Shannon left Grady to it, put a dozing Josh back to bed and took Jarrod shopping for the batteries and wire he needed for his science project. He was so much fun to be with that the two-hour, four-store search was relatively painless.

Home again, it was time to think about dinner, to make sure Evan had everything under control in order to be ready to leave in the morning and to see that the other two boys would be ready for school. Laundry, she thought absently, while another corner of her mind prepared the dinner menu. Lunches. They'd all be up early to see Evan off, then she'd have to drive Jarrod and Grady to school because Jarrod's science project, constructed on a board, was too big to be welcomed on the bus. Pleased she had that under control, she went to check on Evan, failing to notice that, despite the chaotic situation, she felt comfortable, at ease.

Over steak and salad the boys talked excitedly of Evan's future.

"Wouldn't it be great if you got to do a Levi's commercial?" Grady asked. "More milk, please, Shannon."

Jarrod looked upward thoughtfully. "I think you should do something with beer and women."

"I think that would be illegal at his age." Shannon passed the carton across the table. "Maybe for Pepsi or Dairy Queen."

Evan took his dark glasses out of his shirt pocket and put them on, flipping up his collar to affect a sexy, mysterious look. "Or I could model expensive European sunglasses."

The teasing lasted through cleanup, then ebbed as the boys prepared to return to their various projects, realizing finally, Shannon guessed, that tomorrow life would be different for all of them. They harassed one another continually, sometimes playfully, sometimes angrily, but it was obvious that they loved one another, that the trauma of their mother's abandonment had forced them to depend on one another even more than most siblings did. Now that was all going to change, and the three boys eyed each other in the middle of the kitchen.

"You guys going to be up early to see me off?" Evan asked.

Grady's eyes filled, and Jarrod hung his thumbs in his pockets. "If you'll leave me your Eddie Bauer fatigue shirt."

Evan looked at Jarrod, smiling thinly. "It's in your closet."

For the first time Shannon could remember, Jarrod was at a loss for words, but he recovered quickly. He swallowed and cleared his throat. "Then I'll be up."

Evan turned to Grady. "And I left you the Trailblazers hat."

Grady nodded, his eyes still brimming. "Then I guess I'll be up, too."

The boys dispersed, but Shannon needed a moment to collect herself before she checked on Edie and Josh.

By eleven o'clock that night, the invalids had long since gone to sleep and Grady had come down to hug Shannon good-night, an action that pleased her out of all proportion to the casual way it was executed.

Evan and Jarrod were carrying the science project into the living room when the telephone rang. Thinking it might be Marty, Shannon reached for it eagerly.

"Hale residence."

There was a pause on the other end of the line, then a husky voice Shannon identified as Monica's said excitedly, "May I speak to Marty, please?"

"I'm sorry. He's out of town," Shannon replied.

Monica sighed, then said somewhat reluctantly, "Then let me speak to Evan."

Shannon called him to the telephone, ignoring her premonition of impending disaster. "Your mom," she said quietly as he took the phone from her.

A bright smile lit his face as he put the receiver to his ear. "Hi, Mom," he said eagerly. "I'm all ready. I've just got to—" Evan stopped, his smile freezing. The color drained from his face, and he turned away to the wall, listening to the voice on the other end of the phone.

Shannon knew her premonition was confirmed; something had changed Monica's plans.

"Sure..." Evan said in a voice as devoid of color as his face had been. "Yeah, sure."

Shannon was suddenly aware of Jarrod standing beside her. "Is it Mom?" he asked quietly.

Shannon nodded, probing her mind for words of comfort and sage advice to offer Evan, but nothing would come. Grady, in the gray sweats the boys all preferred to sleep in, wandered into the kitchen rubbing his eyes. "Is it Dad?" he asked. "Is Grandpa all right?"

Evan hung up the phone and remained staring at the wall. Shannon tried to shepherd Grady and Jarrod toward the stairs, but Evan suddenly started off in that direction, cutting off their route. Then, apparently changing his mind, or too upset to know what he was doing, he paced back to the counter again, obviously trying to hold himself together against a force of grief and anger stronger than he was.

Grady, never subtle, took one look at his face and asked quietly, "Aren't you going to Hollywood?"

Evan continued to prowl the kitchen, his hands clenching and unclenching, his eyes unfocused. "Susan Sarandon broke her leg on the third day of filming. Mom's been asked to replace her. She has to be in Morocco tomorrow afternoon."

"You can still go afterward," Grady suggested.

"Afterward," Evan said, a dangerous break in his voice, "she's going on tour to promote the film. She said maybe . . . maybe next year."

Jarrod approached his brother cautiously and put a hand on his shoulder. "I'm sorry."

Evan shook him off, his eyes focused now and filled with pain and anger. "You don't care!" he screamed at Jarrod. "You never care. You don't love her!"

"Because she doesn't love *us*!" Jarrod shouted back, his cheeks flushing with temper. "She doesn't love you. You just make her look younger."

The boys flew at each other like angry tomcats. Evan grabbed Jarrod's shirtfront and pulled his fist back while Jarrod grabbed both sides of Evan's collar and began to throttle him.

"Stop it!" Shannon moved between them, dodging fists, to push them apart with a hand on each chest. She had to employ more muscle than she'd anticipated and tried to support her punier strength with an authoritative glare. "Stop it," she repeated more quietly, breathing deeply with the effort. "That's no way to solve anything." She looked scoldingly at Jarrod. "You could be more understanding." Then turning to Evan, who strained against her hand, she said gently, "Evan, I'm sorry. We all are. Let's sit a minute and talk about it."

Evan spun away from her, his handsome face still a mask of pain. He paced across the kitchen again, then, in a gesture of impotent rage and frustration, drew his fist back and let it fly. Shannon watched the window in the back door shatter as though it were happening in slow motion. It seemed to hang suspended for an instant, then crumble to the floor in a shower of glass and broken frame. Slowly Evan withdrew a bloody fist and forearm.

For an instant the four of them were absolutely still, Evan as shocked as anyone by what he had done. Her heart in her throat, Shannon ran to him, drawing him toward the sink. Rich, claret-colored blood flowed out of a five-inch long gash on the inside of his forearm, staining his shirt, his jeans, the sweatshirt Shannon had borrowed from Marty's closet.

"Jarrod, get me a clean dish towel!" Shannon ordered over her shoulder. As pale as Evan, Jarrod immediately complied. The blood was gushing so freely, Shannon wondered worriedly if Evan had cut an artery. Taking the towel Jarrod handed her, she folded it into a long, narrow pad and pressed it hard against the wound. Gratefully she saw that the pressure slowed the bleeding.

"What's happened?" Awakened by the commotion, Edie came to peer over Shannon's shoulder and was shocked by the blood collected in the sink. "My God!"

"Edie, I need something to tie this with," Shannon said, still pressing the pad to the long gash.

"I've got first-aid tape in my room." The housekeeper stepped gingerly through the glass near the back door, then ran to her room.

Shannon turned to Jarrod and Grady. "Get your jackets. You'll have to come to the hospital with me. If he begins to feel faint, I won't be able to handle him by myself." The boys ran off. "Get Evan's jacket, too!" she called after them.

Gently Shannon turned Evan's fist under the running water. She could see small pieces of glass in his knuckles.

"How are you doing?" she asked, gently picking out what she could easily dislodge.

"I feel sick," he admitted grimly.

Shannon hooked a kitchen chair with her foot and drew it behind him. "Sit," she said. She put his hand over the pad. "Hold that." Pulling another dish towel out of the drawer, she ran it under the cold water, then bathed his face with it.

Then she noticed Josh, standing near the refrigerator, sobbing. Beside him, Tulip whined. "Come here, Josh," she said calmly, rinsing out the cloth again. He came to her, and she picked him up and sat him on he counter, as though this were any other conversation they'd had while she was cooking. Tulip followed, sitting beside Evan with a worried frown.

"Is he gonna die?" Josh asked between gulps.

Shannon applied the cloth to Evan's face again and noted that, though he still had very little color, his eyes were clearer. "No," she assured him. "He's going to be fine."

Edie returned with the tape and helped her secure the pad in place. Jarrod and Grady helped her get Evan on his feet and put one arm in his jacket. Jarrod attentively hung the other side over his shoulder. Grady handed Shannon her jacket, and she noted absently that he'd thought of that detail himself.

"I want to come!" Josh cried as they started for the door.

"No, you have to stay with me," Edie said, picking him up and following the small parade.

"No, I want to come!" Josh leaned out of Edie's arms and reached for Shannon, crying. "I want to come with you, Shannon!"

Shannon handed Jarrod the keys. "Put Evan in the back seat where he can stretch out. One of you sit with him." She turned her attention to Josh, taking him from Edie for a moment to hug him. "You can't, Joshua. We have to go to the hospital where people are sick, and you've got the flu."

"Then I should be there, too!" he reasoned.

That was an angle on the problem she hadn't considered, she thought wryly. "Your flu germs will make the people who are sick even sicker. You wait with Edie, and when we get back I'll wake you up and tell you all about it."

"You promise?"

"I promise."

Josh went back to Edie without complaint, and Shannon hurried to the van. Edie grabbed Tulip's collar before she could follow.

MARTY DROVE HOME from the airport, smiling at the darkness through the windshield as he thought about the nurse his father had agreed to hire. Alice Fuller was tall and pleasantly plump, probably ten years Henry's junior. She reminded him of a cross between Helen Hayes and George Patton, unalloyed sweetness with a will of steel. She also reminded him vaguely of his mother.

"I can cook as well as nurse," she had said, standing at his father's hospital bedside and taking his pulse. "And I've cared for single men before. I understand you're the chairman of the Hale stores."

"That's right," Henry had said, watching her suspiciously.

"Well, you look pretty sound to me. Your pulse is strong and your color's good. I imagine you're anxious to be home to get some work done. I also take dictation."

Henry had darted Marty a look of amazement. "You're hired."

"Well, thank you, Mr. Hale. I think we'll get on well. I've been widowed for twenty years, and there's nothing like congenial companionship to keep a body's wits together." She'd fluffed his pillow. "There. You're to be released in a few days and your son's arranged to have a car pick you up and take you home."

"If you'd rather I wait, Dad, I will," Marty had put in quickly while the nurse had paused for breath. "But I think you'll be in good hands here with Mrs. Fuller."

Henry had seemed to have had difficulty pulling his eyes away from the nurse. "What? No, no. Go ahead. If you leave now, you'll be there to see Evan off in the morning."

Before Marty could reply to that, Henry's attention had once more focused on Alice, who was making a list of things Henry wanted laid in at home for his arrival. Marty had known it was time to leave his father's bedside.

Turning off the main highway into his neighborhood, Marty let his mind form the image of Shannon in his bed. Perhaps he could lie beside her for a few hours, he thought with a grim sort of acceptance, before he had to face the morning and watch her and Evan walk out of his life.

Marty slowed and pulled into his driveway, thinking it curious that the kitchen and living room lights were still on after midnight.

Chapter Fifteen

While a doctor and a nurse prepared instruments at a nearby table, Shannon held Evan's hand as he lay supine on a bed in the emergency room of Mid-Portland Community Hospital. "Is the anesthetic starting to work?" she asked, worried by his continued pallor.

"I can't feel my arm at all," he said, closing his eyes and heaving a deep sigh. "I'm sorry. That was a stupid thing to do."

Shannon laughed softly. "I'd probably recommend punching something that wasn't going to bite back." She sobered, tightening her grip on his hand. "But I think I understand how you felt. It's hard to be that hurt and angry and not want to hit something."

A tear ran from the corner of Evan's eye into his hairline. "Jarrod's right," he said, his throat flexing as he swallowed with apparent difficulty. "Mom doesn't love us. I was selfish enough to think that maybe she didn't love my brothers, but surely she loved me. We'd been together longer. I remember how great it was when I was little and she was home all the time. I guess I thought I could have that back. I never understood that those times weren't as great to her as they were to me. God, I wish Dad was here."

Shannon dabbed at the tear with a tissue and smoothed the damp hair back from his face. "I think she does love you, Evan. All four of you. She just loves herself more. I recognize the type. I had a father like that.'' She talked and stroked his hair, keeping her touch and her voice quiet. "All the time I was growing up, I thought there was something wrong with me because he didn't love me more. But that wasn't it. I let that ruin my life for a long time. Don't let it mess up yours, Evan. All I had was my father. My mother had left and I had no brothers or sisters. You're handsome and smart, and your father and your brothers love you. That's a lot of good to hold up against just a little bad.''

"All right, young man.'' A doctor who didn't look much older than Evan kicked a rolling stool beside the small table on which he had rested the boy's arm. Surgically gloved, he sat down and inspected the gash. Then he grinned at Evan. "We got all the glass out of your knuckles. Now let's get a zipper on this arm so that if you're ever tempted to do that again, it'll go a little easier on you. You shouldn't feel anything, but you'd better keep a grip on your mom there till we're finished.''

Evan and Shannon exchanged a smile, neither of them bothering to correct the doctor. The fact that Evan did exactly as he suggested made Shannon forget that the doctor was under a misconception.

MARTY BURST THROUGH the emergency doors and found his arms suddenly full of Jarrod and Grady.

"God, Dad!'' Grady said, his eyes wide, his cheeks flushed. "There was blood everywhere! Mom changed her mind about Evan going to live with her, and he kayoed the window on the back door and tore his arm to pieces! He looks like Freddy Krueger got him!''

Jarrod punched Grady's shoulder impatiently. "Scare him to death, why don't you?'' To Marty he said calmly, "It wasn't that bad, Dad, but it was a good thing Shannon knew what to do. He's going to be okay. She's with him in one of the rooms back there where they're sewing him up.''

"Okay." Marty led them back to the metal-and-leather sofa they'd been occupying when he walked in. "You guys wait here, and I'm going to see how he's doing."

A nurse pointed him through double doors to a partially open curtain across the room. He walked toward it, unable to see anything of Evan but the soles of his large cross-training shoes. Shannon held his hand in both of hers and leaned over him, smiling. Still unnoticed, Marty stopped within a foot of the curtain, his heart filled by the picture they presented.

In jeans and a baggy blue sweatshirt that looked curiously familiar, her auburn hair tied back in a small ponytail with loose tendrils at her neck and ears, she looked nothing like the woman who knew every detail about the running of the Portland Hale's. It was as though she were stripped down to basic woman, all sensitivity and strength, offering comfort and courage and the promise of endless support.

Evan raised his head. "Dad! Hi."

Shannon freed Evan's hand and moved back to allow Marty to get closer to his son. Marty put an arm around her shoulders while taking Evan's hand and smiling at him. "I hear you lost a confrontation with the back door."

Evan shook his head. "It wasn't much of a contest. I'll pay for it."

"We'll worry about that later. Right now Edie and Josh are nailing a board over it. How do you feel?"

"Stupid. Nerdy." He sighed. "Sort of like Grady at his worst."

Marty smiled. "That bad."

"You're fidgeting, son," the doctor scolded gently, his eyes on his work. "There's going to be zigzag stitches here we won't be able to explain."

"Sorry."

While the doctor continued to tease Evan, Marty turned his attention to Shannon. She wrapped both arms around him and sank against him with a sigh of relief. She couldn't recall ever being so happy to see anyone in her entire life. All that was unresolved between them was forgotten in the simple pleasure of his unexpected presence.

He kissed the top of her head and rubbed her shoulder. "I owe you an entire carousel for this one," he said softly.

She looked up at him, her eyes weary and distressed. "I'm so glad you're home."

Marty was confused by the emotion in her eyes and the strength of her grip on him. He tried not to let himself believe that it meant more than simple relief that he was home to take over his brood and she could get on with her life.

The more he heard the boys talk about the weekend, the more he became convinced that nothing more accounted for her reaction.

"After Shannon spent all day Saturday doing his laundry, and most of Sunday ironing it," Grady said when they all walked out to the parking lot, Evan wrapped from fingers to elbow in white gauze, "he isn't even going."

To everyone's surprise, Evan smiled. "You don't have to sound so disappointed about it."

"Do I have to give you the hat back?" Grady asked.

"No."

Grady put an arm on his shoulder. "Then I'm not disappointed."

"We didn't really want you to go, anyway," Jarrod said as they reached the station wagon. In the harsh glare of the parking lot light, he looked uncharacteristically serious. "You just seemed so excited. We didn't want to douse it for you. I'm glad you're staying."

"Thanks."

Shannon helped Evan into the middle seat, and Marty looked at Jarrod, proud of what must have been a difficult admission for him. Jarrod whispered by way of explanation, "I'd have to pass algebra on my own. Ugly thought." He and Grady got into the back.

Marty put a hand to Shannon's mussed hair, thinking she'd never looked more beautiful to him. "You okay to drive home?"

She pulled her unzipped jacket closed against the cold, midnight wind and leaned against him again. "Couldn't you come with us?" she asked. "I could come back with you in the morning to get your car."

Reluctance to be parted from him, he wondered, or an unwillingness to face the boys alone now that her reserves of strength were sapped and the kids were getting a second wind?

"Sure." He put his hands out for the keys. She handed them over with a weak smile and climbed into the passenger seat.

Shannon made cocoa for seven while trying to cope with her feelings. At the table the three older boys regaled their father with the events of the weekend and the details of Evan's round with the back door. Then they all listened, Edie and Josh particularly, as Evan described what had happened in the emergency room.

I'm high on adrenaline, Shannon thought, wondering at the warmth that had begun to build in her when she'd been sure Evan would be all right and he had taken her hand. It had begun to flame when Marty arrived and took her in his arms; it was a positive conflagration now as the family she had come to love so much talked and laughed behind her, Tulip running among them, begging cookies.

Think about what you'd be in for, she reminded herself sharply. You survived tonight, you might even have done yourself proud, but it could be an isolated incident.

"Want some help with that?" Marty's voice startled her out of her thoughts, and she handed him the tray on which she was placing steaming mugs of cocoa.

"Yes," she said, still somewhat distracted. "You can carry this to the table."

Marty took the tray, wanting to take her in his arms and kiss away that confusion in her eyes. He wished he knew which was gaining favor in her mind, second thoughts about leaving him or eagerness to get away.

When Shannon sat at the table, Josh vacated Edie's lap for hers and promptly fell asleep as Marty filled everyone in on Henry's condition and described the nurse he'd hired to care for him. Edie went to bed shortly after 1:00 a.m. Jarrod got up from the table and stretched, slapping a hand on Marty's shoulder. "Glad you're home, Dad. Night, Shannon." As naturally as though he'd been doing it all his life, he leaned down and kissed her cheek.

"Me, too, Dad." Grady hugged Marty's neck, then Shannon's. "See you guys in the morning. Come on, Tulip."

Chapter Sixteen

When Jarrod and Grady disappeared, Evan turned to Marty, his eyes tired but suddenly free of the constraint that had existed between them for so long. He glanced at Shannon, then looked down at the table, tracing a line in the linen weave with his finger. "I know you guys are probably really beat, but I'd like to tell Shannon something, okay?" He glanced up at his father again.

"Sure," Marty replied. "Would you like me to leave?"

"No. It involves you, too." Evan pushed away from the table and stretched both legs out as though being physically comfortable would help him reveal something he found emotionally *un*comfortable. He looked at Shannon and said abruptly, "Thanks for all you did for me tonight." He heaved a sigh as that admission seemed to ease the way for the rest of what he had to say.

He stretched his good arm to the table and retraced the line he found so fascinating. "When we visited Mom after Christmas," he said, "her cook cooked for us, her chauffeur took us places and we swam in the pool and watched television while she talked with her agent and people came and went. She hugged us a lot and made a big fuss, but she didn't spend much time with us." He raised sad eyes to his father. "I didn't think about it until I saw Shannon running around here like crazy all weekend. Mom has all this

reat stuff, but she didn't *do* anything for us. The people
ho work for her did." He prepared to fold his arms, then
inced when his injury protested.

"If that's starting to hurt," Shannon said, "I have your
rescription in my purse."

"I'll take it when I go up," he said, cradling the ban-
aged arm in the other one. "Anyway, I guess I understand
at Mom figured it might be something different to have
e live with her while she didn't have anything exciting to
o. But when the role came up I was in the way." A frown
ulled between his eyebrows as he looked at Marty. "I fi-
ally understand how you must have felt, Dad, how the
her guys feel. I don't know why I didn't see it before."

"Maybe you didn't want to," Marty suggested gently.
We all turn away from what we'd rather not face."

"Well..." He sighed and gave his father a slight smile. "It
els better to understand it." He shrugged, his expression
onfused. "I still love Mom, but I think we're probably
etter off without her. At least on a regular basis. Vaca-
ons once in a while would be all right. Know what I
ean?"

Marty nodded. "I had a hard time admitting it, too,
nce."

"Shannon makes a lot less noise than Mom," Evan said,
smile brightening his face, "but she's always there when
u need her. She's been more of a mom than Mom was.
nd she doesn't even live here." He grinned from Shannon
Marty. "Shouldn't you do something about that, Dad?"
Evan stood, put an arm around Marty, then around
annon, then went to the end of the table where Shan-
n's purse stood open.

"The..." Shannon had to try twice to clear her throat.
The little yellow envelope. Just one with a glass of wa-
r."

"Do you think I should go to school tomorrow?" he
ked her, standing in the doorway between the dining room

and the kitchen. "I mean, I don't know if it'd be more fun to sleep in because I have a good excuse, or go to school and look heroic with my bandage."

Shannon turned to Marty for an answer.

He shrugged. "Evan asked you," he said.

She grimaced at him, then turned to the boy. "See how you feel in the morning. Ah . . ." She beckoned him back as he headed for the sink and a glass of water. "Could I have one more hug? I kind of liked that."

Smiling, he hugged her again, kissed her cheek, winked at his father, then downed his tablet and went upstairs.

Marty leaned his forearms on the table and studied Shannon while the early-morning quiet settled around them. "I don't want to alarm you," he said finally, "but you're turning out to be excellent mother material."

"Now let's not get emotional about this," Shannon said practically, her voice breathless because the warmth she felt still appeared to be growing. Marty's satisfied look was contributing to the downfall of her resolve to think clearly. "It's been a highly charged evening, and we're all just—" she made a rolling gesture with her hands "—getting carried away."

"Sure." He didn't sound convinced.

"This is serious," she said, wondering why he didn't see the gravity of it. "Your children's happiness is at stake."

Marty looked into her eyes, delighted to see concern there. She wasn't certain anymore. He was winning, but he could still blow it if he wasn't careful. "All right," he said, adopting a solemn demeanor. "Go ahead. Refute Evan's argument."

Shannon dismissed that with a wave of her hand. "He was hurt and I took him to the hospital. Anyone could have done that."

"That's not what I'm talking about."

"You mean about doing more than his mother. Well . . ." she said, shrugging. "There was a lot to do. I was standing in for you. I was just—"

"That's not what I'm talking about, either."

Shannon looked into Marty's eyes and found that he was suddenly, genuinely, dead serious. "What?"

"Evan just gave us the most concise yet all-encompassing description of the perfect mother that I've ever heard."

Shannon thought back over what he'd said and frowned. "I didn't hear it."

"He said—" Marty paused to quote Evan correctly "—'Shannon makes a lot less noise than Mom, but she's always there when you need her.'" He reached out to cup her head in his hand and repeated slowly, "She's always there when you need her. That's the important thing. I don't think God made parents to perform perfectly. He made them to be there. You don't have to be brilliant, or make Solomon-like decisions, or even be sunny all the time. You just have to show up on the job whether or not you know what to do and do the best you can. Let the kids see that there's security in life and continuity and that even when they do things wrong you'll still be around to help them get it right next time. My kids have adopted you, Shannon, whether or not you're ready to adopt them."

Shannon pulled away from him and got to her feet. She paced the length of the table and back again. Not entirely sure what she was thinking, Marty sat and waited. "Can this really be happening to me?" she asked, apparently of no one in particular. "I mean, I want to be talked into it." She stopped near Marty's chair and looked down at him, her eyes troubled and a little frantic. She put a hand on his shoulder. "I'd love to know that this would work out for all of us, that I could stay with you and the boys forever, but are we sure it's right?"

Marty pulled her gently into his lap. "If you want to know what parenting is like in terms you'll understand, it's much more like life on a merry-go-round than Sunday afternoon on a carousel. If you want to decide whether you should do it, I think the best approach is to forget all your problems and my problems, forget all the practical arguments and consider how it feels to you."

"You can't make a decision about children on how it feels," she protested, looping her arms around his neck.

"Yes, you can. You always make love decisions on how it feels. Close your eyes, think about all you went through this weekend, good and bad, and tell me what you feel above all else."

Though his voice was calm, Marty considered that he might be bravely slitting his own throat. It must have been a pretty awful weekend. But he remembered how she'd looked bending over Evan, how she'd looked when Josh had curled contentedly in her arms, how she'd looked when Jarrod and Grady had kissed her good-night as though it were the most natural thing in the world.

Shannon did as he asked and tried to concentrate. First she had to blot out how right it felt to be in his arms, how warm and deliciously solid he felt. She was trying to consider the children.

She'd been harried, she remembered, busy every moment, stretched to the limit. But she'd laughed with Jarrod, been amazed by Grady's perceptions and touched by Josh's eagerness to love her. She'd gained Evan's affection. She was filled with a warmth, a sense of being a woman the store had never given her.

"Mostly," she said quietly, opening her eyes. "I remember being scared . . ."

His heart sank.

"Being tired . . ."

That was it. Garroted by his own plan.

"Feeling warm . . ."

He looked at her cautiously.

"And feeling needed." She smiled at him. "I think I liked that most of all. There were a couple of times when, had you been here, I'd have felt as though I..." She paused, looking at him, then looking down at her lap, afraid to make the admission, afraid to reach for it.

"Say it," he prompted, reading her mind. Hope, strong and resilient, came back to life.

"Well...I sort of thought I could...maybe...have..."

He kissed her ear. "What?"

She leaned her head on his shoulder and tightened her grip on his neck. "Everything. I felt as though I could have everything. Do you want to share it with me, Marty?"

Marty raised her head and took her lips, breathing life into her, drawing it out for himself. Love, so long in coming, washed over and over him as Shannon clung to him and kissed him back with all the passion and promise of forever for which he'd dared hope.

"I'll try so hard Marty," she promised as she dotted kisses along his neck.

Marty shuddered, his body coming alive despite the hour and the traumas of the day. "I think it'll be easier for you than you imagine. And you'll have me and Edie. We'll be fine."

Shannon looked into his eyes, the confusion finally gone from hers. She smiled, her expression filled with the warmth that now fueled her body. "I missed you something terrible. I hate the thought of ever leaving you again, even for a day."

"You're not going to," Marty said with resolve, lifting her in his arms as he got to his feet. "You're staying here. We're getting married tomorrow or the next day, as soon as we can get the details together."

Shannon clung to Marty as he wound his way up the narrow stairway, laughing as he had to turn sideways at the landing. "I could walk," she suggested, then leaned out to nibble at his ear. "Though this is very nice." Her voice became a whisper. "In fact, maybe I'd better. What if the boys are still awake?"

"They think of you as their mother already," Marty whispered back. "Anyway, maybe we'll get lucky and sneak into my room without being noticed."

"Be serious," she said. "I've been around here long enough to—"

A door at the far end of the hall opened, and Grady erupted from it, sturdy, hairless chest bare, sweatshirt clutched in his hand, Tulip at his side. He looked up at his father, holding a flushed Shannon in his arms and asked reluctantly, "Is this a bad time to tell you I'm supposed to bring three dozen cookies to class tomorrow morning for Teacher Appreciation Day?"

Recognizing one of the favorite words in her vocabulary, Tulip barked loudly.

Marty looked down at Shannon, his expression dry. "Fairness demands that I give you an opportunity to re-consider."

Shannon tightened her grip on his neck, happy enough to burst. "Not a chance."

HARLEQUIN
American Romance®

COMING NEXT MONTH

#341 IMAGINE by Anne McAllister

Frances Moon was a woman of the '90s. The 1890s, that is. At least she was convinced she'd have been more comfortable back then. She had everything she needed in the wilds of Vermont. And if she'd wanted a man, she could create one. Then Jack Neillands showed up. Inch-for-masculine-inch he embodied her perfect man. But fantasy heroes were safe and predictable . . . and Jack was anything but!

#342 LUCKY PENNY by Judith Arnold

Syndicated columnist Jodie Posniak got all sorts of household hints, recipes and questions from her readers. Until now she'd never gotten a love letter. Into Tom Barrett's missive, Jodie read an aching over lost love. Though his words were simple, she envisioned a man who would charm her with his tenderness . . . and ignite her with his passion.

#343 SPIRITS WILLING by Leigh Ann Williams

New Yorker Angie Sullivan flew off to the Coast to collaborate with a Hollywood living legend on her autobiography and found her employer distracted by a New Age mystic who'd spellbound Tinseltown. Angie suspected she was being hoodwinked California-style. Angie's own mental energy was being diverted by guru biographer Lance Wright, who definitely enhanced Angie's aura—on a purely sensual plane.

#344 BEST BEHAVIOR by Jackie Weger

Willa Manning longed to give her beloved adopted daughter the grandparents she dreamed of, but not at the risk of losing her forever. Nicholas Cavenaugh understood Willa's reservations, but he'd promised to bring his friends the child their lost daughter had borne so far from home. Fate, which had brought Nicholas and Willa together, had put them on opposite sides in the only struggle that could tear them apart.

In April, Harlequin brings you the
world's most popular romance author

JANET DAILEY

No Quarter Asked

Out of print since 1974!

After the tragic death of her father, Stacy's world is shattered. She
needs to get away by herself to sort things out. She leaves behind
her boyfriend, Carter Price, who wants to marry her. However, as
soon as she arrives at her rented cabin in Texas, Cord Harris, owner
of a large ranch, seems determined to get her to leave. When Stacy
has a fall and is injured, Cord reluctantly takes her to his own ranch.
Unknown to Stacy, Carter's father has written to Cord and asked
him to keep an eye on Stacy and try to convince her to return home.
After a few weeks there, in spite of Cord's hateful treatment that
involves her working as a ranch hand and the return of Lydia, his ex-
fiancée, by the time Carter comes to escort her back, Stacy knows
that she is in love with Cord and doesn't want to go.

Watch for *Fiesta San Antonio* in July and *For Bitter or Worse* in September.

JDA-1

H A R L E Q U I N
American Romance®

Live the

Rocky Mountain Magic

Become a part of the magical events at The Stanley Hotel in the Colorado Rockies, and be sure to catch its final act in April 1990 with #337 RETURN TO SUMMER by Emma Merritt.

Three women friends touched by magic find love in a very special way, the way of enchantment. Hayley Austin was gifted with a magic apple that gave her three wishes in BEST WISHES (#329). Nicki Chandler was visited by psychic visions in SIGHT UNSEEN (#333). Now travel into the past with Kate Douglas as she meets her soul mate in RETURN TO SUMMER #337.

ROCKY MOUNTAIN MAGIC—All it takes is an open heart.

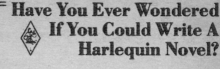

Have You Ever Wondered If You Could Write A Harlequin Novel?

Here's great news—Harlequin is offering a series of cassette tapes to help you do just that. Written by Harlequin editors, these tapes give practical advice on how to make your characters—and your story—come alive. There's a tape for each contemporary romance series Harlequin publishes.

Mail order only

All sales final

TO: **Harlequin Reader Service**
Audiocassette Tape Offer
P.O. Box 1396
Buffalo, NY 14269-1396

I enclose a check/money order payable to HARLEQUIN READER SERVICE® for $9.70 ($8.95 plus 75¢ postage and handling) for EACH tape ordered for the total sum of $_____*
Please send:

☐ Romance and Presents   ☐ Intrigue
☐ American Romance   ☐ Temptation
☐ Superromance   ☐ All five tapes ($38.80 total)

Signature_____
                                                  (please print clearly)
Name:_____
Address:_____
State:_____ Zip:_____
*Iowa and New York residents add appropriate sales tax

AUDIO-H